LET THE GUILTY PAY

A BARTHOLOMEW BECK THRILLER

RICK TREON

FAWKES PRESS

Cover design by Fresh Design

Print ISBN 978-1-945419-56-0

Ebook ISBN 978-1-945419-57-7

LCCN 2020930226

PRAISE FOR LET THE GUILTY PAY

"...cleverly plotted, deftly paced page-turner with complicated, deeply relatable characters. Everyone has a secret, everyone has an agenda, and Rick Treon dispenses the well-earned twists and reveals with the stiletto precision of a master."

- Heather Young, Strand Award winning author and Edgar nominated author of The Lost Girls

---

"...invites you in like a glass of sweet tea, then knocks you off your feet like a fifth of whiskey. This is dirty Texas noir where no one walks away clean."

- August Norman, author of Come and Get Me

"...a sharp, mesmerizing thriller weaving together two murders, two decades apart; the connections between these crimes become evident through unexpected twists and revelations. Featuring complex, well-rounded characters and vivid settings...begs to be finished in one sitting and left me eager for another installment."

- K.P. Kyle, author of Sync

For my brother Jesús, and all the other pipeliners who welcomed me into their world.

PROLOGUE

Excerpt from *Cold Summer,* **John Beck, First Edition, 2002**

Residents of Hinterbach, Texas, woke up in a new place. The quiet Hill Country town had been stained by Summer Foster's blood.

1

She was in pain, and that was my fault. I always misjudge my strength when I'm upset.

But the fact that I had her by the elbow while asking what the hell she was doing? That was hers.

"Sorry," I said, softening my grip and my tone. "But I can't let you walk away."

She took advantage and jerked free. "Sure you can. Just pretend you didn't see anything." Her eyes narrowed. "Why were you following me, anyway?"

I didn't want to admit the truth. We were both new to the job and spent most of our breaks talking and smiling at each other. The other pipeliners assumed I was sleeping with *the hot girl*.

I felt like there was a chance, though, so I kept getting to know Jillian through intelligent discussions during stolen moments. It was a tried-and-true method. I was lonely. She was lonely, too. That's what she told me anyway.

But there were some days when I couldn't get that alone time, when she would lose me among the dozens of other workers, enormous earth-moving machines, and maze of steel pipe. That was the case a few minutes ago, and I shouldn't have cared. But at 3:15 p.m. on the Saturday before Labor Day, I'd wanted to spend as much time as possible with Jillian before our rare two-day weekend.

Rather than answer her question about my motives, I deflected. "It doesn't matter why I came over here—I caught you. How long have you been doing this?"

To say I was upset with Jillian would be a massive under-statement.

We were welders' helpers. As the title suggests, our job was to do the bidding of our welders. Fetch their tools. Bring them water. Clear their pickups of empty beer cans in the morning, then fill their coolers with new eighteen-packs covered in convenience store ice.

Each helper had one welder—I worked for my best friend Jorge, she helped my old friend, Paul—and everything we did affected their reputations.

That's why I was angry. Jillian had just pulled out a cheap battery-operated grinder from the end of a pipe and gashed the rusted steel like a cutter on the inside of his thigh.

Leaving grind marks is one of the worst sins a helper can commit. When we were caught leaving scars, that section of pipe was supposed to be cut out and the ends re-welded to ensure the line didn't have any weak points.

But beyond posing a safety issue, grinding on the pipe could postpone a job—the greatest sin of all. Money flows through pipelines, and those who keep companies from their cash aren't pipeliners for long.

Six welds had been cut out the last three weeks, and the bosses were on edge. Jillian and I were the only helpers who hadn't been accused of severe ineptitude. Our welders had no repairs, so the four of us showed up every day in relatively good moods. Everyone else was mad as hell.

"So what?" Jillian pushed past me and hoofed it toward the rest of the crew. I'd followed her to the lay-down yard, where finished sections of pipe waited for inspection and transportation. Everyone else was parked about a hundred yards away, with most taking shelter in their air-conditioned trucks.

I jogged after Jillian and confronted her head-on, grabbing her shoulders.

"I can't let you keep doing this." I was talking too loudly, so I stepped closer and lowered my voice. "I have to turn you in."

Her focus shifted to a spot over my left shoulder. I turned around and saw several labor hands and welders walking toward us.

Jillian took advantage of the bad optics. She slapped me across the face and ran a few steps before turning around, hands on her hips and forced tears leaking from the corners of her brown eyes.

"I told you, we're over." She pointed at me, continuing to play the distressed damsel. "Don't text or call me again. If you do, so help me Bartholomew Beck, I'll get you kicked off this fucking job."

I tried walking toward her, but the crowd—which by now was nearly everyone—began closing the gap and yelling at me to back off. Jillian retreated into the mob and found Melissa, a fellow helper and the only other woman on the job, who rushed her toward the collection of jacked-up trucks.

Melissa lowered a tailgate and gave Jillian a boost so she could sit. Welders liked to have their trucks ride as high as possible, despite how hard it was for us helpers to climb inside and retrieve their tools. I watched as Melissa, an ex-Marine who had won several arm wrestling contests against other helpers, gently rubbed Jillian's back.

Our weld boss, Zak, stepped between me and the rest of the crew and whistled to shut everyone up. "Welders, get a head start on the weekend. Go home with ten. We'll see y'all on Tuesday."

I needed to tell Zak what I'd seen. I stomped toward him, but he held up his right hand.

"I don't know what that was, but it looks bad." He was calm, but I could tell he was in no mood to hear excuses. "And I don't need it on top of the other shit going on around here."

I opened my mouth, but Zak cut me off. "I don't want to hear anything from either of you until Tuesday. And if you make another scene like that, I'll run both of you off."

He didn't let me respond before marching toward his truck, which was being swallowed by dust as a dozen pickups raced for the gate.

I waited for the air to clear and found Jillian. She gave Melissa a quick hug before shutting Paul's passenger door.

Melissa immediately turned around and marched to Jorge's truck. She jumped up into his bed and flipped open her pocketknife, then proceeded to scrape off one of the stickers on the side of his gray welding machine.

Jorge hopped out of the cab and pointed at her. I walked their way but still couldn't hear what they were arguing about. I also couldn't read which decal she was removing, but I knew by its location.

Melissa was attacking the silhouette of a naked woman and the words labeling his rig *The Panty Dropper!*

———

THE BITTER SMELL of cheap beer and tomato juice poured from the opening of Jorge's can. It was his second chelada. The first had gone down in five long pulls.

I didn't approve of his drinking and driving. But since I rode to work with Jorge every day, I also didn't have a choice. I'd offered to drive once, telling him it should be part of my duties as his helper, but Jorge was proud of his hunter green truck and the welding machine in its bed. If we were going to crash, it would be his fault and nobody else's.

I reached across the cab to turn down the cumbia music. Jorge stopped dancing in his seat. "Dude, what the hell?"

"I need to talk to you." I tried to convey the seriousness with my stare but knocking Jorge off his party pedestal was never easy.

"You always want to talk." He paused to take another swig from the tallboy. "You're worse than my wife."

I shook my head, unsure how to get him to listen. "That fight with Jillian a few minutes ago, it wasn't about—"

"It was about the fact that the hot girl doesn't want to fuck you. Melissa already yelled at me about it. She's scary, bro."

I clenched my jaw to keep myself on track. "That's not why we were arguing."

"Oh yeah? What's the matter then? You can't get it up for her?" He laughed and turned the radio back up.

I muted the music again. "Look, I'm serious. I caught her leaving grind marks next to a weld. She's been causing all the cutouts and repairs."

That finally got his attention.

"Holy shit." Another, longer drink. "Did she tell you why?"

"No." I turned to look out the windshield. "I was trying to talk to her when it all went sideways. And Zak was so pissed he didn't let me tell him."

"Good. We should handle it ourselves."

That didn't make any sense. I was new to pipelining and didn't know all the unwritten rules yet, but shouldn't Zak be the first to know if someone was sabotaging the job?

Jorge read the confusion on my face. "You know that would come back on me and you, right?"

"How?"

"The bosses look at us all like a team. Us two, you, and Jillian. And Paul's your best friend, so it's like you vouched for them."

"Not best friend. *Old* friend." I was constantly correcting Jorge on that point. The position of best friend belonged to him. Paul Schuhmacher, on the other hand, was an old high school buddy. Until a wild night in Oklahoma a month or so before the job started, I hadn't heard from him in more than a decade. Paul

7

was a year ahead of me at Hinterbach High and went to Tech on a football scholarship. Then he dropped off the map. At this point, I knew more about Paul's father, a U.S. congressman from the Texas Hill Country who was constantly in the news.

We told Zak we knew each other, so he paired Paul and Jorge together. Jorge would weld one side of the pipe and Paul the other. That made Paul and Jorge brothers-in-law—a pipeline term that hadn't made much sense to me. But apparently it meant we were like family, and Jillian's actions were to be treated as a family matter.

"So how do we handle it?" I asked.

"We probably won't have to do anything. You know what she's been up to, so I bet she'll just stop."

"And if she doesn't?"

Jorge shook his can to see if any was left. He was putting it to his lips when I heard a deafening thud. The truck rocked to the right, then lunged like a bull trying to buck us.

When the pickup was safely parked on the side of the county road—Jorge always took the back way home to avoid police— we jumped out of the cab. He immediately inspected his side for damage, while I looked back to see what we'd hit.

A deer was sprawled out across both lanes. It was a doe, with at least one broken leg and a slick, heaving chest. My heart sank.

Jorge, as usual, knew what I was thinking. "Hey, I've been drinking. Forget the deer. We have to get out of here."

"You know we can't do that." The right thing to do was to put the animal out of its misery. "Come help me."

"I'll drive off and leave you, bro. I swear to God I will."

"Calm down. I'm sober, so we can say I was driving if anyone comes along. Just toss out the empties."

Jorge nodded and got back in the cab. I walked over to the deer and stroked her neck. She kicked violently and let out a haunting—almost human—death scream. Though she was breathing, her side was crushed, the light brown hide soaked in blood where a rib had penetrated her flesh.

I turned back expecting to see Jorge. He wasn't there. I called for him again, but all I got in response was a middle finger from the passenger-side window.

I jogged over. "What are you doing? Come help me."

"I can't do it, man. Just get in so we can go."

We all turn into cowards in some moments. For Jorge, it was here, now, confronting certain death.

I, on the other hand, had known for many years that death didn't faze me.

I was sixteen the first time I took a life.

I'd been riding back to town with Dad after watching my sister run at a track meet. We'd seen that deer, but he couldn't swerve in time. My job had been to control the buck while my father slit his throat. We then drug him to the ditch, where myriad insects and animals waited to feast on the carcass.

I would have to do both jobs this time. My knife was not sharp enough for the task, and I couldn't get that close to the deer given how much fight she'd shown. I jumped into Jorge's bed and opened the stainless-steel toolbox. After sifting through the grinders and hammers, I emerged with the machete he kept to chip off the teal-colored epoxy that coats underground pipelines.

I tried ineffectively to slow my shallow breathing as I approached. She could sense what was coming and began writhing and screaming louder with each step. She managed to get on two legs but fell, the pain of her broken hind leg and ribs proving too much to bear.

"I'm sorry girl." I repeated the phrase as I lifted the machete, still trying to reconcile dueling truths. I was about to take the life of another living, sentient being, which is inherently terrible. But I was also putting an end to her suffering, which I knew would continue for hours unless she was hit by another vehicle.

I couldn't look at her while I did it. I'd never been proficient with hand tools, and my new occupation had only slightly improved that skillset, so I kept swinging at where her neck should be until the screaming stopped.

I only had a moment to think about the life I'd taken before hearing an oncoming truck. We were still in the middle of the road, so I slid the machete between my belt and jeans like a marauder and drug her body off the blacktop, still asking her for forgiveness.

2
***

I spent the holiday weekend with Jorge and his family. I was no longer upset with him, and the deer's screams had faded and been replaced by the laughter of Jorge's children.

But as we parked among the rest of the welders, I realized my ill feelings toward Jillian hadn't diminished. I was anxious after more than forty-eight hours of radio silence, so I scanned the groggy faces. I found Paul. Not Jillian.

Paul stuck out his hand for a morning handshake, revealing the hint of a red tattoo that ended at his wrist. "Hey Big Nasty, how was your holiday?"

I smiled. My nickname from high school was Beck, and that had sufficed until my foray into pipelining. Though it started after an evening I came to regret, the new nickname also described my scraggly beard and brutish, undisciplined strength.

"Not bad." I checked over Paul's shoulder and tried to see if Jillian was sitting in his pickup. "Spent the weekend in Borger with Jorge."

"Gotcha. I stayed around here, too. That drive is too damn far for two days."

I nodded, though distance hadn't kept me from traveling

from my temporary Texas Panhandle home to Hinterbach. I'd been there once this year. That was enough to last a couple more decades.

I was about to ask why Paul hadn't stopped by Jorge's, but it was nearly seven a.m. No more time for small talk. "Where's Jillian?"

"I don't know. She didn't show up at my trailer this morning, and she's not answering my calls. Guess she got too tore up last night to make the drive."

Jorge tapped me on the shoulder and handed over the clipboard with the daily Job Safety Analysis, which detailed the potential hazards awaiting us that morning. For the bosses, the JSA was a way of covering their asses if anyone got hurt. For us, it was an attendance sheet, proof we showed up and deserved our ten hours of pay.

I wanted to ask more questions about Jillian, but the site superintendent began speaking as Paul was signing, signaling the start of another day.

I was thankful when Zak announced break time. The heat had already climbed into the nineties, and I was helping a group of labor hands haul equipment. The bosses had warned us it would be hotter than usual.

Zak must've been reading my mind. "Could one of you grab me a bottle of water?"

Though it seemed obvious, not everyone heeded the constant warnings to stay hydrated. On my first job in late July, I'd seen two other pipeliners pass out, one of whom fell face-first into the side of his pickup while trying to reach the sweet relief of his truck's AC. That was one of the times I'd asked myself, out loud, what the hell I was doing out on a pipeline.

But I remained eager to please. I nodded and started walking toward Jorge's truck before Zak grabbed my arm. "Not you, Big

Nasty. I need you to go get me a sky hook. We're going to need it in a few minutes."

"Yessir."

I'd never heard of a sky hook. Thankfully, I spotted Jorge leaving one of the job site's three portable toilets and heading toward his truck. "I need to find a sky hook for Zak."

"Oh shit," he shouted into the wind. "You better go get it."

My head swiveled out of reflex more than anything. I didn't know what a sky hook looked like, and I wasn't going to spot one in the next three seconds.

"Do you know where one is?"

Jorge shook his head as he kept walking.

"What do they look like?"

"Dude, just think about it while you're looking. You'll figure it out."

While it was fun hanging out with Jorge for ten hours a day, at moments like these I wanted to tell him to shut up and help me find the damn thing. But that was literally my job, not his. And thanks to the man who pronounced his name "George" or "Hoar-Hay" depending on his audience, I was gainfully employed and had avoided begging my parents for money.

"Fine," I huffed. "I'll be back in a minute."

Jorge checked his invisible watch. "Better hurry."

I hustled to an area where shared equipment was either stacked on pallets or laying on the dead prairie. There were chain clamps, which secured two ends of pipe while welders tacked them. Flames from the six weed burners—long torches attached via rubber hoses to grill-sized bottles of propane— would then warm those ends before being fused. There were several other pieces of equipment I'd become familiar with through on-the-job training. Nothing resembled a hook.

I searched my brain for other places a sky hook could be hiding. I remembered Jillian pulling out her cheap grinder the previous week. Perhaps this elusive sky hook was in a similar hiding spot.

Testing that theory meant hiking to the other end of Site One —the official designation for our job site, located on the outskirts of Fritch, about forty-five minutes northeast of Amarillo. Sweat rolled down my arms and soaked the wrists of my leather gloves. I took them off and stuffed them into my back pocket as I approached the lay-down yard.

I was staring at the spot where I'd caught Jillian—I still had no idea why she would sabotage the work—when Paul sidled up to me. "What are you looking for?"

"A sky hook." I turned to face him. "I have no idea what that is. Have you seen one? Or can you at least tell me what I'm looking for?"

"I'm pretty sure someone set one down over there." He pointed at the other end of the yard, near the area for equipment designated for Site Three. "It just looks like a big ol' hook. Let me know when you find it. I'll give you something for my character to say in your next book."

I thanked Paul without telling him there was no next book. Not that he would know or care. Before finding myself in this new vocation, my adult life had been about words. Long words, short words, ten-cent words, words fancier than Whataburger ketchup. But after two unpublished true crime manuscripts and one unsold work of fiction, I no longer thought of myself as a writer.

I neared the edge of the area and searched the ground. No hooks. There was a pig launcher we'd completed two days earlier, and that seemed promising.

On one end was an open piece of rust-brown pipe that extended nearly twenty feet. On the other was a blue door concealing the hole into which a giant tampon—that's how Jorge had described a *pig* to me—would be pushed for periodic cleaning of the pipes that crawled underneath the High Plains.

Someone had probably left a sky hook inside the launcher. I leaned down a few feet and peered into the open end. I didn't see anything, but it got pitch black about two feet inside the pipe. I needed to open the gate and let light shine through.

My nose detected a foul odor as I walked to the other end. A skunk? No. One of the hundreds of prairie dogs that littered Site One had crawled inside and died.

It was a solid hypothesis, though I hadn't considered how a prairie dog might get into the launcher. The enormous pipe—twenty-six inches in diameter on the open side, which would later tie into the existing pipeline, and thirty inches across on the gate side—wasn't laying directly on the ground. It was propped up on three-foot square columns built out of railroad ties. A rodent would need a hell of a reason to make that climb, and under normal circumstances there would be no prize waiting for it.

But that realization didn't hit me until long after I opened the gate and saw Jillian's misshapen head. I could only assume it was Jillian because her face was severely discolored and lumpy. Half of her dirty blonde hair was nearly black from dried blood and matted against a temple that had been caved in. That's all the detail I could absorb before turning away and gagging.

I looked toward the rest of the crew. Nobody had seen me, so I jogged until my left foot found itself ankle-deep in a prairie dog hole. After standing and replacing my white hardhat, I decided to walk, though part of me felt I was disrespecting Jillian by taking the extra time. My thoughts were broken by the sound of a dozen welding machines firing up, a chorus of combustion engines fighting to be heard. The crew was resuming work, though Jorge and Zak were talking as I approached.

They started laughing when they saw me coming. Jorge leaned toward me. "Did you find that sky hook, buddy?"

"What?" I struggled to find the right words. "No, I didn't, but—"

"Did you look everywhere?" Zak asked. "I told you I need that thing right now."

We contracted our huddle as a large yellow digging machine,

known as a track hoe, rumbled by. "I know," I said. "I'm sorry, but—"

"Dude, we're fucking with you," Jorge said. "There's no such thing as a sky hook. We wanted to watch you lose your shit trying to find one. It's like an initiation. You should put it in your next book."

"Yeah, maybe," I said. "But right now, I need you two to come with me."

"Dude, I told you, we're messing around, there is no—"

Jorge finally shut up when I started walking back toward the yard. He grabbed my arm. "Bro, we've got to get back to work. What's going on?"

"I was looking for the sky hook and—"

"For the last time, there is no such thing as a sky hook." Jorge's eyes flashed in a rare moment of frustration.

"Okay, I get it. But you and Zak need to come see this."

"See what?"

I needed to say the words: Jillian is dead, and I found her body. But I wasn't ready, so I pointed toward the launcher.

"Jillian," I whispered.

Jorge yelled at Zak and sprinted across the yard when it sunk in. Zak asked me what was going on, and I finally articulated the words "hot girl" and "dead." He took off after Jorge. I walked behind them, in no hurry to return to her corpse, but knowing I should.

Jorge had a growing beer gut but remained nearly as athletic as the intramural softball star he'd once been. I'd never seen him out of breath. I'd never seen him throw up either, but his five-nine frame nearly folded in half as he vomited fermented sugar and scrambled eggs. Zak skidded to a stop beside Jorge and had a less visceral reaction. He took off his sunglasses and put his hands on his narrow hips. He stared at Jillian for what seemed like half an hour, though it was probably about ten seconds. He eventually dropped his head, his freshly shaven chin trying to burrow into his sunken chest.

I stood farther back, the wider view revealing details I'd missed earlier. Jillian's bellybutton faced up, her bloated, blue-gray arms squeezed tightly to inflated sides. Her hands were lying flat, palms against the steel. She was in street clothes, a tight-fitting tank and jeans struggling against her torso and legs, her toes pointing to the left.

But my eyes were drawn to the thin, deep gash in her neck. An inch or two more, and whatever made the cut would've severed her head. That and the crushed right half of her skull were more than enough to have killed her, but her head bore one more disfigurement—a one-foot screwdriver sticking out of her right eye, also pointing to the left.

I fixated on the yellow-and-black handle and struggled to breathe. How had I missed it the first time? The shock and the smell, I suppose. But with this new perspective and time to process the image, a terror from deep inside reached up and squeezed my throat shut.

I'd seen this before.

3

The Fritch Police Department arrived first. The middle-aged chief rummaged through the back of his Explorer before emerging with a roll of crime scene tape. He summoned his officer, and the pair created a perimeter. They clearly hadn't done it in a while, if ever, which said more about the quiet bedroom community of about 2,000 than their effectiveness as policemen.

"Well, I'm going to Dairy Queen," Paul said. "Y'all want anything?"

Jorge reached for his stomach. I shook my head.

"How can you be hungry right now?" I asked.

"Hey, I didn't see her. Besides, we're not getting any more work done today."

He was right. And in their haste to secure the crime scene, the chief and a wide-eyed officer—a pair who likely comprised the entire on-duty contingent of the FPD—hadn't told any of us to stay.

Zak called out to Paul and the others walking away. "Just be back before too long."

They left just in time. A Hutchinson County Sheriff's Office truck and a Texas Department of Public Safety SUV arrived next.

The sheriff's deputy, who'd turned on the lights but not the siren, drove straight to the crime scene tape. The less-hurried DPS officer angled his vehicle across the road leading out of Site One, symbolically locking the rest of us in. Our superintendent, Captain Redbeard, approached the SUV and spoke to the driver. He returned a minute later and gathered everyone as a second state trooper drove past.

"Listen up," Redbeard said. "We're done for today. Everyone goes home with ten, and we'll report to Site Two tomorrow morning. I'll have more information by then, and we'll figure out where to go from there. Jorge, you and Beck stay behind for a minute."

We watched the rest of the group disband. They remained respectful and solemn as they walked to their trucks, but their masks fell away quickly. They'd been given more than half a day off with pay, including their usual two hours of overtime.

Jorge checked his phone while we waited. "Everyone's going to the bar. You coming this time?"

I didn't want to have this conversation again, but I had no excuse to avoid it. "I don't think so."

"Look, I know you're still kind of new to this, but the guys are starting to think that *you* think you're too good for them."

I'd explained to Jorge at least a dozen times that I was not interested in getting drunk and hitting on barflies. Jillian had never gone out with them, either. "Even if I liked going to the bars around here, I sure as hell wouldn't be going today."

"See, that's where we're different," Jorge said. "All I want to do is drink until I forget about it."

We heard bootsteps and turned around. A DPS officer was walking beside Zak, who motioned for Jorge and me to join them on their way to Redbeard.

"Sergeant, this is Jorge and his helper, Beck," Redbeard said. "Beck found her, then called Jorge and Zak over."

The sergeant took off his beige cowboy hat and shook our hands.

"Gentlemen, I know you probably want to get out of here after what you saw, but I have to get your statements before we can let you go." The sergeant pulled a notebook from the breast pocket of his khaki uniform. "I'm sure you understand."

He asked to speak with me first, so we stepped a few yards away from Jorge and Zak. Redbeard had already left in his pickup to fetch a cold thirty-pack at the nearest convenience store.

"I take it Beck is your last name?" the sergeant asked.

"Yes. My full name is Bartholomew John Beck."

He chuckled. "Well, that's a new one. I'll need you to give me that first name one letter at a time."

"I get that a lot." I spelled it slowly, then raced through my worst morning in twenty years.

MY BLACK SEDAN was parked along the curb next to Jorge's house. There was a slight disconnect when I thought about the bachelor I met in college now paying a mortgage. He had talked me into making my liver work overtime on the weekends during my final years at a North Texas state school. I was still trying to write the next *In Cold Blood* and thought earning a bachelor's in English lit and an Iowa Writers' Workshop MFA would bolster my credibility. I never made it to Iowa City.

Jorge didn't share my academic ambition. He was attending a two-year technical school nearby but hung out with the university students. He got to know campus intimately by doing the walk of shame, though he rarely felt the shame. How we met was a matter of debate, but we spent the better part of my junior and senior years tearing up that college town.

Despite his responsibilities, vestiges of the party boy I once knew remained. In the fifteen minutes it took to get to his house, Jorge took three calls from other welders asking why he wasn't at the bar yet. He pulled up next to my car and didn't bother to park. He needed to make a clean getaway before his wife got home.

I told him I was going inside to nap on the couch, which was now doubling as my bed—a massive improvement over my previous accommodations in Jorge's travel trailer. I wanted to tell him what was on my mind, but I also didn't want to burden him.

He could put it together if he'd bothered to read my first true crime bestseller. Jorge was a loyal patron and had paid for a copy of all four books I'd written—he and my parents were just about the only people to buy the last one about a love triangle gone wrong in Lubbock—though I knew he hadn't cracked any of them open.

Earlier that year, he'd asked me when the next one was coming out. I hadn't had any bites in more than two years, and my agent no longer took my calls. Jorge had much better career news. Texas and Oklahoma were in the middle of an oil and natural gas boom, and companies couldn't hire enough welders. He said he could help me get out of my financial hole—and the general funk caused by a writer's isolation, combined with the lack of a social life—and offered me a job as his helper. I'd said for years that I trusted Jorge with my life. And even though I wasn't proficient with them, I'd grown up around power tools thanks to my father. The prospects seemed brighter than writing another manuscript that wouldn't sell.

Jorge sped off, and I walked to the back of my car. I always kept some paperbacks in the trunk to sell for cash, and I still had about sixty dollars in my wallet from sales at the job site.

I dug down to the bottom of a cardboard box and pulled out my first book, *Cold Summer: The true story of a murder that rocked the Texas Hill Country.* On the cover was an Associated Press photo doctored to appear black-and-white except for a red tool shed—a wood structure built to look like a miniature barn—to the right of a dilapidated doublewide trailer.

I flipped to the third chapter, the one where I described the crime scene. I skimmed the pages until I found the relevant paragraph.

Det. Roland's eyes scanned Summer Foster's body. They started at the feet, which were both pointed to the left, toward the shed that held Butch Heller's tools. The veteran lawman's eyes drifted up her calves until they met at her knees, which were covered by her thin, flowery dress. She was laying on her side, like she was merely sleeping one off after a long Fourth of July celebration. But as Det. Roland's eyes got to her face, the images caused his stomach to turn. The right side of her head had been bashed in—crime scene investigators would later find a short, two-pound sledgehammer covered in blood spatter—and a screwdriver was sticking out of her right eye, pointing toward the shed from which it had been removed.

I could never forget those crime scene photos or the conversation with Detective Jimmy Roland, now retired from the Hinterbach Police Department. But memories deteriorate. I'd seen that evidence, conducted that interview—and dozens of others—and written those words nearly two decades ago. I was barely eighteen and had not yet graduated high school.

I had one more passage to read, from the third-to-last chapter. Most of the book was in the third person, but I slipped into first-person when the narration included my own experiences. In this passage, I described my participation in the trial that put Butch Heller on Death Row. I was eighteen.

I had never been on a witness stand. I'd never even made a speech at a podium or been questioned in the principal's office. Though District Attorney Martin Gamble had asked all the questions before, prepping me for the moment, I was so nervous I nearly forgot my full name.

I'd gone by my last name only, Beck, for several years. Even my parents had dropped my first and middle names. It was a family tradition. I only heard my full name when my mother was scolding me.

Remembering that led me to the correct "answer" to the DA's question: Bartholomew John Beck.

Much of the early questioning established who I was. We concluded that, at the time of Summer's murder, I was a sixteen-year-old, soon-to-be junior at Hinterbach High School, where she was the librarian. I was also Summer's neighbor, and our family had known her since before I was born. I also knew Butch Heller, Summer's off-and-on live-in boyfriend for years, and I was able to identify him sitting at the defendant's table. They seemed to have been mostly off leading up to the events of July 4, 1999, but I remembered seeing Heller around for a week or so before that night.

I had been prepared to give the next answer, but I still took a few deep breaths after being asked, "What do you remember about the night of July 4, during the town's fireworks celebration?"

I looked up from the page, my adrenaline making it hard to focus. But I had a feeling someone would question me about Summer's murder soon. I needed to make sure the memories were fresh.

"I wasn't in the mood to celebrate," I said. "My parents had gone to a twelve-pack party across the street. I'd stayed behind at our house, but I eventually decided I needed to stop being such a shut-in. I wanted to enjoy the fireworks, and maybe go over to Miss Foster's house to hang out with my friends. They were going to come back after the show to sneak beer. I was watching the fireworks from our front lawn when I saw Mr. Heller drive up. He drove up on Miss Foster's front lawn and almost hit her fence. Then I noticed Miss Foster smoking a cigarette in the side yard, next to her tool shed. I watched Mr. Heller walk up to her, though it took a while because he was swaying a lot. I could hear Mr. Heller yelling between fireworks going off.

"I had seen this sort of thing a few times, and I never got in the middle of it. But then I saw Mr. Heller grab her and throw her to the ground. That was new to me, though I'd heard my parents talk about how Mr. Heller would sometimes 'get physical' with Miss Foster. I

guess I decided that I should go help her. I started walking over and lost them behind the cars parked by her house. When I got past the cars, I saw that he had her by one of her ankles and had dragged her half into the tool shed. I kind of freaked out and froze. I'm not proud of that. Then I saw her leg drop like he'd let it go, but then he came out of the shed and swung down on her with something, like a hammer or a hatchet. It looked like he'd hit her in the head, but she was able to crawl. Mr. Heller stood over her and hit her in the head again a couple more times before she stopped moving.

"I stayed still, and I guess he couldn't see me. He went back into the tool shed, and I heard noises like he was throwing stuff around and screaming. Then I saw him come out and kneel beside her. I think he was crying, but I can't be sure. The fireworks got real loud at the end. I'd finally worked up the courage to walk over when I saw Mr. Heller raise both hands and stab Miss Foster. He stood back up kind of wobbly, then took off running.

"Once he was gone, I went over to Miss Foster to try and help her. But it was too late. She wasn't moving, and there was a long screwdriver sticking out of her right eye. I ran inside her house and found a phone to call 911."

Before my testimony, the medical examiner said Summer died almost immediately after the sledgehammer's final impact with her temple, so she probably didn't feel the screwdriver penetrate her cornea. That made me feel better.

As I closed the cover, I hoped the same was true of Jillian.

4

Site Two was closer to Jorge's house, so the next morning's ride should've been shorter. But even the quickest route was far from direct, and more than half of it was along a winding trail through hilly ranchland. The gate separating that path from the nearest county road was secured using a rotating contraption with eight padlocks. We'd missed our 6:30 to 6:45 a.m. window, when one of the bosses was posted at the gate to let workers onto the private property.

Part of me would've been fine with missing some work. I hadn't held regular work hours in years, and the last few months had not converted me into a morning person. But we didn't want to face the humiliation of showing up late. "So, what do we do?"

"Relax, bro. It's not a big deal. Get out so you can hold the gate." Jorge jumped down and shuffled in his flip flops. I trailed behind but couldn't see what he did to open the gate, though it looked like he was working a novelty-size combination lock.

Jorge clapped at me like a football coach trying to encourage his team. "Come on. I'm going to have to haul ass to get there on time."

Jorge barely slowed down enough for me to close the gate

and jump into the passenger seat. He revved the supercharged engine so hard it sounded like a jet as we climbed over the first of two hills, leaving a sandstorm in our wake. Jorge liked to take advantage of the crisp morning air by driving with his windows down in the morning, but I rolled mine back up when the dust made me cough.

I tried to grab a few more minutes of shut eye, but as we raced down the hill the truck rocked so hard the side of my head smacked the window. Jorge laughed when I started cursing.

We crested the second slope about three minutes later. More than twenty trucks were parked in the middle of the patchy pastureland. There were also two large track hoes, black King Kong arms with their fists resting on the ground, flanked on each side by piles of painted pipe fittings—red ones bent ninety degrees while green ones had a forty-five-degree tilt—and similarly colored valves resting on pallets.

The vehicles were facing a gathering crowd of welders, helpers, labor hands, inspectors, straw bosses, bosses, and supervisors. We stopped near the back of the impromptu parking lot and began walking. Even several rows from the epicenter, we could hear the murmur from dozens of conversations in English and Spanish. The chatter died down as we approached the huddle and Redbeard started speaking.

"Listen up. By now, I'm sure y'all know that a helper was found dead at Site One yesterday. We don't know what happened yet, but the police have told us we're no longer allowed there because it's a crime scene. So, for now, everyone's going to report here in the morning."

He turned and motioned toward the new yard.

"The police let us bring all the pipe and fittings we need here. We'll spend most of the morning getting it all organized. Some of y'all might have to go talk to the cops. I have no idea if or when that'll happen. But we *will* do everything we can to help them, understand?"

The demand was met with a collective nod. Redbeard started

sending groups off with new instructions until it was just the welders and helpers left, except for Zak. Jorge and I hurriedly found the clipboard and signed our names.

"Zak's not here today," Redbeard said. "He went straight to Site One to talk with the police. I don't know if he'll be back today, so you're all getting ten hours of ass time while we get things situated."

The news was met with a collective groan, and we meandered as slowly as possible to our respective trucks.

"I hate days like this," Jorge said. "They go by so slow."

I was thankful I would get to sleep through the morning. I tossed my phone onto the center console, climbed into the cab, and leaned the seat back in preparation for a long nap.

"Hey asshole, don't go to sleep. Stay up and keep me company. What movie do you want to watch?" Jorge had unlimited data that was connected to his satellite TV service. Many welders had the same setup specifically for this situation.

I kept my eyes closed but knew I had to answer. Otherwise, he'd keep screwing with me and keep me awake anyway. "What're our choices?"

Jorge rattled off titles as I drifted to sleep. He had what seemed like a hundred movie channels to get through, and I'd already picked one. Sleep had nearly taken hold when I heard Jorge answer a phone.

"Hello, Beck's phone."

My eyes shot open. I reached toward Jorge, but he pulled away. "Yes, he's right here. Hold on a second."

"Dude, what are you doing?"

Jorge covered up the bottom half of the cellphone. "It's a girl. Who's Veronica Stein? She sounds sexy."

I motioned for him to hand me the phone, which he did while nodding and mouthing, *Hell yeah.*

"Veronica, hi. It's Beck."

"Did you get a new job or something? I thought I called your cell."

"You did. That was... don't worry about it." I shot a look at Jorge. He was pulling up the movie and didn't look at me, but he smiled.

"I read your story when it was published in July. I liked it," I said. "Was there something else you needed?"

Veronica was a reporter for the *Lone Star Ledger*, a nonprofit journalism website based in Austin. She was young, but a hell of a writer. Just before going to work with Jorge, I was her source for a story about the twentieth anniversary of Summer Foster's murder.

"I'm working on another article," Veronica said. "Last time we spoke, we talked about Butch Heller's execution date."

"I remember."

"My editors have asked me for a deeper investigation into the case. It has to run in a week at the latest. I've already done most of the interviews, but I'd like to get your voice in there, for obvious reasons."

I opened my mouth but stopped short of agreeing to another interview. The rights to *Cold Summer* had reverted to me long ago, and I'd self-published a second edition. I stood to get a much larger cut of any spike in sales, like the one right after her article ran in July.

The same was bound to happen with any new stories about the case. People still remembered the murder. And more recently, Butch Heller had been in the national news for being the next to die on Texas' Death Row. As the presidential election loomed, liberals had decided to make the death penalty a major social issue. The state, as might be expected, was vigorously defending its policy, and national news outlets were feeding on the debate.

But I suspected Veronica had a different hunger. She'd be trying to prove Heller was innocent, hoping her work would lead to a stay from the governor. A story casting doubt on Heller's guilt would go viral, and she might get her own book deal, then a documentary if her story was successful. Everyone covering crime these days wanted their own Netflix or HBO docuseries.

"Mr. Beck?"

Veronica was trying to prove I was a liar. I had to stall. "You caught me at a bad time. Can I call you back later today? Tomorrow at the latest, I promise."

"No problem at all. If you could make it today, even if it's late, that would be best."

Jorge barely let me end the call before bombarding me with questions. Who was she? Was she hot? Had I slept with her? Did she have any hot friends? Why didn't I keep talking to her? Was she hot?

I deflected and told him to start the movie from the beginning. He let my conversation with Veronica go undiscussed for the moment, but we both knew he'd interrogate me later.

As we sat watching an aging rock star and a future pop icon fall in love, I weighed the pros and cons of calling Veronica back.

WE PULLED up to Jorge's house at 5:25 p.m. after spending all ten hours at Site Two and grabbing a twelve-pack—and two cheladas—from a convenience store on the way. I followed Jorge into his cozy home. He needed every square inch, especially with me on his sofa. Jorge and his wife had three girls, all under five years old and as hyperactive as he still was. Each girl had her own dog, and the family shared a cat and a potbelly pig named Hambone. I called him Hammy, which always caused a playful argument with Jorge's middle daughter.

Hammy was relegated to an addition Jorge was building in the back of the three-bedroom, two-bathroom house. Some part of the house had been under construction for more than two years, but he swore this addition would be the last. We both knew he was lying.

I flopped down on my side of the leather sectional while he

took up his post on the matching loveseat. He cracked open one of his cheladas and handed me a beer as all three daughters dogpiled him.

I took the beer out of courtesy, but I was already staring at my phone. I'd pulled up the story Veronica had written a couple months ago. It was published on the third of July, one day shy of twenty years. I needed to read the story again, to get a feel for the type of reporter Veronica was, before calling her back.

Even on the mobile version of the *Ledger*'s website, the design was slick. The headline—MURDER ON THE FOURTH OF JULY: SUMMER FOSTER, BUTCH HELLER AND THE DEATH THAT TURNED HINTERBACH INTO A CULTURAL LIGHTNING ROD—was superimposed on the same AP photo that adorned my cover.

That photo remained the background as I scrolled to read the opening paragraph.

Hinterbach was still a quiet town during the first week of July 1999. City Hall had no sanctioned fireworks show planned for Independence Day, but the volunteer fire department and city council had a long tradition of teaming up to produce a short program just after dusk. Like every other year, it would take place near the banks of the large creek that runs through town. Those who hadn't traveled to Kerrville for its larger show often gathered outside to watch during their private celebrations. Summer Foster, the town's beloved high school librarian, was doing just that on July Fourth. But as the rockets' red glare streaked across the Hill Country sky, Foster was brutally killed by her live-in boyfriend outside their trailer near the heart of Hinterbach. The murder landed Butch Heller on Death Row and thrust the sleepy municipality into the national spotlight, sparking changes to both that are still felt two decades later.

I was jealous. Though she had more hindsight, and an education from The University of Texas, I liked Veronica's introduction better than mine. I still think I had the better title, even if it was derivative.

The rest of her first section laid out the events of that night as given by police, prosecutors, and me. They were essentially the same as in *Cold Summer*. Some of the paragraphs were lifted from my book, properly credited and used with my permission. I also provided a couple of fresh quotes, though they were purposefully dull.

Scrolling down to the second section revealed a new background: the most recent AP mugshot of Butch Heller, supersized and given a black-and-white filter, with the subhead 'IT WASN'T ME' superimposed below his doughy, mustachioed face.

Heller admitted to being nearly blackout drunk that night, breaking a brief brush with sobriety, but said he drove up to Summer's trailer and found her already dead. He said he stumbled to a neighbor's house and incoherently asked to call the police. It was a version of events he'd been repeating for twenty years. But with me—a solid eyewitness—and the physical evidence he left at the scene, it never held much weight.

Next, Heller's defense attorney laid out a plausible alternative suspect. The lawyer, boisterous Austin attorney "Action" Jackson McGrady, was much more convincing. He provided "evidence" that Summer's ex-boyfriend, Franklin Jones, had been the jealous man who bashed in her skull and left a screwdriver in her eye. First, McGrady pointed out that Summer had taken out a restraining order against Jones two years prior. It expired the day of her murder. A photo of the court document was embedded next to that paragraph. McGrady then claimed to have dug up a purchase order from a body shop in Kerrville, where Jones had been living, showing the prominent banker had taken his new BMW coupe there for fender work and new upholstery. The order was expedited for a hefty fee, according to another document that was also embedded next to the text. I used my index finger and thumb to zoom in on the image. The name of the body shop didn't sound familiar.

McGrady argued that Jones had lost control of his Beamer as he sped away after killing Summer, then got the interior redone to get rid of physical evidence. Finally, Action Jackson pointed out that Heller is right-handed, while Jones is left-handed. Summer's fatal injuries were to the right side of her head and face, indicating the killer was a southpaw.

None of it could be used in court, but it was compelling circumstantial evidence. Veronica followed McGrady's comments with a line stating neither Jones nor any member of local, county, or state law enforcement commented when she asked whether Jones was ever a suspect. The FBI offered a one-liner saying all evidence gathered during the investigation had been turned over to the district attorney's office, which would have to provide any further information.

All those agencies had commented to me just after Heller's trial. I pointed out in *Cold Summer* that the DA's office and the FBI had ruled Jones out as a suspect, but Veronica had left that out. She'd already started her own narrative, subtly hidden in what had otherwise been a straightforward breakdown of the case.

Heller's section of the story ended with a more personal touch. Veronica broke the fourth wall and told readers she visited Heller on Death Row at the Polunsky Unit in Livingston. She'd been allowed to film the interview, in which he talked about his life there for nearly two decades.

Heller then described what he thought would be his final day on Death Row, the drive from Livingston to Huntsville, and final hours just outside the execution chamber, where he spoke with a chaplain and ate his final meal.

He was saved by an eleventh-hour stay from the U.S. Supreme Court ten years after his arrest.

"I went through the whole dog and pony show," Heller said. "I had my last visitors, was read my last rights, was served my last meal.

"They did everything but kill me."

Heller's last meal feels like it was ordered off a menu of favorites from each region of Texas: chicken fried steak, a salad with ranch dressing, fried catfish, three barbacoa tacos with refried beans and rice, a barbecue bacon cheeseburger, and a comically large chocolate milkshake. (In 2011, the state revoked the right to a custom last meal. They are now given the same chow as the rest of the inmates in the Huntsville Unit.)

Heller said he ate the meal while sneaking glances into the chamber. He could see the cross-shaped table and restraints where he was to spend his final moments.

"I could see my own ghost while I picked at my salad," he said.

The man convicted of killing Summer Foster was about 10 minutes from having his death sentence carried out. One of his final acts was calling four people from his cell with the aid of a prison chaplain. Among those who received calls from Heller were two unnamed women he'd corresponded with through prison letters, an Ethel McDonough in rural Nimitz County, and newly sworn-in U.S. Rep. Grant Schuhmacher.

Heller, who claimed to be a born-again Christian, was read his last rights and said he'd taken "at least three steps" toward the execution chamber, which would've been about halfway there. Texas Department of Criminal Justice officials said he was never let out of his holding cell.

The Supreme Court granted his stay so more DNA testing could be done. The justices unanimously agreed with the Innocence Project's argument that a significant amount of testing was skipped during the original investigation, though DNA had been the hot new scientific advance of the decade.

I thought back to the original trial. The prosecution brought in an FBI expert to explain the concept of DNA to the jury. It was easy to see that none of them understood the science, but they didn't need to. All the jury needed to know was that Summer's blood was found covering Heller's hands and clothes when he was found on a neighbor's porch that night.

But that was the only testing done. Heller's advocates had pointed to several items at the crime scene, and an untested rape kit performed on Summer's body. The Supreme Court agreed.

But two years after the testing was completed, a judge from the Western District of Texas denied the appeal again. Though the judge didn't explain his decision publicly, state prosecutors later leaked that most of the items tested were inconclusive, and a few items had Heller's DNA on them.

The rape kit, however, showed she had sex with Heller and another man that day. Experts found no evidence of rape, so the existence of another partner strengthened the state's proposed motive for the murder—that Heller thought Summer was cheating.

The third and final section of Veronica's story was about the transformation of Hinterbach from small Hill Country town to a cultural hub and tourist trap. The screen's background changed from Heller's mug to a side-by-side comparison of downtown Hinterbach in 1999 and its present state. One side was desolate with a lonely stoplight and a couple of cars. The other was a bustling street that included hordes of foot traffic on sidewalks beside wall-to-wall shops. I didn't love the section's subhead—FORGING THEIR FUTURE—but the information below it interested me more than any other part of the story.

Veronica first dove into the municipality's history. She even broke down the name in German, and explained the legend of that name, according to town elders.

The name Hinterbach is the collision of two German words: hinter, meaning behind, and bach, meaning creek (or brook, as many would argue based on the phonetics). The name seems geographically appropriate, as the later-named Freddy's Creek bisects the town. However, if you ask about the name's history at the few truly local coffee shops left, older members of the community spin a different yarn.

An octogenarian named Fern, who didn't want to give her last name because "everyone already knows it," said the town's identity was borne from the Hinterkaifeck massacre of 1922 in the German state of Bavaria.

"You know the town wasn't always called Hinterbach, right sweetheart?" Fern asked.

I smiled. Fern was right, both about the town's name and everyone knowing her identity. Fern Falkner had been running a German bakery since my father had been a kid, so there was nobody left in town more qualified to explain the history of Hinterbach. I could hear her asking Veronica that question, like a matriarch about to share a secret family recipe with her daughters and granddaughters, then spending an hour asking more rhetorical questions and waving her graying hands.

The village was originally known simply as Neu Deutschland, or New Germany, until after World War I ended in 1918. According to local legend, many of the returning soldiers didn't want to be reminded of Europe or the war they'd fought there. The town was hit hard by The Great War, with seven of its young men dying overseas. At some point, the creek that runs through town became an informal memorial to one of the village's most popular fallen heroes, Frederick "Freddy" Fischer, and the young men took to calling their hometown Bachland, referencing the brook.

This struggle persisted for years, and Texas maps made between 1918 and 1922 use both names. The fight got heated enough that it was taken up by the state Legislature in late 1922.

By then, six people had been brutally slain at the farm in Germany known as Hinterkaifeck.

The family and their new maid were killed by blows to the head with what Texans would probably call a pickaxe, though the technical term is mattock. The months leading up to the murders are shrouded in possible supernatural events—if you believe that sort of thing—and the murders are still unsolved.

Several suspects have emerged, including two men rumored to have been sleeping with the widow of Hinterkaifeck's owner, Viktoria Gabriel. Perhaps the most intriguing suspect was her late husband, Karl, whose body was never recovered from a World War I battlefield.

No matter the killer, the murders were the stuff of horror movies. In fact, films were made depicting the murders, and the Hinterkaifeck massacre has been made famous again in recent years via the podcast and television series Lore.

I knew the story well and had heard several versions of it in high school. When my friends and I were fourteen and fifteen— when we were trying to make out with girls but none of us could drive—the cool parents would let us have movie nights. During these gatherings, any newcomers were told the story, the details becoming gorier and more terrifying with each version.

When *Lore* featured the Hinterkaifeck massacre, I was one of many who listened and later watched. I wondered if my class-mates also compared the evils that existed in that town to the one that existed in Hinterbach. Was it the people who were bad, or had the towns infected them?

The Bavarian story was so shocking that, in theory, a Neu Deutschland resident or member of the Legislature could have heard about the murders. If they wanted to honor the war heroes' wishes and include "bach" in the official name, marrying "hinter" and "bach" may have seemed reasonable.

"Now, doesn't that make more sense than anything you've ever heard?" Fern asked.

"Yes, ma'am," I said out loud. "It sure does."

Official records indicate Hinterbach was suggested by several members of the town and voted the official name in a close decision.

But it's almost too tantalizing to consider Fern's version, given what happened on July 4, 1999.

Veronica then recounted Hinterbach residents' reaction to the crime in the days following the discovery of Summer Foster's body, as chronicled by the local daily paper. That segued into the general media coverage, which was swift and mountainous. The story even made it to *The New York Times*, which sent a reporter to recount the "blundering investigation" and "rushed" arrest of Butch Heller. The reporter also criticized the town itself: "its appearance, its atmosphere, its general vibe. Hinterbach might as well have a billboard on the highway into town that reads, 'White trash ONLY' and one on the way out saying, 'So glad you decided to leave.'"

The journalist, who was more courteous in person than his writing suggested, had naturally conducted a lengthy interview with me for his piece. I couldn't remember much about him, except that he was wearing a corduroy jacket and a long-sleeved shirt in the middle of July. Even though we spoke inside my air-conditioned house, beads of sweat dripped from his forehead, smudging the notes he'd scribbled in blue ink on his bright yellow legal pad.

In an obvious response to this negative press, and to rid the town of its black eye, the city council—led by Mayor Schuh-macher—began a campaign called *Taking back the Bach*. They immediately passed resolutions to revitalize downtown. Part of the initial series of ordinances outlawed trailer houses within two square miles of what had suddenly become an historic courthouse. That meant Summer's dirty yellow doublewide, which had remained vacant after it became a crime scene, was moved. The town also went all-in on its German heritage, granting massive tax breaks to any business using a German name and peddling German goods and food.

I was an unofficial part of the city council's reformation effort. The mayor essentially organized the group that encouraged me to write *Cold Summer*. He led a contingent of locals—my parents, our high school counselor, and Hinterbach High's junior and senior English teachers—in convincing me to talk with an agent he met after the murder. The book would have to have a happy ending that included the redemption of Hinterbach, thus repudiating the earlier negative accounts of the town.

I probably should've asked more questions, but they were offering me As in all my language arts classes while I worked on the book. It violated state education standards and common sense. But with a hundred-thousand-dollar advance on royalties, which all but assured me a college education and money to get my writing career started, that seemed like a small concession to my family and me.

Two decades later, Hinterbach is one of the top tourist spots in the state, particularly when folks are on their summer vacations. Main Street now has five places to taste locally brewed beer, four storefronts occupied by local wineries, three places to get a bedazzled pet rock, at least two local candlemakers, and a full art gallery.

That stretch of road is where I re-entered Veronica's story. I was a source that could speak about the murder and subsequent investigation. I was also a resident who could discuss the town's changes. I indulged her and, to remind the world that I still existed, went back to Hinterbach. I walked alongside her as we discussed the massive transformation with a *Ledger* cameraman a few yards in front of us. Though my quotes were once again measured and benign—a practice I found safest when speaking about that summer—I made one joke as we walked near downtown.

I skipped ahead to my favorite part of the video.

Will you look at that, I'd said as I pointed to a row of cars parked next to each other. *One Porsche, two Porsche, red Porsche, blue Porsche.*

The camera focused in on a line of four Porsche Boxsters— white, then black, then red, then blue.

When I lived here growing up, we couldn't spell Porsche, let alone imagine seeing one drive down the street.

Most of our conversation got cut, and I caught some flak from the Hinterbach Chamber of Commerce for those comments. But they didn't sue, and neither did the Volkswagen Group. And even if they had, I'd said the cars are synonymous with wealth. That ought to make them happy, right?

I scrolled to the last line of Veronica's article. It was a decent way to wrap up the twentieth anniversary, though this time I read it with an eye toward her future intentions.

Many current and former residents of Hinterbach are waiting for one last chapter before they can close the book on Summer Foster's brutal murder: the mid-September execution of Butch Heller.

The piece seemed to end with some finality. She didn't ask whether Heller was innocent or hint that another stay of execution was possible. I assumed a principled news editor would take that kind of opinion out, though she'd said an editor had assigned her this new investigation. And she'd be looking deeper.

But why did she and the *Ledger* feel the need to re-investigate what had been—no matter how heinous or savage—an easily solved murder?

5

I woke up to Jorge shaking my right shoulder, which had been sore to the touch for months. I was an old man in my new line of work. Exacerbating my age was the fact that I'd led a mostly sedentary life for more than fifteen years.

"Beck, didn't you tell that chick you'd call her back tonight?"

I took in a deep breath and opened my eyes wider to try and focus. "What time is it?"

"It's almost eleven."

It took a moment for his words to register. When they did, I sat up and put on my glasses, which had fallen on the matted carpet. "Yeah, thanks."

"Tell her I said her voice is sexy."

I shook my head. Veronica was going to expand upon the theory that Franklin Jones, not Heller, had killed Summer Foster —a theory that completely ignores my eyewitness testimony. I helped put Heller on Death Row, and I needed him to stay there. I also could not allow Veronica to use her platform to write anything negative about me or *Cold Summer,* whose sales had already nosedived again after the anniversary bump.

I'd fallen asleep working out the details, but there was a chance I could avoid both of those bad scenarios.

I picked up my phone and saw that I had a text. *Hi Mr. Beck, it's Veronica Stein with the Lone Star Ledger. Wanted to remind you about getting back to me tonight. Thank you.*

I tapped on her name.

"Mr. Beck, thank you so much for calling me back."

"Not a problem. And it's just Beck."

"Of course. Have you thought about what we discussed?"

I wanted to tell her that I was upset about being called a liar. But that wouldn't help my cause. More than anything, I needed her to stop working on the story. "I have, and I want to pitch an idea that might seem radical, but it's in your best interest."

"I don't understand. Are you going to provide a comment for my story, or not?"

"No, and it should be obvious why. But, if you give me a few minutes, I think you'll like my idea."

"Why would it be obvious? You don't even know what angle I'm taking."

"It doesn't matter what angle you take. If you're investigating the case any further than I already did, you're saying I am lying, or that I don't know what I saw that night, or that what I wrote was untrue or inexhaustive in some way."

Fingers tapped computer keys. "Hey, we're not on the record," I yelled. "I already said I'm not commenting for your story."

Jorge peeked his head into the living room and put his finger to his lips. The girls were sleeping. I mouthed *sorry*, and he disappeared back into the hallway.

"That's not how it works," Veronica said. "When you're talking to a reporter, you're always on the record unless we *both* agree you're not. I should also let you know that Texas is a one-party consent state, which means I don't have to tell you if I'm recording our conversation."

"You know, shit like that makes people hate journalists."

"Okay, you know what? I don't have to take this." Now she was the one yelling.

I turned my head away from the phone and took a deep breath. I needed to keep her on the line, or my idea was shot. I tried hard to sound sincere. "You're right. I apologize. Can we talk off the record, please?"

"See, was that so hard?"

"You didn't say yes. Are we off the record or not?"

Veronica laughed. "You're a quick learner, Beck. Yes, we are now off the record."

"Thank you. I want to reiterate that I have no comment for any story that will contradict what I wrote in *Cold Summer* and points to any killer other than Butch Heller."

"That sounded fine. Why wouldn't you want that on the record?"

"Because it makes me sound defensive. And, if you're out to prove someone else killed Summer, it'll make me look like I'm involved in a coverup."

"Writing that you declined to comment will have the same effect."

"That's what I wanted to talk to you about."

Veronica paused. "I'm lost again."

"I want to dissuade you from writing whatever story you have in mind about the murder. But, in return—"

"Are you freaking kidding me? I'm done with this conversation."

I blurted out my idea as if it were one long word. "There was a copycat murder yesterday where I work, and I can get you inside access to the investigation."

Silence. I pulled the phone away from my ear and checked the screen. The call timer was still counting. "Are you still there?"

"Yes. I'm trying to see if I have this right. In return for telling my editor I don't want to write the story she *assigned* to me, you claim you can get me, quote, inside access to another murder that just happens to have taken place at your job—though I thought you were essentially self-employed as a true-crime author."

"I understand it sounds radical. But if you'll indulge me for a few minutes, I think I can convince you."

A shorter pause. "I'm listening."

I explained what happened on the job site, minus a couple of details—the fight, the fact I'd discovered Jillian's body, that her murder mirrored Summer Foster's—and began describing what a welder's helper does. I could hear her typing on her computer and imagined her pulling up local news stories. I'd done that earlier, and there were a couple of short articles online. All they said were that local and state authorities were investigating a death on private property near Fritch, but they were enough to lend credibility to my story.

"Assuming you're telling the truth, I still have one question," Veronica said. "How do you plan to give me this golden ticket into the investigation?"

"That's the best part. A welder can bring you onto the job as their helper with no questions asked. Literally none. He gives them your name, you show up to fill out paperwork so they can pay you, and you're in. No background check, no references, no resume—nothing."

Saying it out loud made working on a pipeline sound illegal. "It's all legit, though. I swear."

"You want me to work out there? Using those power tools and doing all that stuff you were talking about?"

I understood why this would scare her, especially if she'd never worked with her hands. But I hadn't touched a power tool since high school and was handling myself well enough. "It's not as bad as it sounds. I bet a third of the helpers on our jobs have been women, and most are better at it than I am." I was fibbing a bit. Maybe a fifth were women, and *all* of them were more competent helpers than me. "Plus, I know a welder. We'll tell him you're desperate for money and that he'll have to do some of the harder work. He'll be thankful to have anyone there to hand him rods and run his temperature."

"See, I don't even know what that means. And would I be replacing the woman who died? This all sounds insane."

"Yes, you'd be helping Paul," I said. "He's our welding partner. He's also an old friend of mine, and he'll be fine with it."

I had no idea if that was true. But Paul needed a warm body to help him, and Jillian had been new, too.

"Okay, let's say all of what you've told me so far is true, and you really can get me out there like you say. How does that help me?"

I smiled as I set the hook. "I see you doing a sort of Gonzo Journalism piece with it. You can do your best Hunter S. Thompson impression, minus the drugs" —though if she wanted some, there was plenty to be found out on the pipeline— "and you can give the details about what kind of work she was doing, ask people what they thought of her, that sort of thing. And I can feed you what I learn from the investigators."

"Why would they talk to you?"

It was my turn to pause. I didn't see any harm in telling her I was one of three people who found the body.

"Me, my welder, Jorge, and our boss found her. I gave one statement to a state trooper yesterday, but I was told the detectives in charge of the case would probably need to talk to me, too. And, though I'm not a journalist, I do have experience interviewing people and will be able to get details out of whoever is in the room."

Even through the phone, I could tell she was close to giving in. "Here's what I think," she said. "I will admit, a fresh investigation will probably be a better story. But, like I said, I was given the Butch Heller assignment and have done a lot of work on it, so I don't know. Let me call you tomorrow."

"Perfect," I said. "Oh, by the way, I forgot to mention that the job pays sixteen dollars an hour for sixty hours a week, including overtime after forty. And seven hundred dollars a week per diem."

What I heard next—a cough and tapping as she crunched the numbers on her computer's calculator, coming up with $1,820 a week before taxes—was the sound of me reeling her in. "And you'll be making all of that on top of whatever the *Ledger* pays you since you'll be on assignment. That also means you'll be expensing things."

"More like they'll use getting paid as an excuse to *not* reimburse me, but I get what you're saying."

I could tell by her voice I'd convinced her of my idea's merits. That's why I saved the bit about the outrageous pay for last. It was a sure way to push any young writer, journalist or otherwise, onto my side of the fence.

We finalized her plan to call me with an answer in the morning. I hung up feeling wide awake, certain that I'd gotten Veronica's mind off Summer Foster and onto Jillian's murder.

Princess, a tiny mop-creature that resembled a miniature dog, pawed at my right hand. She began whining for me to pet her, and the other dogs joined her. Even Hammy chimed in from his kennel in the kitchen, which was covered with a blanket to help him sleep.

I felt bad for causing so much noise but was glad for the company. I'd accomplished my goal, but it was hard to keep out thoughts of the two dead women, and of my own morality. After all, I'd just traded Jillian's death to keep someone from further investigating the murder of Summer Foster.

But I desperately needed to keep Veronica from exhuming that case. Digging up the truth would set Butch Heller free, and that kind of upheaval might be too much to handle.

6

EXCERPT FROM COLD SUMMER

If someone wanted to shine a positive light on Butch Heller, they might call him quixotic. He imagined himself the knight of Hinterbach, perhaps even all the Texas Hill Country, fighting police and small-town corruption. To everyone else, he was a public nuisance, a frequent resident of the city jail's drunk tank, and a man described by many in the community as common trash.

But to Summer Foster, he was the handsome former sports hero, and the only man to ever earn her love. And during the weeks leading up to her death, many neighbors and observers reported positive changes in Heller, including regular attendance at twelve-step meetings held at a church in nearby Kerrville.

Because the Fourth of July is one of the biggest drinking holidays of the year, Heller attended a special meeting at 8:30 a.m. As events would reveal, his short time being a friend of Bill W. was not enough.

According to witness statements, the only thing Heller said after he was found on a neighbor's porch was one simple phrase, repeated several times: "I need to call the police." He offered no confession or claims of innocence before police arrested him. With the exception of asking for a lawyer, Heller remained silent during the initial interrogation, which took place a few hours later after sleeping off the considerable amount of alcohol he'd consumed that evening.

By the time prosecutors presented the case in front of a grand jury, the Hinterbach Police Department, Nimitz County Sheriff's Office, Texas Department of Public Safety, and Federal Bureau of Investigation had gathered enough physical and circumstantial evidence to secure a conviction without any input from Heller.

7
___

BUTCH HELLER

July 4, 1999, 7:45 a.m.

Heller lifted the straight razor, stopping just before it reached his neck. It was a holiday. Maybe shaving wasn't necessary. Plus, by the time the party was wrapping up and Summer was getting in the mood, he'd have that nice two-day stubble she liked. Thoughts of his younger girlfriend mixed with the heat of the shower, and Heller wanted to wake Summer with a kiss between her shoulder blades.

He shook off the feeling and focused on the task at hand. He was up early on the nation's birthday for yet another congregation of former drunkards in Kerrville. Heller didn't want to go, but attendance was mandatory if he wanted to remain with Summer.

Though he wouldn't admit it publicly, Heller was enjoying the benefits of sobriety. His body and face were thinner. His skin had shed its reddish hue. Summer had complimented him on his looks the day before, though the comment was sandwiched between a *you should've stopped drinking a long time ago* and an *I told you so*.

He hadn't argued Summer's decision to kick him out six

months ago—a first for him—but instead started getting clean on his own. Heller had been sober when he returned twenty-three days ago, but he knew she was far from convinced he could stay that way. He had suggested the meetings, not expecting her to believe it would work. But if he attended the twice-weekly meetings, along with completing other honey-do's like rebuilding the rotting front porch, he could move back in.

Heller had been faithful. He'd even been getting dressed up for the meetings—he'd once heard a man say people should *dress for success*—and he was shaving daily, revealing the strong, cleft chin that had helped him get laid so many times as a younger man. Now he wished the facial hair would instead grow on the top of his head.

He walked naked from the bathroom to the closet in their bedroom. Part of him hoped Summer was awake and would appreciate his body. A morning quickie wasn't in the cards, though, as she was still dead asleep on their queen bed. He took a moment to enjoy the sight of a sky-blue comforter exposing her sculpted shoulders and left arm, which she was using as a pillow to support a head of short blonde hair—a new haircut he was still getting used to. No matter the length of her hair, she was stunning. He would've taken her picture if they owned a camera.

He tiptoed around the bed to the closet instead, reaching inside to pull a plain blue T-shirt and a pair of jeans from the shelf above the hangers. Heller slid back around the bed to the dresser, where a pair of socks waited in the bottom drawer—his only drawer, which also held the underwear he wore in winter and whatever else he could fit. Though she'd relinquished some closet space, Summer hadn't given him an equal share of the dresser. He still had to earn that, which was fine for now. Summer's house, Summer's rules.

After dressing and slipping into a pair of sneakers, Heller tried his best to open and shut the door quietly, though that was next to impossible in such an old trailer. As he stepped onto the porch he'd agreed to fix, Heller looked at the lawn he needed to mow again. He didn't know why Summer insisted on that chore. It was just a patch of overgrown weeds.

He kicked up a cloud of dust on his way to a cherry red 1987 Firebird that used to be his pride and joy. He'd gotten it repainted a couple years ago and had an old high school buddy put flame graphics down the side. It still looked perfect, though he hadn't bothered to wash it in months.

———

HELLER SQUIRMED IN HIS SEAT. He'd never felt comfortable in churches, though he wasn't there searching for the Lord and had no reason to feel guilty.

As a boy, Heller's parents had dragged him to a Baptist church, where he slept with most of the girls and women who attended, many of them in darkened rooms during Sunday and Wednesday services. They were in their holy place, and he was in his. Plus, there were few better alibis to give lazy boyfriends and husbands.

He'd attended different churches for the same reasons in his twenties and thirties, but by his early forties he was a devoted boyfriend—except for drunken parking lot hookups when he and Summer were fighting. She'd given up on salvation long ago, so church wasn't a part of their deal.

A man who said his name was Greg led Heller's new meetings. Heller didn't have a sponsor, but Greg would do the trick if Summer ever demanded to meet one. Most of the guys there were regulars, but Heller noted several new faces searching for strength at the only Fourth of July meeting for at least fifty miles.

Heller didn't consider himself one of them. He drank for fun, but everyone else blamed it for some of his most recent troubles.

Greg had been droning on for a while before he said something that caught Heller's attention. "Okay, everyone, we haven't had much participation today. You regulars know I can't let y'all go until we have some speakers. Otherwise, we might's well be going it alone, and we're here because that's not an option. So, who's going to volunteer to speak so we can all go celebrate with our families?"

Twenty seconds of silence passed before Greg shook his head. "All right then, looks like I'm going to have to pick someone. Butch, you're up."

Heller had spoken a few times. He enjoyed holding court and could always make folks laugh. And if it got this thing over with sooner, all the better. He walked to the front of the bland room—which stunk of sweat mixed with that terrible body spray that had become so popular—nodded at the crowd, gave the standard greeting, and got the standard reply.

"You know, I hadn't realized it until the drive over this morning, but today is the six-month anniversary of... well, anniversary isn't the right word for it. Damned if I know what the right word is. Anyway, six months ago this morning, something terrible happened."

Heller had his audience hooked, so he paused for effect. "There I go, using the wrong words again. Six months ago this morning, I *did* something terrible. I won't bring up the details, except the fact that I'd been drinking."

He clenched his fist until the shaking stopped. He'd fibbed—the six-month mark had not snuck up on him—but the feelings bubbling to the surface were real.

"Of course, even that terrible thing wasn't enough to get me to stop cold. I felt guilty, so I drank more. I tried to relieve my guilt by telling my old lady what happened, and she kicked me out. Y'all know what happened then."

Heller saw several heads nodding at him, so he nodded back. "Exactly. I started drinking even more. I started walking around with a bottle. You know what made me finally go a day without drinking? My boss threatened to fire me. I wouldn't've cared, except I didn't want to run out of money to buy more booze. When I started shaking by the end of my shift because I wanted a drink so bad, *that's* when I decided I needed help. *That's* when I started coming here."

A murmur spread through the crowd. "And now I'm staring down the barrel of being sober one month. And I'm damn proud of that."

Heller looked down as the crowd applauded. He'd told the truth for a bit. Every good lie needs to start that way. He had gone on a bender after it happened. The confession to Summer was also real, which had led to her kicking him out of their house. He took some liberties with the story after that, though. Heller didn't fall deeper down the rabbit hole, and his boss never threatened him.

He stopped drinking because he loved Summer.

Heller was Hinterbach's Good Time Charlie, and he knew giving up booze would be a grand gesture, the kind that gets the girl. And getting the girl had been Heller's specialty since he was twelve years old.

HELLER LET SUMMER SLEEP IN. He knew she would be up until well after two a.m. hosting her annual Fourth of July party. They were legendary in the Bach. As the high school librarian, she was one of the most beloved, trustworthy members of the community. Adults would come over before the city fireworks show to pre-game for the festivities, then return afterward to finish off the night.

There would also be plenty of high schoolers there to celebrate with Summer's son, Sammy. Their parents didn't know—or didn't care—that she enjoyed being fawned over by the boys once a year.

Giving her the extra hours was a nice gesture, though any kindness was canceled out by using it as an excuse to slip away without accountability. The meetings sometimes went ninety minutes or longer. But he'd been there less than sixty. It seemed everyone was eager to make the most of their holiday. She wasn't expecting him home for at least another hour.

Heller felt the smallest rush of adrenaline as he passed the turn for Hinterbach. He wasn't going to drink. No drugs would be involved, either. Still, he felt guilty about lying to Summer. But he knew it was for the best.

She wasn't ready to know about the house at the end of County Road K.

8

A buzzing phone disturbed my morning daze. The clock on Jorge's dash read 6:52.

"That was fast."

"Yeah, I emailed my boss last night, and she got back to me early." Veronica was obviously a morning person. Or her coffee had a few extra espresso shots. "I need to work out the details with you and get up there ASAP so we don't miss the exclusive."

I yawned in response. "We're about to get started out here. Can I call you back at ten?"

"I'd rather not wait."

Another yawn. "Fine. What details do we need to work out before you leave?"

"Where I'm staying and what all I'll need to bring to get the paperwork done. I can figure out the rest when I get there."

I hadn't planned on being her babysitter. "The *Ledger*'s not going to put you up in a hotel?"

"Not when I'll be making a per diem there."

"Okay, so use your per diem to get a hotel." I thought Veronica was in her late twenties, but maybe she was younger than I remembered. Why else would I have to walk her through this?

"Yeah, I thought about that. Then I thought about the fact that I'm doing you a huge favor, and how I'd like to keep that seven hundred every week."

Nope. She was no kid. "What are you saying? That if I don't pay for your hotel, you'll talk your boss out of the assignment? How's that going to look?"

Veronica paused. "How about a compromise. You pay for half of a room. But at a decent hotel, not one of those thirty-dollar-a-night roach motels."

I didn't like it. I wasn't making a second income, and I *also* enjoyed pocketing the per diem every week. But I had one more counteroffer I could live with. "Tell you what: We can go half on a decent hotel room, but only if I get to stay in it, too. Two beds, of course."

"Why? Where are you staying?"

"On my friend's couch. He lives nearby, but he doesn't have a spare room."

She responded with a sigh, then silence.

"Hey, if you want me to pay for half a room, I'm going to stay in half that room," I said.

"Fine."

Jorge opened his door. It was 6:59 and everyone was meandering toward the bosses.

"Hey, I have to go. All you need is your driver's license, your social security card, and a blank check for the direct deposit. When will you be here?"

"Tonight."

I opened my door. "Sounds good. I'll text you the address of the hotel around ten." I slipped the phone back into my pocket and hustled to catch up with Jorge.

"So, are you two going to start fucking or what?" he asked.

"Shut up."

"What? You just said you're going to be staying in the same hotel room."

I shook my head. Flashes of us lying in bed together had run through my head after Veronica agreed to the deal, but that wasn't the point. Plus, after the way she'd played hardball, sleeping with Veronica seemed nowhere in my future.

We walked up to the group of about thirty men and Melissa, who'd stayed after learning that Jillian had died. It was murder, though nobody had said it out loud, and the guys figured she would drag up, pipeliner parlance for leaving with no notice. But she could kick most of our asses and liked to present herself as fearless, whether she was or not.

"Listen up," Redbeard said. "We're back to work today. With things on hold at Site One, we're going to work on all the fabrication out here and ramp up excavation out at Site Three. Operators—see me after this meeting so you know who's going where. Labor hands—go holler at Jameson. Welders—Zak is back today, and he'll get you straightened out. Okay, that's it, have a good day out there and stay safe."

We were all about to break up when Zak cleared his throat. "I have something I need to bring up."

Several welders hung their heads and reluctantly began walking back toward the gathering. Zak liked to talk about the same safety issues at every meeting. Even a newbie like me was getting annoyed. It took about a week to get the basic safety rules down. Wear your personal protective equipment, known as PPE. If you're rigging something to be lifted by a hoe or fork truck, do it correctly. Helpers had to worry specifically about making sure disc guards were on the grinders unless they had permission from Zak or a welding inspector. And the golden rule: If you're not sure whether something is safe, ask.

"We had something pretty serious happen that we need to talk about," Zak said. "Now, I know it was crazy yesterday, and it's going to be that way for a little while, but someone left the gate back there wide open. And that's a huge deal."

The group stopped stirring. Zak wasn't reading from his usual script, and we might be in store for a serious ass-chewing.

"There's a lot of cattle and other livestock out on these

ranches, and we are guests on their property. Not only is there money to be lost if any animals get loose, but it's unprofessional. There are only a few of us here with keys, which helps. But from now on, if you open a gate, you stay there and lock it up. No more telling the last guy through to shut it for you. You open it, you're responsible for closing it. Got it?"

We all nodded or mumbled acceptance. Zak began walking toward the collection of welding rigs, and we let him get a few steps ahead.

I thought back and was pretty sure I wasn't responsible. But as tired as I was in the mornings, I couldn't be sure.

"That wasn't us, was it?" I asked Jorge.

"I don't know if it was *you*. But it doesn't sound like they know, either. Or, if they do, nobody's getting fired this time. Don't worry about it."

Zak did not look pleased as we approached. He was about four inches shorter than me, which seemed typical of welders and their helpers. Being tall meant it was harder to get under the pipe. He was still cleanly shaven below a University of Oklahoma ballcap. The lack of his short beard—he must be keeping it off for meetings with the gas company executives, which he no doubt hated—took thirteen years off his thirty-year-old face.

"Look, we're behind," he said. "We don't have the trailers yet to move the hoes from Site One, so we're going to share these. Things are going to be slower than we want, so we'll be working Sundays from now until I say otherwise."

That last bit was met with a mix of groans and excited whispers. Some of the older welders, especially those who lived nearby, valued their days off. The younger ones who traveled in their fifth-wheel campers were happy to get more overtime.

"As for today, Jorge and Paul, y'all go set up on that thirty-inch pipe," Zak pointed about a hundred yards north. "I'll have them bring over a ninety for you to weld on. Everyone else, go to your trucks and I'll come by and let you know when we have you set up for a weld."

Jorge and I walked back to his truck to put on our PPE. It was an unwritten rule that our fire-resistant clothing—referred to as FRs—steel-toed boots, hardhats, gloves, and safety glasses weren't required until after the tailgate meeting.

"Sometimes I wish we weren't teachers' pets," I said.

"Says the kid who used to ask for extra credit."

It was true. I had turned down a party or two when we were younger so I could finish an extra essay assignment. "But Zak doesn't give a shit if I suck up to him. You're the one with the brown nose now."

"Shut up."

I laughed. Jorge knew I was right, but he would never admit it. Flouting authority had been part of his persona. But he now welded as well as possible, seemed grateful to stay busy, and cared about things being precise. He was a craftsman, not just a hired arm like many of the welders. As a result, we were often put to work first and chosen to stay late if needed. On the other hand, we were also given the welds Jorge and Paul preferred. That usually meant bigger pipe and, occasionally, only finishing the weld.

Jorge began slipping on his boots. "You realize you didn't mention anything about FRs or PPE to your new girlfriend."

I was digging in the back looking for my hardhat. "That was on purpose. She'd've tried to get me to pay for half. And she's not my girlfriend."

"Dude, you could get her. Hell, you almost had Jillian. When was the last time you had a girlfriend?"

Jorge did a lot of good-natured shit talking when it came to women, but it was usually soaked in machismo. He rarely asked me such pointed questions.

"I don't know. Maybe a year." I had lied, as I suspected many men did when confronted with their romantic and sexual deficiencies. The real answer was more than three years. She and I broke up right before I sat down to write my last unpublished manuscript, a domestic thriller in which a struggling male writer kills his fiancée after he finds out she's cheating. Let's just say the setup for that novel was eerily similar to how our relationship ended.

My time without companionship was no doubt why I'd seemed desperate to create a spark with Jillian, when all she'd done was be friendly.

Jorge began buttoning up his starched navy shirt. "See, it's time. Anyway, do you need me to take you to my FR hookup? I'm not sure if he has jeans small enough for her, though."

"No, I remember where he lives. Does he sell boots, too? If not, I need to look up how late RedBoots stays open."

"Nope. Just shirts, pants, and overalls. And don't take her to RedBoots if she's a short-timer. Walmart boots will last a week or two."

"Maybe I want her to spend some of that pipeline money early."

We laughed, the seriousness of the conversation giving way to our typical bullshitting.

"You have no idea how to get a girl into bed, do you?"

"Shut up."

We finished putting on our gear, then removed the foil from our breakfast burritos. Jorge bought us breakfast from a convenience store every morning. He bought two for himself, both sausage, and shoved a handful of hot sauce packets in the bag. I always ordered a bacon and potato and could not handle any spicy condiments. But for Jorge, more important than the food was the coffee. He had to get a large cup, infused with French vanilla creamer and sugar. I preferred a tallboy of Arizona sweet tea.

We sipped our drinks and watched a rigger walk up to a large nylon strap—a thick, green loop that looked like a coiled snake—and threaded it through a short piece of orange pipe angled at ninety degrees. Two more riggers attached the strap to the end of a hook on the arm of a track hoe, which lifted the pipe off the ground.

Getting it to us took several tries because the riggers were inexperienced. It was unwieldy, and they had no idea how to handle it. When it arrived, the riggers and welders—with some assistance from me—got the pipe ends mostly matched up using a chain clamp, a spiked collar we used to tame the uncooperative tubes.

That brought us to about 9:15 a.m., followed by an hour of squaring the ninety, which was frustrating for everyone involved. The precision required, combined with the size of the pieces, meant incremental angle adjustments accompanied by constant clanging of metal.

Much of the work was done by the riggers and a group of labor hands. They swarmed to the ends of the pipe, talking quickly in Spanish and giving directions to each other. One gave hand signals to the operator in the hoe, though the uninitiated might think he was attempting shadow puppets.

As a helper, I should have been in the scrum. But I was little help in large groups and always seemed to be in the way.

"What a clusterfuck," Paul said.

"Yeah, these guys don't know what they're doing," Jorge said. "I've got some good news, though." He turned to face Paul. "We found you a helper."

"Already?"

Jorge nodded. "One of Big Nasty's old girlfriends."

"The stripper who sucked him off?" Paul turned to me and laughed.

"Not her." For the first time I was thankful my face was constantly red from sun and arc burn, disguising my embarrassment. I lied smoothly. "We had a thing over the summer, before I started working with y'all. She's green like Jillian was, but she'll be fine."

"You two getting a hotel room?"

"Yessir."

Paul nodded. "Hell yeah. You're finally going to get laid without having to pay for it."

"Well, he *is* paying for half of the room," Jorge said. We all laughed, causing irritated looks from the labor hands who didn't have the luxury of standing around cracking jokes.

I scanned the job site and found Zak explaining a schematic to a pair of welders. I yelled his name and waved him over. Jorge and I told him about Veronica, and he said he'd go get the ball rolling with Captain Redbeard.

"Bring her to the tailgate meeting in the morning and you should be all set," Zak said.

A labor hand got Jorge's attention. They spoke in brisk Spanish and wild gesticulations.

"They're ready for us," Jorge said. "You got everything ready?"

I nodded. I was wrong. I'd laid out six of the tools we usually used. But, as usual, I forgot something. Four somethings. I ended up climbing into Jorge's bed to retrieve items from the toolbox.

First up was a thicker wedge, which was hidden beneath his spare set of welding gloves and the machete. Next was the larger of his two sledgehammers, which was necessitated by the larger wedge. Then came a larger square than the one I'd started with, followed by the even bigger aluminum drywall square, both of which I should've had from the beginning.

After finally getting everything aligned, Jorge welded about five inches on the top while Paul did the same on the bottom. They then tacked their respective sides after banging on the wedge a few more times.

It was only 9:48, but we wasted a few minutes until our government-mandated ten a.m. break, giving me the chance to use my phone and book a hotel room in Borger, the only town in Hutchinson County big enough for the kind of chain hotels Veronica would be expecting. That was fine by me. I chose one close to Jorge's house to reduce the amount of sleep I'd miss driving there in the morning.

It seemed silly, but I felt nervous before composing my text to Veronica. I was tapping out the address of a hotel, which felt like

I was setting up a taboo rendezvous. Then there was the underlying secret of our agreement. The police investigating the crime wouldn't be happy if they found out I'd brought in a reporter to cover the murder. Neither would our bosses.

But the plan was already in motion, so I put my thumbs to work.

Booked a room in Borger. Try to be there as close to 5:30 as possible. We have a few errands to run before tomorrow morning.

I looked at the screen for a few seconds, waiting to see if she would respond right away. I was about to put the phone down when three dots appeared.

Errands?

I smirked.

Need to pick up a couple of things for you to start work right away. No big deal.

Veronica responded almost immediately.

OK. I'm only in Round Rock, but the timing should work out if I speed a little. I'll call when I'm close.

RedBoots closed at six, so we'd be cutting it close. Otherwise, we'd be going to Walmart. I wanted her to spend more money. I normally wasn't so vindictive, but I wanted to get her back for making me spend nearly half of my per diem. I comforted myself with the knowledge she would only spend twenty-five dollars an item for her FR clothes through Jorge's connection, so she'd still come out ahead.

My concentration was broken by the sound of Jorge opening his door. "All right, buddy. Break's over. Go start the machine."

I nodded and put my cellphone face down on his center console, still unsure if bringing Veronica out there was the right course.

I was still contemplating my choices when things started to unravel.

A loud yell carried through the pollution of grinding and welding machines, and we all turned to see Billy James—who wore a gray but well-manicured Fu Manchu—barreling toward Zak.

Billy pointed at Jameson, the young foreman in charge of the riggers and labor hands. "You too, motherfucker." Billy swiped his finger in Zak's direction, telling Jameson to join our boss.

Jameson complied and jogged toward Zak, who looked surprisingly calm in the presence of an angry man who liked to brag about his days as a defensive end at Angelo State. Jameson, who was at least six-foot-four and was easily thirty years younger than Billy, looked like he wanted to duck behind Zak.

A dozen people sprinted toward the commotion, and two other welders were holding Billy back by the time I got there. He was still pointing, his anger directed mostly at Jameson.

Zak was trying to diffuse the situation. "Billy, I agree that it was partly the riggers' fault."

"Riggers? Riggers?" Billy yelled. "I haven't seen any riggers on this fucking job. I see a bunch of kids who don't know what the fuck they're doing. And the one in charge is younger than my goddamn machine."

Jameson was usually cocky and full of bluster, but he had given in to his instinct and was standing behind Zak.

Zak, however, was used to dealing with angry welders. And, as it turned out, he was the one who'd set Billy off. "Look Billy, the decision to run off your friends was mine. Were they brought the wrong fitting? Yes. But they also welded it on the wrong direction, and I'd just got done explaining it to them."

"So what? That's not enough to run them off, and you know it."

Zak held up his hand, like he'd done to me the week before. "That's going to be their third cutout and repair. And as many welders as there are looking for work out there, that's all I can allow."

"Those other two were bullshit. One was his helper not knowing how to work a fucking grinder."

"And the other was an arc mark."

Billy lowered his finger and voice but remained loyal to his friends. "They don't know how that happened. It's bullshit and you know it. But whatever. I guess they didn't suck the right boss' dick."

Zak walked over and patted Billy on the back. "I understand why you're pissed. Go take a walk and calm down. Then, if you're still upset, we can talk about it."

The bystanders all began gossiping. Who got fired? What happened? Was Billy next? Speculation was rampant, and nobody seemed to have solid answers. I was so engrossed I barely felt the tap on my left shoulder.

"Beck, they need you back over at Site One," Zak said.

"Okay, let me go get Jorge, and we'll drive over."

Zak shook his head. "No, they said to only bring you. Go tell Jorge he won't have you until at least after lunch. Tell him to find a labor hand who can help him for a while."

"Sure thing. But did they tell you why they only need me?"

"It's the Texas Rangers this time. I think they're doing that thing where they talk to us one at a time. Stupid cop bullshit. Anyway, run and tell Jorge, then meet me at my truck."

SITE ONE WAS a sprawling patch of land that had been a working compressor station a few decades ago. The skeletons of the old compressors looked like a parade of giant, square elephants with their trunks turned skyward. The trunks were large exhaust pipes, and the bodies were enormous engines once used to push oil downstream. The crude ended up at one of the major refineries in the Panhandle, West Texas, or Oklahoma.

The compressors were in the distance as we rocked in our seats while his pickup crossed a cattle guard. We continued down the dirt road that led to a large tin building surrounded by vehicles, including an SUV with Texas Department of Public Safety written across the side.

"The cops have set up shop in the main building," Zak said. "They interviewed me in here this morning before sending me after you. I have to go get Jorge next. I'm going to spend all damn day driving back and forth."

I liked Zak, but I felt no sympathy for him. I had my own problems. "You said it was the Texas Rangers?"

"Yep. I guess they figured even the sheriff wouldn't be able to handle it. Or maybe the sheriff called them. Either way, they're the ones who grilled me this morning, though there wasn't much to say. I hope they're done with you quick, too."

I didn't bother to tell him it would be a while.

Zak led me into the building, which looked like a normal office on the inside. I shook my head at a sign that read *Employees are our most important product!* on the drywall, which was painted that pale blue meant to make workers feel like they're outside and not in a corporate coop. We wound our way through a corral of drab, gray cubicles to a small conference room in the back corner.

I peeked my head inside the open door and saw a man and a woman sitting at the far end of the long table. They were dressed like a rich oilman and his tomboy daughter—western in theme, but formal enough to be doing million-dollar deals at a downtown bank, their beige cowboy hats resting on the table. They stood as Zak and I walked around the table toward them.

The woman, who looked about my age, met me with a warm smile and an outstretched hand. "Mr. Beck, it's a pleasure to meet you. My name is Caroline Walker. Let's avoid the Chuck Norris jokes if we can, please."

That got me smiling. I loosened up a little, which I suppose was the point. "Yes ma'am. A pleasure to meet you."

I turned to the man, a portly balding gentleman who looked to be in his early fifties. He wasn't holding out his hand. He must be playing Bad Cop. I glanced behind me to see if Zak was still there, but he'd already left and shut the door behind him.

"Bart, please take a seat. My name is Lieutenant Owen Johnson. Most folks call me OJ."

"Yes, sir. By the way, most people call me Beck." What I didn't say was that I loathed being called Bart.

"Noted," he said. "So, Bart, why'd you kill her?"

9

I f I'd been hooked up to a lie detector test, Lieutenant Johnson would've cuffed me on the spot. I tried to ignore the adrenaline and focus. Despite how my body was reacting to his question, I hadn't killed Jillian.

My brain couldn't find the man's name. For some reason Agent Orange sounded right, but I thought twice about calling him that. "I didn't, sir."

He smiled at Walker, who slid him a dollar. "I told you he wouldn't make it easy on us." Agent Orange pocketed the bill. "No matter how dead to rights they are, killers never just confess when I ask."

Walker opened a leather portfolio and acted like she was reading notes. "The reason we ask, Mr. Beck, is we have half a dozen witnesses who saw you assault the woman they knew as Jillian Rogers less than four hours before she died."

Shit. I was going to end up in handcuffs without the polygraph. "I know how that looks, but it's not what you think."

Agent Orange leaned in. "So, you didn't grab her and yell at her before she slapped you in the face and told you—" he lifted the top page of his pad "—we're over."

I lowered my gaze and shook my head. "Yes, she did. But it was an act. I'd just—"

"It's okay, Bart, no need to come up with a story. It doesn't matter why you two fought. We've got plenty more to discuss." He looked back down at his notes. "It says here after discovering the body, you immediately told Zak and your friend Jorge that you'd found the woman everyone called Jillian."

"Right, Jillian."

"How did you know it was her? The injuries and decomposition of the body made it nearly impossible to ID her by sight."

Walker slid two pictures over to me. I felt the knot in my stomach slide up my throat. Seeing the photos side-by-side, I understood his question. "I was assuming. She hadn't shown up for work that morning and nobody could reach her."

He and Walker stared at me, content to let my weak explanation hang between us. I was familiar with the interview trick, but I had no idea how effective it was.

I broke first. "Look. I don't know how, but my brain made the connection. I mean, I was right, wasn't I?"

Agent Orange nodded. "You were. And that's a red flag for me."

I opened my mouth to protest, but he cut me off. "Where were you Friday night?"

I finally calmed down a bit. I had an alibi with five witnesses. Ten if I counted the pets. "I was with Jorge. I'm staying with him and his family, and I'm there every night."

"So, one of your oldest friends and his family are your alibi. No other corroboration."

I wanted to ask if he was seriously accusing me of killing Jillian. "Yep, just Jorge and his family," I said instead. "Check my cellphone records. The GPS will show me at his house, and it was connected to his internet the whole time."

Agent Orange's lips parted, revealing yellowing teeth and the remnants of his morning dip of snuff. "You're smarter than most of the killers we deal with. We're checking all that, but those records don't come in a day. I'm sure we'll have you locked up long before we get that information." He leaned back. "Besides, a smart true-crime writer like you would know to leave your phone behind."

Heat rushed from my chest to my hands and face.

"You know, I read that book of yours when it came out," he said. "It was good. People usually get a lot wrong when they write about an investigation, but you got close."

If he'd read *Cold Summer*, Agent Orange knew about the similarities in the bodies. But I was going to make one of them say it. "I appreciate that."

Before he could respond, Walker took back her photos and slid them neatly back into her portfolio. "Let's say I believe you, Mr. Beck. Even if you weren't angry at her for turning you down, and even if your phone indicates you were at your friend's house all night Friday, how do you explain finding her body in almost the same way you found *another* dead woman twenty years ago."

I took a moment to think, then told them the truth. "I've been asking myself that question, and I have no idea."

Agent Orange's gross smile returned. "Well, I guess that's all she wrote. Or he wrote, in this case."

I shook my head. "You'd've already arrested me if you could. I know you don't believe me, but I didn't do this. I hope you're looking into other suspects."

Orange opened his mouth, but Walker cut in. "You're right, we don't believe you. But at this early stage, we do need to investigate multiple possibilities. If you want to get on our good side, you could start by being cooperative."

I searched her eyes. She wasn't as hellbent on arresting me as her partner. I needed to cultivate Walker as an ally. "Okay. What else do you want to know?"

"Who on the job site knows you wrote that book?" she asked.

"A lot of people. Jorge knows, and he's been telling everyone about me and my writing. He's even helped me sell copies to some of the guys."

"By sold some copies, do you mean in person, here?" Walker nodded through the walls to the stalled site.

"Yes, ma'am. I keep paperbacks in my trunk."

"So, they were cash sales?"

I started chewing the inside of my lip. They probably didn't care I was ducking the IRS and state sales taxes, but I still didn't like admitting it. "Yes."

"I'm guessing you didn't give out receipts we could see, so we would have a record of who might've read about the screwdriver?"

I lowered my eyes. "No."

"That's okay. We'll let you and the IRS work that out." Walker pulled a white pad from the portfolio and slid it to me with a pen. "But can you write down the names of everyone you can think of who got a copy of *Cold Summer*?"

I did as she asked, though some of the names were misspelled and included descriptions like *the short labor hand with the tattoo on his neck* and *the track hoe operator with the long beard.*

When I looked back up, Walker asked how well I knew Jillian.

"Not very," I said. "She was Paul Schuhmacher's welder's helper, and we all worked together during the day. I was trying to get to know her better during our breaks, but we only talked at work, and she'd only been there a few weeks."

"How did Mr. Schuhmacher know her?"

"He told us he found her on the Internet. I think she'd put out an ad on Craigslist or Facebook."

Walker started taking notes. "What else did you know about her?"

I thought for a moment. It made me sad to think about it, but other than the fact she was sabotaging the job, she hadn't revealed much to me. I thought about telling them why we fought that afternoon, but they seemed to be backing off. No need to add any other suspicious elements to the mix. "She seemed nice, but I only know her name and that she was from the Austin area."

"Well, at least you finally told the truth about one thing," Agent Orange said. "She is from Austin."

It took me a moment to process what he'd said. One thing. And they'd kept saying people knew her as Jillian. "Was her name not Jillian Rogers?"

"Stop playing dumb," Orange said. "You know her name was Sylvia Davenport."

Orange smelled blood again, but I was too confused to worry about him. "No, I didn't. She told everyone her name was Jillian."

"She did try to hide her identity, yes," Walker said.

I shifted to face her directly. "Do you know why?"

"No," Walker said, drawing a harsh look from Agent Orange.

"Sorry, I don't mean to pry," I said. "It's what I do. Well, used to do."

Agent Orange stood and cleared his throat to stop my conversation with Walker. "We're done for now." He opened the door and they walked out to Zak, asking him to take me back and pick up Jorge.

Orange stared me down as I followed Zak back through the maze of cubicles. Walker's look was softer. But even if her gut believed me, I knew her brain wouldn't let her count me out as a suspect. On paper, I was guilty.

I tried telling myself I was the victim of a set of terrible coincidences. But as I climbed into Zak's truck, I couldn't shake the sinister feeling that someone was framing me by summoning the ghost of Summer Foster.

10

EXCERPT FROM COLD SUMMER

Though Summer didn't work in June and July, she usually woke up early—either with Heller or her son, depending on who was working at the time—but there was no need on July 4, 1999. She knew Heller would be going straight to his meeting, and she could sleep through his morning routine. Sammy had stayed the night with a friend across town, and they'd no doubt sleep in as well. She wasn't expecting to see them until the cookout that afternoon.

Her mornings were usually filled with daily chores. She was known to jog around town in the early morning before thoroughly cleaning her trailer and doing the household laundry. Then she would buy groceries, get the mail, and do any other necessary errands. Cooking dinner for Sammy and Heller would start almost immediately after. Evenings were when she had downtime, usually to read or watch television, while Sammy hung out with friends and Heller tinkered with small chores around the house, such as rebuilding the front porch or tightening a loose screen door.

But Summer had spent the evening of July 3, 1999, preparing for her morning of slumber. The house had been prepped and the shopping was done. All she needed to do was get up by eleven a.m. to get ready for the festivities.

11

SUMMER FOSTER

July 4, 1999, 9:30 a.m.

Summer sat up in bed, sticky, craving a shower and a cigarette. Not that she was complaining. Things finally felt normal. Well, close to it. The pangs of depression remained, but they were lessened by a new distraction.

She took a few steps toward the bathroom, passing her vanity. It was an antique and no longer shined like it had when she was a girl. But Butch had re-varnished the wood last year and she'd replaced the large round mirror, which caught her eye when Paul began stirring.

He usually didn't fall asleep afterward, but they'd spent nearly an hour in her bed. She'd also dozed off, which was risky, but her body wasn't used to mid-morning naps and only allowed her ten minutes. It had been nice not having to talk. Paul had the energy of a seventeen-year-old and was trying hard to form a real bond with her via constant pillow talk. She was nice to him and always engaged in conversation, though she only needed him for his tongue and his cock.

Paul rolled over to face her. He was only a sandy-blond senior-to-be at Hinterbach High, but Paul had the body of a full-grown man. He propped himself up on his right elbow, causing his muscles to ripple.

"How's my sexy librarian doing?" The boyish grin and acne on his face reminded Summer he was a teenager.

"You need to stop looking at dirty pictures on the computer."

"I don't do that. Why would I when I have you?"

Summer sighed. "I can look up the sites you visit on the computers in the library. And yes, I know White House dot com is a porn site. The other one is dot gov. If anyone else catches you, you're going to be in a lot of trouble."

The smile melted from Paul's face. "I'm so sorry, Miss Foster."

"It's okay." Summer was still looking at him in the mirror. "I like thinking about you getting hard while you're sitting right outside my office."

Dirty talk had never come naturally to Summer. But she'd known since seventh grade that boys liked it. And she didn't mind it with Paul. He had knocked something loose in Summer, emotionally as well as physically. He'd suggested her haircut, and she enjoyed the idea of doing something for him. Though she knew those dirty photos were where he got the idea, Summer agreed to the stylish pixie haircut so they would have a secret. A dirty, naughty secret.

Her head felt light now, free from the blonde ropes that had fallen to the middle of her back. What remained still had the bright color that returned every summer. She'd spent a lot of time under the Texas sun as a child and teenager. Summer's body rarely had tan lines until Sammy was born, utilizing the roof of the family trailer house as a place to sunbathe when school was out. She always laid out on the side that sidled up to Freddy's Creek. Boys would sneak peeks, and she'd let them, because that's what girls in Hinterbach did.

Paul was constantly complimenting her looks. She knew it was only because that's what boys are taught to do when they like a girl, but Summer enjoyed it. His go-to compliments usually involved her legs, which were long—she was considered tall for a woman at five-foot-ten—but muscular, and Summer had always thought they looked fat.

Most people remembered her as a Hinterbach High cheerleader, but she was also an accomplished high school sprinter and walked onto the Texas State track team after Sammy was born. But the pregnancy had caused her to lose a step. She moved back in with her parents after only a semester and a half but kept up with a running routine. Her legs remained strong, but Summer always felt out of proportion.

Paul, however, said he loved her legs. Compliments like that are what had originally drawn her to him. She wondered if he would sleep with her, or was he just trying to get a rise out of his friends? Was it so implausible that a hormonal teenager would be interested in her? Summer was still on the right side of thirty-five, and she was damn proud of how flat she kept her stomach.

But then there was her face. Her stress level had exploded at the beginning of the year, leaving her with dark bags under her eyes. She'd also been smoking more. A lot more. She'd been inhaling more than a pack a day for almost six months, and she was sure it was yellowing her teeth and causing lines to form around her mouth.

But Paul still called her beautiful. Summer smiled and enjoyed his body for a moment as he slid out of her bed. She closed her eyes as she felt his hands grip her hips. Then came his lips on her neck, followed by his chest on her shoulder blades.

Summer accidentally let a sound slip past her lips. Paul took this as a signal and pressed himself into the small of her back. She usually enjoyed how quickly he recovered—he'd already finished twice—but Butch's meeting would be wrapping up soon, if it wasn't already over. And despite the fact she was cheating on him, Summer still cared about Butch.

On the other hand, she thought about how good Paul felt. Everything about his physicality turned her on. He stood a full head taller than Summer, and he was strong enough to move her exactly how he wanted. And, as crude as it was to admit, Paul's dick was his best feature. He certainly had nothing to be ashamed of in terms of size, but she'd had bigger. Paul's dimensions and shape—the way it bulged in the middle, its slight upward curve—were, as she'd told him earlier that morning, perfect. For her, at least, as though they were built for each other.

The thought of having him inside her was almost overwhelming.

Almost.

Summer took one more moment to appreciate Paul by leaning into him, then took a step forward. "You have to go. He'll be back soon."

"Let him. We both know I can kick his ass, then he'll be out of your life for good."

Paul gripped her hips tighter and pulled her into him. Summer could tell the thought of confronting Butch had put his testosterone into overdrive. This time she was able to suppress any sounds, though her breath caught slightly.

Her body also had another automatic response, which Paul felt when he slid his fingers between her thighs.

She reached down and grabbed his wrist. "Stop. You really have to go."

Before Summer could react, Paul moved his left hand from her hip to the back of her neck, squeezed, and forced her upper body down so hard she barely had time to keep her face from hitting the vanity.

CIGARETTE NUMBER two shook in Summer's hand as she tried to bury those eight minutes. She was searching for a plot among the rest of those that already held moments when men had put themselves where she didn't want them. Hands on her thighs, unwelcome shoulder rubs, even crude jokes and creepy looks—

they all wore on her soul. She would have to dig a long, deep hole for this memory. A full grave.

She knew it had been eight minutes because her nose had almost touched the watch she placed on her vanity every night. She hadn't fought him off, but instead stared at the face and counted the seconds. Four hundred ninety-three. She rounded down. Paul didn't say a word afterward, and neither did she. She stayed bent over until hearing the front door close. Then she'd stumbled to the shower.

As she took another long drag, Summer watched a trio of cats near the dumpster in the alley that bordered Freddy's Creek. An albino female was crouched down as low as she could. Behind her, a black-and-gray-striped male looked ready to pounce. Flanking the female on the left was an orange tabby, which she assumed was male. The female cat—Summer decided to call her Miss Kitty—flinched like she wanted to make a break for it. She was met immediately by a hiss and a swipe from the tabby, who was obviously named Garfield. Miss Kitty backed up, inching closer to the dark male cat, who would be known today as Paul. While Miss Kitty was distracted by Garfield, Paul took advantage and mounted her. Miss Kitty let out that guttural howl that only a cat can make, the one that accompanies the worst kind of pain.

Miss Kitty wriggled herself free and sprinted forward. It took ten seconds for Garfield to wrangle her and for the scenario to begin again, the animal kingdom's version of a rapist and his wingman. Summer shook her head and blew out a heavy cloud of smoke.

As she finished her cigarette, Summer contemplated telling someone this time. She'd developed early and started partying in the seventh grade. Other girls had probably had it worse, though she couldn't be sure because nobody talked about it.

"You fucking idiot," Summer told herself as she walked back inside. She couldn't tell anyone.

Paul was seventeen.

And her student.

Summer was still trying to calm herself when she heard the crunch of gravel under tires. Butch was home. She took a deep breath and walked into the kitchen to make potato salad. By the time Butch walked in, she was making a racket and looking like she'd been hard at work.

"Hey sexy, did you sleep in this morning?" he asked.

Summer turned around as though she hadn't heard him walk in. "Oh, hey. Yeah, I got started a little bit ago. I'm running really late."

Butch started walking toward her. "No, you're not. We have all day."

Summer could feel him sliding up behind her like Paul an hour before. It took everything she had to stay calm as he put his hands on her hips.

12

Veronica had the same question I'd asked Jorge a few months ago.

"Is this legal?"

I had no answer. Reselling clothing is a legitimate industry, but it's usually trendy shirts and designer jeans. But should FR clothing—which is specially treated and required by law at job sites in the oil and natural gas industry—be re-sold? Even if the answer was yes, buying used FRs out of a guy's garage was not on the level.

The more important question: Were the shirts and pants fire-resistant, or were the patches merely sewn onto normal clothes?

But at four for a hundred dollars, everyone hooked up with the oilfield underground was willing to take that chance.

I parked my car in the driveway of a nondescript house in Borger. "Of course, it is. Besides, I'd hate for you to have to spend hundreds of dollars to get on a job you don't care about."

Veronica had been too late to make it to RedBoots, so she'd already bought a cheap pair at Walmart. I was relieved. My animosity about paying for half her hotel room had faded. I was downright giddy at the prospect of sleeping on a mattress instead of couch cushions.

As we got out of my car, I peered into the large window that faced the driveway. A man pulled up the blinds and pointed to the garage like I was being allowed access into a speakeasy. I led Veronica to a heavy steel door that opened as I was about to reach for the knob.

"Hola," an Hispanic man said as we walked into a newly painted and carpeted room, though a slick black pickup was parked in the middle. "You are Jorge's friend?"

"Si." I pointed to Veronica. "We need clothes for her. Dos, uh —" I tugged at my T-shirt and tried to come up with the Spanish name for shirt.

"Camisa," the man said with a subtle shake of his head. "FR?"

"Si." I pointed at my thigh. "Y dos."

The man looked Veronica up and down. She stood taller than us despite being in flats and had shoulders broader than his. If nothing else, she would appear strong enough to do the job.

Veronica knew what clothes fit her frame best, and she was obviously disappointed with the selection when the man came back with two pairs of jeans and two shirts—one blue and one beige—and handed them to her.

"Go behind the truck and try them on," I said.

"You're kidding, right? I'm not getting undressed in some random guy's garage."

She made a fair point, but I doubted our friend would let her return the clothes if they didn't fit. "We won't look. Or you can see if they fit over your regular clothes. You'll want two layers when it starts getting cold in a couple of weeks."

She took a step toward me and held out the clothes. "I'm not doing it."

"If you don't have FRs that fit, you can't be on the job site. Then what was all of this for?" I pointed to the truck. "Will you please go try them on?"

Veronica stood her ground for one more defiant moment before storming off. The man and I exchanged an awkward smile and waited a few minutes for Veronica to re-emerge. The shirt was fine. The pants a bit too loose, which would work in her favor. She didn't know it yet, but Veronica would appreciate looking less attractive on the job.

"I think that'll work once we get you a belt."

"Sure. Whatever."

I used the drive back to Walmart as an opportunity to get her on my side. "By the way, I already have something to help keep up my end of our deal. I spoke to two investigators today."

Veronica turned to me. For the first time since arriving in Borger, she didn't look annoyed.

"Who is investigating?"

"The Texas Rangers. One of them even has the last name Walker. I swear I'm not making that up."

Veronica pulled a notebook and pen out of her purse. "What are their names?"

"Lieutenant Owen Johnson and Caroline Walker. Johnson said people call him OJ. I prefer Agent Orange."

She snorted. "And what did you discuss?"

"They know I wrote *Cold Summer*." I paused before continuing. I didn't want to tell her everything, but she'd find out later if I was lying. "They consider me a suspect."

Veronica kept writing and didn't look up. "Did you kill her?"

I was jarred by the coolness with which she asked the question, as though she wouldn't be surprised if I said yes.

"You're kidding, right?"

She looked up but didn't say anything.

"No," I said. "I didn't kill her."

She turned her attention back to the notepad. "Why do they think you're a suspect?"

"Well, I found the body first and immediately told Jorge and another guy that it was Jillian, even though you couldn't tell by looking at her." I decided to leave out the fight. It was ultimately irrelevant, and I didn't want her to think I'd killed her.

Instead I told her about the injuries, the decomposition, and the side-by-side photos from earlier that day.

"I see why you would make the connection," she said. "I always assume the worst-case scenario, too."

I smiled. It had been a while since I talked to someone else who wrote about death.

"Anything else?" she asked.

"Oh yeah. The woman had told everyone on the job her name was Jillian, but the Rangers said her real name was Sylvia Davenport. They also confirmed that she is from Austin."

"So, the victim is named Sylvia Davenport and from Austin. That's not very helpful."

I bristled but kept my frustration in check. "I know. I tried to get more, but they weren't talking. But you have something to start with. And now you know it's a juicy story. I'm jealous you're writing about it and not me."

I took a few moments to ready myself as we pulled into the Walmart parking lot. Now was as good a time as any to bring up the elephant in the car.

"Thank you for doing this, by the way. I re-read your story, and I know your editors probably think that Franklin Jones may have killed Summer Foster. But I flat-out know that isn't true."

She nodded. "But you have to admit, what his defense attorney said was compelling."

"It's nothing but cherry-picked facts sprinkled into a strong narrative. That's why Action Jackson is such a rich man."

"True," she said. "Telling a good story can be very convincing."

13

EXCERPT FROM COLD SUMMER

Though the early evidence overwhelmingly pointed to Heller, Det. Roland did not want to taint the investigation by failing to investigate other suspects. Ex-lovers are always on that list and, though there were several to consider, one name stood out: Franklin Jones.

After graduating from the University of Texas at Austin's business school and getting his MBA from Arizona State, Jones returned to the Hill Country and was almost immediately made the vice president of a Kerrville bank. His second order of business was reconnecting with the girl he'd been obsessed with in high school. They dated for years, but tensions reportedly increased when she wouldn't move in with him. Then, after catching her cheating with Heller, Jones beat Foster, bruising the right side of her face and cracking a rib.

Det. Roland contacted Jones' attorney and

waited more than a day to hear anything back. The veteran investigator had already been to his house, but Jones was an important man and had said nothing.

"Literally nothing," Det. Roland said later. "He opened the door, saw my badge, and handed me his lawyer's business card. I asked him a few questions, but every time he just smiled and nodded toward the card."

The phone call he received two days later was not from that attorney. It was from an agent with the local FBI office. The agent informed Det. Roland that the feds had an open investigation involving Jones.

"He was cryptic, and wouldn't tell me what the investigation was about," Det. Roland said. "But he provided Jones with an alibi. He said they'd been monitoring Jones, and they knew his whereabouts at the time of Summer Foster's death. The FBI never did tell us exactly where he was, but it didn't matter. We already knew Heller was our doer."

14

FRANKLIN JONES

July 4, 1999, 11 a.m.

He'd been waiting two years. Two long, unbearable years. Jones had taken out that frustration at the gym and was proud of the larger physique he would unveil that evening. But which outfit would show off his swollen arms and chiseled chest most? That was the question Jones considered as he stared at the clothing options laying on his bed.

He'd also been saving himself for Summer. He wasn't going to risk getting another woman pregnant—or possibly falling in love—before their reunion. He'd gotten her once, and he could get her again.

The timing was almost perfect. If the protective order had been lifted a month ago, Jones would have had no problem reigniting the flame. She'd been alone for five months and would be yearning for someone, starving for male attention and needing a strong support system, just like she was when they'd first gotten together. He wanted to provide both in spades.

But then Jones had watched Butch Fucking Heller stand on her front porch again, only this time he was the one begging for forgiveness. Jones was in his usual spot in the courthouse parking lot—which was exactly 119 feet away from her property line—and cursed himself for not breaking the restraining order. But, in the end, Jones knew the restraint he showed would pay dividends. He liked to play the long game. It was always worth it in the end.

Jones settled on a tight red polo shirt, sharply pressed khakis, and his amber aviators. A pair of deck shoes with no socks seemed appropriate for the heat. He carefully put the other choices away, then re-emerged with the more casual clothes he would wear before heading to Summer's party. He wanted a fresh haircut and a shave. He wanted to remind Summer of how beautiful they looked together. No shops were open in Kerrville on the Fourth of July, but Jones had given his barber a nice financial incentive to open at eleven-thirty, just for him.

Jones had nearly twenty-five minutes to kill. He was always running early, a trait he usually liked, but finding ways to waste time that morning was excruciating. He'd woken up at 5:45, like a five-year-old on Christmas morning. He'd spent some time on a long morning workout, followed by cooking breakfast and reading the *Daily Times* over his egg whites and turkey bacon. While reading the paper, he saw an interesting event in the calendar. An alcoholics' meeting would be held downtown.

Jones had known Heller would go. The man who'd caused Jones' two-year exile went to every meeting possible. Jones had also attended those meetings the last two weeks, just to monitor Heller's activities. Jones thought the jig was up the last time he'd gone. Heller had made eye contact and walked over. Jones froze and tried to steady himself for the upcoming fight. Then Heller smiled, and Jones saw no recognition in his eyes. Heller had noticed his Longhorns T-shirt and wanted to chat with a fellow fan. Jones introduced himself as "Francis" and talked about Ricky Williams and his Heisman. They discussed how Texas had trounced Mississippi State in the Cotton Bowl and wondered what new coach Mack Brown would do without the NCAA's most prolific runner.

Jones had followed Heller after that meeting in his less-conspicuous pickup, and Heller couldn't be clever enough to spot a tail. Jones got less confident the farther they got from Kerrville and had to pull into the driveway of a long-abandoned house when he saw Heller turn down County Road K.

Jones got out of his truck and ran to the overgrown street corner. He saw Heller's tacky red Pontiac drive into the dead end and park outside of a dilapidated house. Heller walked inside, but only stayed for about ten minutes. Jones hurried back to his pickup as Heller retraced his path down County Road K. He waited until he heard the car's obnoxious exhaust fade away.

Jones should have let it end there. But the last time he'd neglected his gut for too long, he ended up full of regret. After knocking on the door, Jones had pretended to be with the Census Bureau, just another worker drone there to make sure someone still lived at the house so they could send the new form. It was a good cover story. So good, in fact, that Jones discovered something that would make Summer hate Heller and kick him to the curb permanently.

———

JONES LOVED the smell of his barbershop, always so clean, the hardwood floors swept after every cut and the utensils disinfected religiously. He'd taken years to find the right barber, one that knew how to style his hair and was competent with a straight razor. And, as he'd exploited earlier that week, his barber was easily incentivized by cash. It took so long to find this person because he hadn't considered using a woman barber until last year, when he was in a fix a few hours before the office Christmas party.

"This must be some Fourth of July party you're going to,

Frank," Patty said. "Most people just throw on a ballcap and T-shirt and have fun."

Patty was a bit older than Jones but still attractive. On nights when his discipline wavered, he thought about asking her to dinner. Patty couldn't make much money cutting hair, no matter how skilled she was, so giving in would be inevitable. But he couldn't do that to Summer. Jones did allow her to call him Frank, though, an unrefined nickname he despised coming out of anyone else's mouth.

"You're trying to impress a girl, aren't you?"

"You know me."

Patty turned on her stainless-steel clippers. "Well, she better be worth it to have me out here cutting your hair instead of eating barbecue."

"Oh, she is. The woman of my dreams."

Jones saw Patty shake her head in the mirror. "Well, it shouldn't be hard to win her over. I mean, how many girls have the president of a bank chasing after them, especially one with such a nice head of hair."

Patty wasn't wrong. Jones was even better off than when he and Summer first got together. It helped that his uncle had been the president, and his great uncle the chairman of the board. When the old man had finally retired, everyone got a bump. Jones had been chosen as his uncle's successor in middle school, after it was clear the "eccentric" bank president wouldn't have any children. Jones' college was paid for, from undergrad through business school. Jones—whose mother had been the black sheep of the family and was relegated to Hinterbach—was now a debt-free millionaire with a mansion in the Hill Country and three vehicles, including a brand-new BMW.

"It's nice to talk to someone who gets it," Jones said. "And someone who understands capitalism. So, how much did we agree on?"

"Two hundred."

Jones shook his head. "I'm pretty sure it was one fifty."

"I'm pretty sure I'm only half done. I can stop right now, and you can go looking like this."

He checked his reflection. "Tell you what: I'll give you two hundred, but you owe me a favor."

"And what do you call this?"

"The most expensive haircut I've ever gotten."

Patty smiled. "Fine, but I can't imagine what I could do for you besides cut your hair."

Jones wasn't sure either. He just knew it paid to have people owe him favors. "Who knows? But enough about me. How are things with your boyfriend?"

Patty held up her left hand in the mirror. "Fiancé."

The ring was decent enough, though Jones would've purchased a diamond twice the size and not even checked his bank account beforehand. "Oh, how wonderful. When's the wedding?"

"We're not sure yet. He's still running the body shop and hasn't found anyone to take over the day-to-day so he can focus on the business side of it. But when he gets someone groomed, we want to go get married in Mexico. Maybe take a cruise to get there."

"If he's making that much, I want my two hundred back."

"Very funny. Okay, I think we're done here. What do you think?"

Jones' thick blond hair was cropped close on the sides but left long on top. Patty slicked it back with product, a classic fifties look.

Jones took out three hundred-dollar bills from his money clip. "Perfect as always."

"You don't count so well for a banker."

"Consider it an engagement gift."

Patty took the cash. "Frank, I can't keep all of this. Just remember that generosity when you get the wedding invitation and list of where we're registered."

Jones stood and began walking to the front door. He knew

she was being polite and had no problem pocketing an extra hundred. "We'll see you in a couple weeks."

Jones checked his gold Rolex Yacht-Master, a promotion gift from his uncles, as he walked to his silver Beamer. Twenty minutes until noon. With drive time, five hours was just enough for his last errand.

15

Despite doing the job for months, I woke up in pain every day. I'd gone from a job that required sitting on my ass all day to one that kept me on my feet for hours at a time. It was a shock to my body. During the Department of Transportation physical, which we all had to take before starting, the doctor said she'd detected some protein in my urine, which can happen due to sudden increases in physical exertion. She recommended I monitor the situation with regular tests. A lack of medical coverage for pipeliners guaranteed I wouldn't.

My muscles were angrier than usual as I rolled out of my bed with about fifteen minutes before having to leave for Jorge's house. Veronica was already dressed and sitting cross-legged on her bed, pounding on her laptop's keyboard with a cup of convenience store coffee on the nightstand. I hadn't heard her leave for an Allsup's run. I'd have asked for an apple Danish. I preferred those to the burritos, but Jorge always insisted I eat *real food* rather than processed sugar.

I stumbled toward the bathroom, which was much roomier than Jorge's. "You know, there's a desk and chair right over there."

She didn't look up from her computer. "I hate sitting at desks."

"That's weird for someone who writes for a living."

Veronica didn't respond. I peeked at her screen. It looked like she was reading one of those *Free Butch Heller* websites, several of which had popped up when he was given his first stay of execution, thrusting the case back into the national spotlight.

"Does your editor know you're trolling those sites as part of your *research*?" I made air quotes when I said research, since those sites were nothing but crackpot conspiracy theories, none of which came close to exposing the truth.

"I don't use it, but it helps to know what people are talking about. I sometimes have to ask a source to refute one of the more plausible scenarios."

"I guess that makes sense," I said over the sound of the flushing toilet. I walked toward the dresser, where my clothes were stowed in the bottom two drawers. "I'm going to get dressed. Don't look."

"Go back to the bathroom."

I tossed the clothes onto the bed. "You can go to the bathroom if you want, but I'm paying for half of this room, and I'm going to use it to get dressed."

I didn't give her a chance to argue and pulled off the black undershirt I'd been sleeping in. She snapped her head back toward her laptop.

I wasn't shy about my body. I was no athlete, but I'd never considered myself fat. I was built like the X-Men character Wolverine. I stood five-foot-ten in shoes, short for a Texas man. But what I lacked in height I made up for in strength. Though I was sore, my muscles were as large as they'd been since college. I was still carrying extra fat, but my naturally broad, squatty features masked that. So did the body and facial hair.

I realized how awkward the silence had become as I slipped off my shorts. "Find anything good on that site?"

"Sort of. Someone on the forum is saying they were with

Heller when Summer was killed. That's the first time I've seen that anywhere."

It was also new information for me. I yanked up my boxer-briefs and turned to face her. "Are they staying anonymous?"

"Of course."

I turned back around, hoping to hide my relief. "Yeah. It's not as easy to lie about a life-and-death situation when your name is attached."

"I guess you would know better than anyone."

I froze. "What does that mean?"

"Just that you've testified under oath, so you know what it means to put your name on the line."

I'd never met anyone who understood me like Veronica already seemed to—not even Jorge. I *had* put my name on the line. And in writing *Cold Summer,* along with the associated author events and interviews since, my name had become synonymous with the guilt of Butch Heller.

VERONICA POPPED her head out from the backseat. "Are you sure you know where you're going? We've been driving in the middle of nowhere for ten minutes."

"Yeah, it's a ways out here," Jorge said. "But we're getting close."

As if on cue, we started down the final hill to Site Two.

"Oh wow, there's a lot of people down there." Veronica poked me in the shoulder. "Hey, time to wake up, Bart."

I opened my left eye. She'd found an old ballcap in the back and put it on. "How are you a writer but also a morning person?"

"Because, unlike you, my writing job makes me show up on time and pays enough that I don't have to do manual labor on the side."

Jorge laughed. "Bro, she totally got you." He held up his

hand for a high-five, which Veronica enthusiastically reciprocated.

"Okay, okay," I said. "So, Veronica, what you don't have are a hardhat, face shield, safety glasses, and gloves. They'll have all of that here for you. If anyone gives you shit for not having your own, tell them you left them in your car but got a ride from us this morning. You'll probably go straight with the superintendent to fill out paperwork, watch a video, etcetera. Just fake it till you make it."

"Yep," Jorge said. "That's what Beck's been doing for, what, four months now?"

Veronica laughed. I leaned back and smiled, knowing she wouldn't be laughing for long. Jorge suggested we introduce Veronica to her welder, who was calling himself Paul Henry these days. It was still weird hearing him swap out his last name for his middle. Then again, I wrote under my middle name, so who was I to judge? Paul probably wanted to distance himself from his newsworthy father.

"I apologize in advance for not knowing anything," Veronica told Paul. "And thank you so much for agreeing to all of this."

"Hey, we all had to start off not knowing anything. I'm just glad we could help with your situation."

Veronica's look said far more than words could have. She hadn't heard the story we'd spun for Paul.

"Divorce is tough," Paul continued. "But we'll take your mind off of things and help you get enough money to rent your own place."

Veronica kept staring at me as she spoke. "Yeah, it's been rough."

I tried to apologize with my eyes. "Looks like the tailgate meeting is about to start. We better head that way."

Veronica's presence was felt quickly, and most of the eyes were on her by the time Redbeard started speaking.

"Listen up. You new hires need to get with Jameson after this." He looked over at Jameson, who raised his hand. "Other than that, we're going to keep rolling with the fabrication out here and excavation at Site Three. And, as always, stay safe. Anyone else?"

We all looked over at Zak. He looked like he wanted to speak but shook his head instead.

Veronica turned to me with wide eyes.

"Don't worry." I grabbed her by the shoulders to reassure her. I realized it was probably a mistake as soon as I did. But instead of pulling away or glaring at me, she took a deep breath and nodded.

I maintained my soft grip, excited she was allowing me in, even if it was only for a few moments. "Everyone here's real nice. You're going to watch a boring video but pay attention to the safety stuff. Then you'll fill out a bunch of paperwork and get the rest of your PPE. We'll be here to take care of you after that. I promise."

Veronica took a deep breath and nodded, then joined three other new hires on their way to Jameson's pickup. I wondered if the others knew why there were so many openings in the middle of a job.

"Hey Big Nasty, who's the new girl?"

I turned around to find Zak's helper, Jordan Washington—a six-foot-four black man with the soft voice of a sophomore reading aloud in his English class.

"Just a friend who needs a job. Since Paul had an opening, I figured I'd get her on out here so she could make some quick cash."

"A friend. Right."

Though I knew Veronica would hate it, my persona on the job was that of a horndog, so I had to play along. "I mean, we are staying in the same hotel room while she's here."

Jordan smiled. "You sleeping with her yet?"

"Wouldn't you?"

Jordan's smile faded. "My wife would kill me."

"Hey, what she doesn't know won't hurt her."

He shook his head. "I can't get another girl pregnant or catch something. I mean, not all of us can risk it by getting a blowjob from a stripper."

We both laughed. That story, while not completely true, was how I'd earned my nickname.

Jordan and Zak were with Jorge and I on our previous job in western Oklahoma. We'd gotten rained out on a Thursday and left to run some errands in Oklahoma City. Afterward, when I thought we were heading home, Jorge pulled into the parking lot of a strip club. They left me out of the loop because I would've objected. But, since I was there and captive, I decided to enjoy myself. The girls were beautiful, and Jorge paid for my first lap dance.

The same stripper, who called herself *Kandy with a K*, found me again an hour later and I was more than happy to go back up to the VIP area with three hundred in my wallet. Jorge had paid me back that afternoon for his half of the rent for our RV space— I cut the checks because his wife kept theirs at home—so I had more cash to burn than usual.

I offered Kandy two hundred up front for whatever that would buy me. While she hadn't given me a blowjob, she had used her hand while kissing me on the mouth and neck. When I'd re-emerged ten minutes later, she gave Jorge a kiss on his cheek, so I embellished to get a cheap laugh. I got a few more dances that night, and eventually Paul walked up. He was working on a different job nearby—there were more welders than gamblers in Oklahoma with the oil boom—and we reconnected. Jorge told Paul we were about to head to the job in Fritch, and Paul said he'd think about leaving and coming with us.

"Hey, I got an all-clear from the doctor," I said. "Totally worth it."

Coach Jorge walked over clapping his hands. "Come on Beck, we have a weld to finish."

I looked back toward the new hires, who were staring at a

laptop perched on Jameson's tailgate. For a while, perhaps a few days, Veronica would be caught up in learning what to do out here. But then she would start poking around about Jillian's—Sylvia's—murder. I hoped Veronica would be subtle.

If not, all of this could blow up in my face.

16

Veronica jumped into the back seat during our afternoon break. She had a new hardhat with an orange decal on the side and a clear plastic face shield flipped up overhead.

"Well, that took forever," she said. "Thanks for not telling me about the physical, by the way. I do love this thing, though." Veronica flipped down the face shield hard, like a goalie waiting for the puck to drop. "And everyone's been calling me Ronnie."

"Good, you already have a nickname," Jorge said. "It took Beck a month to get one."

"Shut up."

Veronica leaned forward between Jorge and me. "I thought Beck was your nickname?"

Jorge smacked my chest. "Tell Ronnie your real nickname." He looked at Veronica. "It's a good one."

My face felt hot. I shot a look at Jorge, but it was too late.

"Everyone out here calls him Big Nasty."

"What? Why on earth would they call you that?"

"It's not important." I flipped over my phone and tapped the screen. 10:13 a.m. "Time to get back to work."

She grabbed Jorge's forearm. "Not yet. You have to tell me."

Jorge finally took pity on me. "I'll tell you later. We have to get ready for a new weld."

First up was cleaning the outside edges of the pipe and valve about to be joined. I used our grinder fitted with a tiger pad disc, its overlapping pieces of sandpaper forming stripes swirling around its center. Veronica jumped away from the sparks. I didn't blame her. Though the face shield and safety glasses keep your eyes safe, I'd burned holes in two shirts my first month.

She was also shy when we ignited the weed burners, but Paul handed her the torch and had her finish preheating the steel.

"Why do we have to do that?" she asked after closing the valve on top of the propane bottle. "It's already a million degrees out here."

We all laughed.

"If you think it's hot now, you'd've died out here this summer," Jorge said. "It's got nothing to do with the air temperature. If the pipe's already two hundred degrees when we start welding, it'll cool down nice and slow. If it's cold, the weld will heat up the metal and make it expand fast. But then it'll cool down and contract just as fast, and it could crack."

Veronica looked like she wanted to ask another question, but Paul stopped her. "For the preheating to work, we have to start welding right away."

Paul pulled out a handful of rods from the metal bucket near Veronica's feet and handed them to her. "These are called one-eighth rods, or five-P rods. We'll use them this first time around the pipe. Just hand me one after I toss the old one in the other bucket. Got it?"

She nodded.

"And you remember what I said about running my temperature, right?" Paul pointed to his remote—which looked like a giant kitchen timer, its red face demarking volts rather than seconds—secured to the pipe with magnets a few feet to his right.

"When you say up, turn the dial up five. Down is down five. If you say up or down ten, I move it up or down ten."

"You got it."

Veronica stepped in front of the remote. Paul pulled down his red welder's face shield, put a rod in his stinger—essentially the clamp from the end of a set of jumper cables—and aimed it at the small gap between the end of the pipe and the end of the valve.

"Listo?" Jorge said, asking Paul if he was ready.

"Vamonos," Paul replied. *Let's go.*

Veronica looked surprised at how fluent Paul sounded. She'd yet to learn that Spanglish was the official language of pipeliners.

What followed was a sensory overload. Not only was there a bright blue light emanating from the end of the rod—looking at it could cause blindness—but smoke was rising from the pipe, bringing with it a metallic smell and taste. The chemical reaction caused a sound and the open end of the valve became a megaphone. Adding to the noise were both welding machines, which sounded like a pair of revving semi-truck engines.

I was about to ask Veronica if she was okay, but I heard Paul yell, "up." By the time she remembered what to do, Paul was screaming. She cursed and apologized.

"Congratulations," I yelled. "You're officially a helper."

I UNTUCKED my shirt as I walked into the hotel room, ready to shower off the soot and dirt that always collected on my skin, in my ears, and up my nose. I turned around but didn't see Veronica. I leaned out into the hallway. She was still halfway down the hall, tiptoeing on a bed of hot coals with no end.

I hurried to meet her, remembering how painful it was to walk after my first day. "Here, put your arm around my shoulder."

She nearly fell into my arms. "Can you just carry me?"

"I could, but that wouldn't help you in the long run. You have to walk in them as much as possible until you're used to it."

"Why does this hurt so much?" she groaned.

I helped her sit on her bed. "You've never spent that many hours on your feet, and those cheap boots don't help. Give it a week. You'll be fine."

"I don't know if I'll make it a week."

"Sure you will. After you learn the ropes a little bit, you'll realize it's the easiest money you've ever made."

"I'm not here for the money, remember?"

"I do, but it might be a little bit before you can get anyone to talk to you about the murder."

She let her right boot drop to the floor. "I'm better at this than you think. I'll have what I need in a couple of days."

"Do you have a deadline?"

She let out a loud sigh as the second boot dropped. "No."

"You should take some time. Gather some color for the story."

"You just want to keep staying in this hotel room."

I laughed. "True. But I've also done this writing-about-crime thing, too. You want to impress your boss? Stick with us for a while."

"Why would I do that? My goal is to spend as little time here as possible. I should've just added your no comment to the Butch Heller story and moved on with my life."

I sat down beside her. "But you'd've been printing a lie. You feel good about not doing that, right?"

Veronica nodded but didn't look at me. We sat like that until I got uncomfortable and walked into the bathroom.

"What do you want for dinner?" I yelled as I got undressed. "I'm going to go buy some stuff for the minifridge. It won't hold much, but I can get you a TV dinner or something."

I walked back into the room to find Veronica in a long T-shirt with HARVARD ALUM on the front. I couldn't see anything else, but I assumed she was wearing something underneath.

"Can you pick up some beer? Dos Equis?"

"Wow, you are trying to fit in with these pipeliners," I said. "You'll have to switch to something cheap and domestic, though."

"Baby steps," she said.

I pointed to her shirt. "I thought you went to UT?"

"Oh, I did. This is my dad's. He got a business degree from there. Now he basically runs one of those new tech companies down in Austin. He's hoping this whole journalism thing is just a phase."

"Yeah, my dad was the same way. He's thrilled I'm finally working for a living."

"What does he do?"

I sat down on my bed and faced her. "He's retired. He and my mom didn't start having kids until they were in their late thirties. They didn't think she could have any, then my sister and I came along. Anyway, he was a master carpenter. He worked jobs kind of like this, then started building some of the best furniture in the Southwest. He's had pieces in almost every custom furniture store in Texas, Oklahoma, New Mexico, and Colorado. Now they travel the country in their RV visiting family and fishing."

"Sounds nice. What about your sister?"

I looked down at the carpet. "Ruth Ann died when I was in high school."

Veronica moved to my bed and put her hand on mine. "Oh my gosh, I am so sorry."

"It's okay," I said. "Time heals all wounds, right?"

"That's what they say."

I rubbed her fingers, and our eyes met for a moment before she jerked her hand away. "I'm going to jump in the shower."

I did a terrible job of hiding my disappointment. "Gotcha. I'll go get the beer and some groceries."

17

EXCERPT FROM COLD SUMMER

Heller liked working with his hands. Like many who abuse alcohol and drugs, he changed jobs frequently. He'd been a mechanic, carpenter, plumber, electrician, and construction worker. He liked to use those skills during his spare time. His tool of choice on the afternoon of July 4, 1999, was a hammer, though the one he used to rebuild Summer's porch was not the one he used later that night.

That hammer was a small sledge. He'd stolen it from his most recent job site, which was perhaps the pettiest of Heller's list of crimes.

The Hinterbach Police Department file on Heller was thick well before he was arrested for Summer's murder. His criminal history included breaking and entering, assaulting a police officer, and public nudity. He had also sued the Nimitz County Sheriff's Office once—and HPD twice—for excessive use of force. Neither case was successful, though he did get out of his fourth Driving While Intoxicated charge by successfully proving the arresting deputy failed to properly Mirandize Heller.

18

BUTCH HELLER

July 4, 1999, Noon

As he rebuilt the porch in front of their trailer, Heller thought about the brownie points he was earning with Summer, who thought he was putting in hard manual labor.

She had no idea he was having fun.

Of all the things Heller had done to make money, carpentry was his favorite. He was skilled with a hammer, and pounding nails was an excellent way to work out frustration. Taking a pile of wood and turning it into something solid and useful also scratched his creative itch.

The progress was a bit slower than he'd hoped, though. The heat was oppressive. Heller wanted a beer, preferably one that had been sitting under ice in a cooler. Instead, Summer had given him a pitcher of sweet tea. Though the effect wasn't the same, Heller poured a glass and surveyed the neighborhood. He wasn't the only one in Hinterbach working on his honey-do list. He counted two push lawnmowers and a weed eater, plus one neighbor putting on a new screen door.

Heller was about to down the rest of his glass when Bernard Beck walked out of his house.

Bernard, whom most folks called Bernie, and his family had lived across the street from Summer for more than twenty years. His wife had helped with Sammy after Summer's parents passed. He and Heller had been friendly and collaborated on a few projects, including their respective tool sheds.

They hadn't worked together since his daughter died in that car crash. Ruth Ann had been Bernie's pride and joy. Not only had she graduated the salutatorian in May, but she'd won two gold medals at the state track meet. Ruth Ann was also class president, drum major, captain of the softball team, and a list of other accolades that took about five minutes to recite.

Heller gave his neighbor a cursory nod, expecting little in return. But to his surprise, Bernie jogged across the street.

"Howdy, neighbor," Bernie said. "I see Summer finally talked you into rebuilding that old thing."

"Yeah. And on a holiday. I must really love her."

Bernie slapped Heller on the shoulder. "Funny how it always seems to work that way."

"What about you? I'm sure your old lady has you working on something."

Bernie's smile disappeared. "No, I'm all caught up. I came by to see if you needed help." His eyes were pleading with Heller. The isolation had finally gotten to him. "With me and the boy, you can get this done in no time."

Bernie pointed to his son, who was using a weight rack in the open garage. Heller couldn't remember his first name. It was something strange. Most people just called him Beck, though Bernie usually called him *the boy* or *the kid*.

"He's growing up fast," Heller said. "He'll be able to take his old man soon."

"He already can, but don't tell him that. He has a chance at starting defensive line."

Heller turned his attention back to Bernie. "Really? How old is he now?"

"Sixteen."

Heller looked back at the boy. "Sixteen going on twenty-six." He rubbed his stubble. He's damn near got a full beard. I'm jealous."

"Me too."

They shared a laugh. It was nice to have his neighbor back. Between that and being back in Summer's good graces, Heller allowed himself to imagine being truly happy again.

"So, can we help?"

Heller picked up his favorite framing hammer. "I really am almost done. But, sure, let me go get some more tools."

"Here, you hand me that and I'll call the boy over here for some muscle. If you want, you can go inside and help that beautiful wife of yours while we finish up."

Heller handed Bernie his hammer. "No sir, I'm not going to let you have all the fun. You two get started, and I'll be back in a minute."

Heller walked around to the backyard, where Summer was spreading a tablecloth on one of three picnic tables Heller had built a few years ago.

"What's cookin', good lookin'?" Heller asked.

Summer shook her head. "You're corny, you know that?"

"Yes ma'am." He leaned in and kissed her on the cheek. "And you love it."

She smiled and returned to her tablecloth. "Did I hear you talking to someone out front?"

"Yeah. Bernie. He saw me working on the porch and came over to help."

Summer whipped around to face Heller. "Are you fucking kidding me? How can you do that to him?"

Heller put his index finger to his lips, begging Summer to lower her voice as he rushed over to her.

"Look, he doesn't know. If he's ready to have friends again, isn't that the best way I can help him?"

"How can you be such a monster. After what you did—"

"It was an accident," Heller said through clenched teeth.

Summer turned and stomped toward the back door to their trailer. Heller watched her, then walked into the tool shed. He pulled the string to turn on the overhead light, but it didn't come on.

He tried again. Nothing. He cursed and yanked so hard the nylon string came off in his hand. "Goddammit. Guess I'll add that to my list of shit to get done around here."

Heller fumbled around on the tool bench and found a flashlight. He walked to the back and found the crate that housed his hammers and other hand tools. The first hammer he pulled out was a mini, two-pound sledgehammer. He laid it down on the bench and reached back in the crate. The next two he found were the claw hammers he needed.

Summer was back in the house when he re-emerged. He hurried to the front and readied himself to engage in small talk with Bernie. Anything deeper, and Heller might not be able to keep his shit together.

The rest of the front porch only took thirty minutes to finish. He and Bernie made quick work of the pile of lumber in the front yard. The younger Beck was strong as an ox, though he possessed almost no skill with a hammer and mumbled every time he missed a nail. There wasn't much talk aside from that.

Heller thanked his guests and walked back into the house. He moved quickly to the bedroom, hoping to avoid a knockdown, drag-out with Summer. "We got the porch done," he shouted toward the kitchen. "I'm going to jump in the shower. You're welcome to join if you want."

"Fuck you."

Heller didn't respond. He smelled rank after spending a couple hours in the sun and needed the shower. Summer had laundered the sheets and made the bed. He contemplated taking a nap after washing up. After his early morning, it might help him get through the night with enough will power.

Despite his best efforts, Heller started thinking as he turned on the water. Was Summer right? Was he a monster? Heller still wasn't sure.

HELLER HAD TURNED the New Year holiday into a weeklong bender. He'd been laid off from his job as an electrician at the end of December and didn't want to tell Summer, so he made a bar in Kerrville his temporary workplace. He liked to think he was a day or two away from coming clean. He was also close to proposing marriage, though he had a few things to smooth over with her first.

All that would have to wait after the third of January. Or, to be precise, the first few hours of the fourth. If he'd still been employed, that would be the last day of the holiday weekend, so Heller had been drinking more than usual. It would've been out of character for Heller to be anything less than half in the bag at all times. So, for authenticity's sake, he closed down the bar before making one last stop.

Heller felt fine as he rolled up County Road K on his way back to Summer. But if he was sober enough to drive, how in the hell had he lost control? Part of it was the rush he was in. Heller knew that much. His brain was racing at the thought of what he was doing, of what Summer was going to say when he got back to Hinterbach. Still, had he not been so drunk, Heller wouldn't have ended up sideways on the blacktop.

The next thing he remembered was a rusty pickup smashing into the bed of Heller's work truck. It was one of the few things Heller's piece of shit father left him when he died of cirrhosis. His Dad had never been trustworthy, but the pickup was, and the heavy steel toolboxes on both sides of the bed were like tank armor.

The other truck slid and went up on two wheels. Heller heard shattering glass as he stomped on the brake pedal. It struck his passenger side, so Heller wasn't hurt. Just dazed.

After falling out of his own vehicle, Heller looked back. The front half of the rusty pickup had crumpled like an accordion, and a girl was lying halfway out of an opening where the windshield had been. He stumbled over and brushed back her slick hair. Even in his drunken state, Heller immediately recognized Ruth Ann Beck.

Heller had acted more cowardly than he ever could've imagined that night. It remained his greatest source of shame. He'd never admitted everything that happened. But after Ruth Ann's funeral later that week, Heller broke down and told Summer he had caused the crash.

He'd expected Summer to be upset, but also to console him. Instead, she went silent and sat for what seemed like five minutes. Then she unloaded a series of rapid-fire slaps and screamed until he left.

"HURRY UP IN THERE," Summer yelled through the bathroom door. "It's almost time for you to start grilling, and I need you to help me get the other tables set up before that."

Heller smiled. She may never forgive him, but at least Summer had let him back in the house.

19

Veronica and I watched as a pair of track hoes worked in tandem to carry a long stretch of twenty-six-inch pipe. The bases of the earthmovers looked like black-and-yellow tanks, their top halves swiveled out ninety degrees. Both inched along at the same glacial pace while their mechanical arms suspended the steel tube at least twenty feet above the ground.

"That is so cool," she said.

"Yep. And it never gets old."

Our attention was pulled away from the synchronized slow-motion dance by Zak's booming voice. "Helpers, let's go."

"Go do what?" Veronica asked.

I started walking. "Get railroad ties so we can build skids for that pipe."

"I didn't understand half of those words."

I motioned for her to follow me, and we fell in step with ten other helpers to form a line that snaked through a maze of pipe. Jordan Washington led us around a deep trench that exposed the existing pipeline, then stopped as he reached a massive pile of the wood planks, each one four inches tall, six inches wide, and four foot long. Though we called them railroad ties, they were much smaller than the ones used on train tracks.

"We need to bring a bunch of those pieces of wood over to where we were standing." I said.

I walked over to the pile, but Veronica stayed behind. "You expect me to do that, too?"

The rest of the helpers were already tossing the ties off the top in a schizophrenic beat of wood-on-wood thumps. "You'll only have to carry one. It'll be fine."

"What the hell am I doing here?" Veronica whispered to herself.

I cupped her elbow. "I've been there. But if you're like me, you'll find out you're capable of a lot more than you think."

We approached the diminishing pile of wood, and I stood three on end to show her my lifting technique.

"Get them vertical like this. Then you bend all the way down, so your shoulder is about halfway. Give them a big bear hug, then lift with your legs and balance them on your shoulder." I groaned as they teetered beside my head. "Now you get one of them and try."

Veronica looked at me skeptically but did as I asked. She was wobbly and had to take a step back to steady herself, but she got it up and smiled. "Holy crap, I did it."

"Yep. Now we have to lug them back over there."

This was the bad part. When we first got to the job, much of the pipe and fittings had yet to arrive, so we all had a lot of time on our hands. Jordan had bet me fifty bucks I couldn't carry three of the railroad ties at the same time. Most can only manage two, though Jordan also claimed he could carry three. I won the bet. But from then on, I was accused of slacking any time I carried fewer than three.

I was winded by the time we caught up with the other helpers. Veronica was not, though she was constantly shifting her weight from one foot to the other. The hike had no doubt enflamed the soles of her feet. They were swollen and red by now, with at least one blister on each. Insoles and thicker socks would help. That's what I'd done, though I had to sever the toes from the insoles before my Flintstone feet would fit inside.

"You've got to work on your cardio, Mr. Big Nasty."

"It's just Big Nasty," I said between gulping air.

There was not much aerobic activity built into the duties of a welder's helper. There were opportunities to build strength, and I'd taken advantage of that. But the lack of continuous movement, combined with an aversion to going to the gym after spending ten hours on our feet, allowed many welders and helpers to maintain their beer bellies.

We dumped our logs into one of four piles that stretched parallel to the road leading past the job site. The rest of the helpers started building the skids below the pipe, which was still suspended by the track hoes. When all four were built, the pipe was settled onto the wood. Zak, Paul, and Jorge put four-foot-long levels along the pipe, and wood was added and subtracted to get the pipe exactly right.

"Now what?" Veronica asked.

"We cut it into sections."

"Wait, we have to cut the pipe, too?"

I pointed to Jorge's pickup. "Yep. That's what those bottles are in the back of each rig. The green one is oxygen, and the black one is called acetylene."

"A set of what?"

I snorted. "Acetylene. It's a gas that mixes with the oxygen. It produces a blue flame that cuts through the steel like butter."

Jorge approached us. "Dude, quit trying to explain it. You don't know what you're talking about."

"What did I get wrong?" I asked. "I told her exactly what you told me."

"Yeah, well, I gave you the dummy version because I knew you didn't care. But if she's going to write about us, I want her to get it right." Jorge pulled the glasses off my face and put them on his, sliding the bridge up his nose with his index finger. "First, the metal isn't melting. The acetylene does bring the steel to its ignition temperature, but then we let the oxygen flow in. That interacts with the iron in the steel, changing the molecules and causing oxidation."

"Like rust?"

"Kind of. Only it's a lot quicker, and a lot hotter. The point is, it's a chemical reaction, not heating up the metal and melting it like this guy said." Jorge nodded his head toward me, and they laughed at my expense.

I was a little pissed at Jorge as he handed back my glasses. Why hadn't he explained it like that when I'd asked? Was he trying to impress her, or did he really think she would put that in her story? I might put it in something I wrote one day, or did he think I would never get published again? Though I wasn't planning on it, it hurt to think he'd given up on my writing career, too.

"But here, why don't we show you what we mean," Jorge said. "Beck, you and Ronnie go get the band and crawler. And make sure it's for twenty-six-inch pipe this time."

I motioned again for Veronica to follow me. She was still walking slowly, so I waited a minute for her to catch up, then we trudged to the equipment trailer, which looked suspiciously like a U-Haul that had been painted white.

"You said Jorge didn't go to college with you," she said.

"He didn't. He went to technical school for two years. It was in the same city, though."

"They must teach a lot of science there."

"Yeah, these guys aren't dumb. They earn their money."

She stopped walking. "I never said they were dumb."

"But you thought it." I knew she had, because that was the same misconception I'd brought to the job. Aside from the chemistry, welders also use algebra and geometry regularly—math I'd retained exactly long enough to get through high school, followed by a brief primer before testing out of math for college.

Though Zak walked around with a packet of schematics that detailed every measurement needed for each piece we welded, the previous job site was not nearly as organized. Oftentimes, a weld boss would merely give an overall length to the welders— say, a pig launcher that needs to be forty feet long total, including the ninety-degree fitting at the end—and leave it up to the welders to figure out how to fit the pieces together. That includes finding the measurement to the middle of the angle. Or perhaps the weld boss had done the math and figured out they needed a sixty-five degree turn at the end of the pipe. That required modification of a ninety-degree fitting by cutting one end.

She didn't respond to my barb, choosing instead to ask another question. "So, how much money do the welders make?"

"It varies by job, but generally between forty and forty-five an hour—"

"Holy shit—"

"For their arm," I finished. "That is, that's what Jorge makes. He also gets sixteen an hour for his rig."

"Wait, what?"

I nodded toward the trailer and we started walking again. "The company technically rents his truck and welding machine for sixteen dollars an hour. And he gets the hundred dollars a day per diem like us."

I could tell she was doing the math in her head, but I had it memorized. "Three thousand, seven hundred eighty dollars a week, before taxes. And on this job, they're providing the diesel for his truck and the gas for his machine."

Veronica shook her head. "Where did I go wrong in my life?"

"Well, you also aren't going to lose your eyesight at sixty and have lung problems from breathing in that chemical smoke for decades. That's why a lot of welders and helpers eventually become inspectors, or bosses like Zak."

"Still," she said as we reached the trailer. "So, he said we're looking for a band and crawler. What on earth are those?"

I pointed at a thin circle of stainless steel about a foot wide,

26" written on its side in yellow paint. "That's the band. Go ahead and throw that over your shoulder."

She did, and I looked around for the corresponding crawler, a giant silver scorpion with a fifteen-foot-long black tail. The stinger at the end of its tail was a gearbox that resembled a fishing reel. When its user began reeling, the scorpion would crawl around the pipe on its band.

The band and crawler were supposed to be stored together, but they rarely were. My eyes stopped when I noticed what looked like a small car battery with jumper cables attached to the terminals. But the loose ends of the cables were stripped, the bare wire ends loose on the floor. Not only did it seem out of place, it was probably a fire hazard. I'd ask someone about it later.

I found the crawler and we shouldered the items to the pipe, where Jorge and Paul combined them and attached a bronze torch to the scorpion's head and aimed it at the pipe. Veronica seemed mesmerized as the blue flame cut into the steel at a thirty-five-degree angle, creating half of the V-shaped bevel into which they would weld.

She looked at Jorge when he and Paul were done. "So, you can only cut through metal with that, right?"

"Yeah. I mean, it would burn someone if they put their hand under the flame, but it wouldn't cut them like one of those... how do you say... shit. Beck, what's that sword they use in those space movies."

"Lightsaber," I said.

"Yeah. It wouldn't work like one of those. Why?"

"I was trying to think of why someone would hit a woman over the head to kill her instead of using one of those torches."

It appeared the novelty of the job was already wearing off. Veronica was going to start digging into the murder. That made me nervous, though I was also curious to see what she would uncover.

"So, they told you about Jillian?" Paul asked.

"Well, I asked them why there was an opening after the job had already started," Veronica said. "And you know Mr. True Crime Writer over here, he described all the gory details to me."

"Yeah, he does that sometimes," Paul said.

"If you don't mind me asking, how'd Jillian end up being your helper out here? Was she your friend like these two?" Veronica pointed at Jorge and me.

"No," Paul said. "A friend recommended her to me. Well, I say a friend. Another welder I'd met a while back gave her my number. She started texting me, asking if she could come with me to the next job. When my last helper quit, I had her come test with me. She did okay, so I let her stick around."

I realized I'd lied to Walker and Agent Orange, though I swore Paul had told us he found Jillian—I had to consciously not refer to her by her real name, Sylvia, when she was brought up—on a website.

Veronica had her own question. "What's a test?"

"We don't do job interviews like you've probably had to," Paul said. "Out here, when a company wants to hire new welders, they have them do a couple of test cuts and welds. There's usually like five or ten welders at a time. If you pass, you're hired. The welders don't always bring helpers, but I like to when I can because it sucks testing by yourself."

"What happens if too many welders pass?"

Jorge and Paul laughed. "Out of ten, usually only three or four do," Jorge said. "It's not that the welders aren't good. But sometimes you have a bad day, or the inspector doing the test doesn't like you. And sometimes there are a couple of welders trying to break out, and they've never tested before."

Veronica nodded, taking mental notes. "So, you'd never met her in person before testing for this job?"

"Nope."

"Was she staying with you?"

Paul's eyes widened. "Oh no. I've got a girl back home, and she'd shoot me dead if she found out I was staying with a woman, especially one who looked like Jillian. I mean, I don't know what Beck told you, but she was a good-looking girl. Not that you're *not* good looking. I mean—"

Veronica held up her right hand. "It's okay, I get what you're saying. So, if Jillian wasn't staying with you, where was she staying?"

"I'm not sure. I think she said something about a motel. It might've been the same place as Jameson, but I'm not sure."

Veronica shot me a look. I couldn't interpret it, so I turned around and started walking toward Jorge, who was leaning on his truck after starting it and turning on the air conditioner before lunch. She caught up with me and leaned in. "Don't make plans for tonight. We've got work to do."

I was about to ask her what she meant when I felt a meaty hand on my right shoulder. I turned, only to realize Jordan Washington was leaning in over my left.

"I get you with that every time," he said. "It's lunchtime. Not that y'all need a break."

"Shit, we're working harder than you," Veronica said.

"Damn, she got you good, bro," Jorge said, still standing about twenty feet away from us.

"Whatever," Jordan said, even quieter than usual. "I'm going to go eat some of my girl's homemade tamales. I *was* gonna share, but not anymore."

Veronica started asking Jordan questions. Though I wanted to listen in, I took the opportunity to walk over and ask Jorge about the battery in the equipment trailer.

"I have no idea what you're talking about," he said. "You're sure it wasn't just a spare battery for one of our trucks?"

"No, it was too small." I made a box with my hands to indicate the size, a rectangle about a foot wide and maybe eight inches across.

"And you said there was exposed wire?"

I nodded. Jorge got a thousand-yard stare as he thought. I

knew he'd figured something out when he shut his eyes and mumbled to himself. "That fucking bitch."

I looked over at Veronica.

"No, not her," Jorge said. "Jillian. She was using that battery and wire to make fake arc marks on the pipe."

If leaving a grind mark on a pipe is a helper's worst sin—one Jillian was committing in secret when I caught her the week before—the equivalent for welders is leaving an arc mark.

The act of welding is essentially completing an electrical circuit. Connected to one end of a piece of pipe is a ground clamp, which is attached to a negative electrical lead that feeds into the welding machine. On the end of a positive lead is the welder's stinger. The circuit is complete when the stinger and welding rod touch that piece of pipe, voltage created by the machine flows through the leads and melts the rod.

If the rod touches the pipe outside the bevel, it leaves evidence—evidence that can be faked by completing an electrical circuit with a battery and exposed wire.

"Holy shit," I said, wondering how I'd allowed myself to be so completely fooled by her. We all keep secrets. But she'd been living a double life.

Finding out why might be my key to staying out of prison.

20

Veronica rushed through the door to our hotel room, though her feet had to feel like a bundle of exposed nerves.

She started grabbing clothes, then sat down on her bed and started unbuttoning her shirt. "Hurry up. We've got a date."

I watched her until she reached the last button and her eyes rose to meet mine. I turned around in embarrassment. "Who's we?"

"We're going to Jameson's motel room to drink with some of the guys." Veronica groaned as she flipped off her boots.

"To get more information about Jilli... Sylvia?"

The bed squeaked as Veronica stood, and I heard her step gingerly toward the bathroom. "Yep."

I slowly turned my head to make sure she wasn't visible, then sat on my own bed and unlaced my boots. "And this concerns me how?"

"I need you to drive because I'll be drinking. I also need someone there I know. Going into a strange guy's room, where I know people will be getting drunk, is not something I want to do alone. Plus, I told him you were coming."

I started changing into a shirt and non-FR jeans. "Fine. But we're not staying all night. We've got work tomorrow."

"I don't care. You know that this—what we're doing tonight —is why I'm here, right?"

"I do. Believe me, I want to find out what happened as much as you." I made sure to sound more relaxed than I felt. Though I knew they wouldn't find any physical evidence linking me to the murder, those Texas Rangers might've had enough to arrest me.

I pulled up my jeans and turned around to find the maroon T-shirt on my bed. Veronica had left the bathroom and was already standing behind me.

"Hurry up, we're supposed to be there in ten minutes and his motel is back in Fritch."

"When did you set all of this up?"

She opened the hotel room door. "During the morning break."

"But you were in the truck with us."

"I was texting Jameson. He gave me his phone number the first day I was on the job. He likes to think of himself as a ladies' man."

"I'm pretty sure he's married."

Veronica shrugged. "I didn't say I was going to sleep with him. I'm just going to get him drinking and talking."

WILLIE NELSON and smoke from his favorite flower billowed out of Jameson's motel room when he opened the door. "Come on in, y'all."

"Hey, Jamie," Veronica said. "Thanks for having us."

"I only let my momma call me Jamie."

"If you get to call me Ronnie, I get to call you Jamie."

The flirting was nauseating, but watching it was better than sitting in our room worrying about her.

Jameson's tiny room was difficult to navigate because of the people and the thirty-packs of beer on the floor. All the light domestics were represented, but nothing Veronica would like.

"What's the lady having?" Jameson asked.

"Oh, whatever you're drinking will be fine."

He grinned and pulled a blue can from the nearest box. He handed her the beer then looked at me. "Grab whatever you want. But if you start coming over here every weekend, you'll have to start buying."

I nodded and reached for a beer. Jameson led Veronica to an old loveseat. They sat next to Chris and Redbeard. Jordan sat at a tiny desk, while a couple of laborers sat awkwardly on one of the twin beds. As I meandered deeper into the room, I realized the side door was open, connecting it to the next room, where a few other familiar faces were milling around drinking.

I leaned on the far wall and stared off into space, wondering how I was going to pass the time while Veronica worked her source. I reached into my pocket to grab my phone when I saw Paul emerge from the bathroom.

"Hey Beck, I didn't expect to see you here. Where's Jorge?"

"I don't know. I didn't come with him. Ronnie wanted to come hang out and I said I'd drive her."

Paul smiled knowingly. "She needed a break from the bedroom, huh? But why aren't you sitting with her?"

"You know me—I'm not sleeping with her. I'm just her designated driver."

"You've got to stop being such a nice guy. Chicks don't like it when we're too nice. They say they do, but they don't."

"I'll keep that in mind for a girl I'm actually trying to get with."

Paul was right. I was too nice.

I had worked hard my entire adult life to be nice. It led to a sense of personal satisfaction. It also led to hearing everyone's problems all the time. Women opened up to me because I was nice. They told me things I had no business knowing. I then had to enter into the societal agreement that states I will never use those vulnerabilities to my advantage. There is a subculture of men who do not stick to this contract, a horrifyingly large group to which I did not belong.

Being too nice also led to keeping secrets. As it applied to me, it meant not putting certain things into my books.

True crime writing is often dry. But in my last two rejections, editors had said they couldn't get through my manuscripts because there was not enough "color," the implication being I didn't have enough of the gory details. But after spending months getting to know families of victims, how could I write about the worst moments of their late loved ones' lives? I was too nice to do that to a grieving family.

But what about fiction? I had a hundred anecdotes from friends of both genders that would make tragic stories for characters to overcome. But, even after changing some facts and obscuring identities, I couldn't do it. Acquiring editors said my story "didn't have enough tension and conflict," and that I hadn't "put my characters through enough to make their transformation matter." I could easily fix those problems, but how could I betray the confidence of my friends and live with myself? I was too nice to do that. And proud of it.

So, there I stood, a failed writer, waiting for a woman to get done flirting with another man so I could drive her back to our shared bedroom.

"You know, I almost believe it when you say you're not trying to get with her," Paul said. "But I don't."

I turned and looked at Veronica, cozied up against Jameson, laughing at something Jordan had said. I allowed myself to wish I could switch places with Jameson. Would I prefer that? Absolutely. To deny it would be as believable as denying the earth was round. Some people did, but the rest of us knew they were either full of shit or had a loose grip on reality.

I needed to change the subject. "How's your dad? Last I read he was running an energy committee out in Washington."

"Energy and commerce. Funny how our government

connects those two." He finished his beer and crushed the can. "It's like, if nobody's making money, they don't care about it."

"When did you get so philosophical?" I remembered Paul being the perfect stereotypical jock in high school. If his thoughts had ever transcended football, girls, and beer, I never knew it.

"I've seen some shit. I mean, my dad's a congressman, and I'm drinking cheap beer in a cheaper hotel instead of partying on a beach somewhere."

He brought up a good point. I wanted to ask more, but I'd learned a while ago how impolite it was to inquire about some pipeliners' pasts. Though I'd never had to do it myself, most good-paying jobs required extensive rounds of interviews and background checks. None of that was required in this world. We all had to pass drug tests, and sometimes prove we could handle ourselves physically, but that's where it stopped. I'd met more felons in the past few months than the rest of my life combined —and I used to talk to criminals for a living.

While discussing sordid pasts was taboo, I'd yet to meet someone on a job site who didn't like talking about their ink.

This was the first time I'd seen Paul in a T-shirt since high school. Other than a sandy blond beard, the biggest physical difference were his arms, which were somehow even larger and covered in tattoos. His sleeves were a mishmash of shapes and words. A mermaid. An ace of spades. Something tribal that seemed homemade. Three black hearts.

"When did you get into tattoos?" I asked.

Paul paused, considering how much to tell me. "I guess it started in college, though most of these came after." He looked down at his arms. "I spend too much money on them. But hey, I might's well spend it while I have it, right?"

I thought about giving him my lecture on starting a Roth IRA, but before I could he slapped me on the shoulder. "I think I'm going to get going. We'll see you two tomorrow."

I watched Paul walk toward the door, then turned my attention back to Veronica and Jameson. I had no reason to care how she got information out of Jameson or anyone else. But that didn't mean I had to watch it. I took my unopened beer, which only served to keep the other guys from handing me one, and went into the other room, hoping I had enough battery left to spend the rest of the evening distracted by my phone.

VERONICA'S ENTRANCE into our hotel room was much less direct after a night of drinking. She weaved her way to her bed and flopped down, her legs hanging over the side.

"So, he didn't admit it, but ol' Jamie was definitely sleeping with Sylvia."

"If he didn't tell you, how do you know?"

"A girl just knows."

I laughed. "Even if you're right, that has nothing to do with why she was killed."

"Sure it does. He's married, and he told me his wife comes one weekend a month. If wifey found out, that's motive."

"But could wifey have done that to Sylvia? Bash her head in? And where did she get the screwdriver? No, that's not right. There would've been a hell of a catfight, but it doesn't explain Sylvia's death."

Veronica propped herself up on her elbows. "What if he did something to piss off Sylvia, and she threatened to tell his wife about the affair? Maybe Jamie killed her to keep that from happening."

That was a scenario worth considering. But I had a hard time believing Sylvia's secret identity and sabotage weren't connected to her death. I still hadn't told Veronica about that—or our resulting fight last week—and now was not the time. Though our interests were temporarily aligned, she had been looking to expose me as a liar and fabulist writer less than a week ago. She had good instincts. I didn't want to give her a reason to turn her investigative spotlight away from Jameson and onto me.

Perhaps Jameson had also caught Sylvia scarring and burning pipe. He'd be angry. He had a key to Site One and, in theory, knew his way around a toolbox. So, whether it was jealousy or sabotage, Jameson was a likely suspect.

But when I tried to picture Jameson doing the deed—bashing in the side of her head, which he nearly took off with a power tool of some kind, then stabbing her in the face with a screwdriver—I drew a blank. Instead, I saw the man who'd shielded himself from a welder twice his age.

No. Jameson was not the killer. I relayed the story to Veronica, who considered what I was saying but seemed unconvinced.

"Fine, Mr. Big Time True Crime Writer. What's your theory?"

I sat down on my bed and faced her. "I don't have one. That's why you're here."

"Bullshit. Bull Fucking Shit. You're playing it cool, but I know you're scared out of your mind about going to prison for her murder. You want to figure this out more than I do."

She was right. But that didn't mean I had to admit it. "You're getting loose with your language, young lady."

"Oh my God, how naïve can you be? I am not a good girl. You assumed I am because of how I acted when I interviewed you the first time."

"I see. Well, *I* assume people are genuine and honest until I find out they're not."

"And that's why you haven't written anything good in a decade."

I should've erupted in self-defense. But I couldn't. She'd put into words a truth that haunted me for years. I was a one-hit-wonder, and that's only because I was directly involved in something so horrible that everyone wanted to read about it, no matter who did the writing. I also had a team of people who knew that, if they could help me enough, we would all cash in.

Instead of arguing, I started finding clothes to change into after my shower.

"Oh God. Beck, I am so sorry. I'm drunk. I don't know what I'm talking about."

I shuffled through my underwear drawer, unable to face her. "Yes, you do. And it's okay. If you were wrong, I wouldn't be here. I'd be at a desk writing something."

"No, I'm sorry. Tell me why you think Sylvia died. I bet it's a much better story than mine."

I turned around. Veronica was sitting up now, cross-legged again, but staring at me with a softness that had been missing up until then.

"Well, it has to be someone who's read *Cold Summer*. I know the investigators are taking that into account. They asked me for a list of people on the job site who bought a copy of it. I gave them a dozen names."

"Were they mostly welders and helpers?"

"Yeah. And one operator." I sat back down on my bed. "So, the way I see it, it's kind of like a Venn diagram. In one circle are the people who know about Site One. In another circle are people who know how Summer Foster was killed. In the middle are the people on that list I gave to the Texas Rangers, which I would say doubles as our suspect list."

"Would you be willing to re-write it for me?"

"Sure. But it's basically everyone you've met on the job so far."

"Okay. So, the question is: Of the people in the middle of that diagram, who would've wanted Sylvia dead? And why would they try to copy how Summer was killed twenty years ago?"

"I don't have those answers. But we do know she was lying to everyone about who she was. She must've been running from something."

"Right. Jamie did say something interesting to me today. He said that every time they, quote, hung out, Sylvia was always ignoring phone calls and texts. He asked who it was, and she said it was her family. But he looked one time when she was in the shower, and the missed calls were from a blocked number."

I had a hard time believing family members would block their numbers. "Maybe an ex?"

"Maybe. I'll have to think more about it when I'm sober."

I looked at the alarm clock on my bedside table. "Good idea. It's already almost one o'clock. I'm going to take a shower. See you in the morning."

As I turned on the water, I wondered who Sylvia really was —and who'd left her for me to find.

21

EXCERPT FROM COLD SUMMER

Summer Foster was happy in the hours before the murder. She smiled and laughed with neighbors as she prepared her annual Fourth of July celebration.

Jeremiah Schmidt, a sanitation worker for the city who lived two houses down, was walking his dog and asked her to recommend a book for his son, Chris.

"I'll be honest, I liked stopping and talking to Summer because she was beautiful. I mean, how often does someone like me—a guy who basically wades through shit all day—get to talk to someone like that? But mostly we talked about my son and school. Everybody loved her. That's why her death was one of the worst things this town ever experienced."

Before the murder, violent crime in Hinterbach was almost nonexistent. It was far from Rockwellian, but the town's criminal element was mostly limited to drugs and petty theft. Kids would steal beer coolers out of the back of pickups on the weekends, and a car might be taken for a joyride outside of the convenience store on Main Street.

After the murder, four religious leaders in Hinterbach called a community meeting. Hundreds packed into the Broadway Church of Christ. The topic of discussion: how evil can overtake a community.

A priest, a minister, and two preachers—those of other faiths were akin to atheists and therefore not represented—warned residents of the sneaky danger posed by small sins. They argued that the collective evil of hundreds of those infractions—drinking alcohol to excess, experimenting with drugs, sex outside of wedlock—could infect a town. They used verses from their varying versions of the Bible as evidence. In summation, the holy men told Hinterbach residents their collective hedonism had led to Summer's murder.

It was their fault. And only a swift correction could keep it from happening again.

22

SUMMER FOSTER

July 4, 1999, 1 p.m.

Summer could not stomach Jeremiah Schmidt. He'd never intentionally done anything negative to her. But the way he looked at her, the way he spoke to her—the way she could sometimes see him get an erection if they talked too long—it was almost too creepy for her to handle.

But their sons were friends and teammates. So, even though she never ran by his house and checked her front window before stepping into the yard, Summer had to engage him a few times a year, including every Fourth of July.

She drew in a deep breath and forced a smile as he approached with his family's dog, a half-canine, half-grizzly that lunged toward her and promptly began sniffing around her crotch.

"Howdy neighbor. Getting ready for tonight's shindig?"

Summer scratched the top of the dog's head and tried to redirect its nose. "Hi, Jerry. How are Delilah and Christopher?"

"Lily and Chris are good." Jeremiah leaned in far too close for Summer's comfort. "Speaking of Chris, I was really, really hoping you could help me out with something."

Summer stood her ground, refusing to step back. It helped that she was a fraction of an inch taller. "Of course. What can I do for you?"

"Well, I want to help Chris keep his grades up this year. You know, for football and basketball. I saw something on the news about how reading books over the summer can help kids do better in school the next year."

"That's all very true."

"Good deal. So, I'm sure you can tell that I don't read a whole lot. Lily does, but I thought maybe I'd come see what you think Chris should read to keep his mind sharp and all."

Summer was surprised by Jeremiah's thoughtfulness, at his concern for his son's education. He still creeped her out. But, for once, Summer was thankful Jeremiah had walked her way.

"Well, you could have him read *Seabiscuit*. It's about a race-horse, one that won the Triple Crown way back when. The book has some bad language, but it's an amazing story of hope and triumph. It was just released, so I don't have a copy in the school library, but you can get it at the bookstore in Kerrville next week."

"*Seabiscuit*. Got it." Jeremiah took a step back and looked her up and down, stopping briefly when his eyes got to her chest. "I love what you've done with your hair. Brains and beauty. You're the whole package."

Summer closed her eyes and forced her facial muscles to cooperate. "Thank you for the compliment, Jerry. It's been a pleasure as always, but I have to get back to setting up."

"Okay, Summer. I'll see you at the party tonight."

"Looking forward to it," she shouted over her shoulder.

Summer saw Butch dragging a picnic table to the middle of the yard, a decent distance from its usual home under the awning. He'd built that the previous July. Butch was a good man. Dealing with Jeremiah—and remembering what Paul had done that morning—gave her some perspective.

But every time she thought about Butch, she thought about Ruth Ann Beck.

————

SUMMER HAD SUCKED Butch off the morning after he killed Ruth Ann. Six months later, she still couldn't understand how a man who'd taken the life of another person could think about sex less than twelve hours later. But he'd finished on her tits, then made them coffee as though nothing had happened.

On her morning run, Summer had noticed the fresh dents in his truck that stretched from the rear of the passenger-side door to the middle of the bed. When asked about it later, Butch said someone else had backed into it. The story sounded believable enough.

He let Summer mourn over the next few days without acting out of the ordinary, though the smell of whiskey on his breath might've been a bit more potent. But then Butch came back to her house drunker than she'd seen him in months. He began crying and told her they needed to talk. He told her about getting fired from his job and going to the bar during the day instead. Then he told her about getting a little too drunk, about losing control of his truck and ending up sideways across both lanes of the Kerrville highway.

Butch said he'd passed out, probably from the spinning, and woken up to the sound of a honking horn. He told her how he couldn't get out of the way in time, and how Ruth Ann had T-boned him. Through his sobbing, Butch said he got out to help her, but that she'd gone through the windshield and was dead by the time he reached her. He admitted to his cowardice and said he never called the police.

In retrospect, Summer was sure Butch had been expecting her to be shocked, but also forgiving. He had obviously not been expecting her to start hitting him and calling him every terrible thing she could think of. He'd asked her twice why she reacted

so angrily that night. Butch knew Ruth Ann had been Summer's
neighbor for all eighteen years of her life, and that the two occasionally ran around town to help the girl improve her track
times.

But what Butch didn't know, what nobody knew, was that
Ruth Ann Beck—the neighbor girl with blue eyes and the
warmest smile in Hinterbach—was the love of Summer Foster's
life.

UNTIL RUTH ANN, Summer had only slept with older men.
Sammy's father was a former Hinterbach High School star quarterback who'd been home from college. He'd gotten a scholarship to play for Texas A&M, though he wasn't a starter. He and
Summer fooled around some when she was a sophomore and he
was a senior. They later hooked up during a party while he was
home from College Station. She'd written him a letter telling him
he was the father, but she never heard back and didn't know if
he ever got the message.

From there it had been a string of experienced men. Seniors
during her freshman year at Texas State. Men in their thirties
after she'd come home, one of whom seemed disappointed she
was older than eighteen. She read later that he was caught with
dozens of photos featuring underage girls. Then there was
Butch, who was seven years her senior.

The only man her age she'd ever slept with was her piece of
shit ex, Frank. Summer had admittedly been with him for financial security. And, although she now knew it was an obsession,
the man had showered her with adoration and seemed to
genuinely crave her affection.

Since Ruth Ann's death, Summer had often considered how if
one or two things hadn't been happening at the same time—if
only a couple of circumstances had been different—she wouldn't

have entertained the notion of pursuing a sexual relationship with the girl.

But after Frank had beaten her for cheating, Summer wandered into a strange place. She was still with Butch, who was sweet and a good boyfriend. He was fun and probably loved her in his own way, but he was also a loafer and a drunk. And, while Butch was fine in bed and ate her pussy like no one else, he was never going to ignite the passion in her that every person craves, whether they know it or not. At the time, Summer didn't know what that passion felt like.

Meanwhile, Bernard Beck was looking to help his daughter live her dream of being a high school track star. Or, perhaps it was Bernard's dream. In either case, he approached Summer in June, right after Ruth Ann's seventeenth birthday, seeking her advice on sprinting. Ruth Ann was good at the 100-meter and 200-meter sprints. Everyone in town knew that Summer had come close to setting the Texas high school record in the 200. Summer was happy to help her neighbor.

It began with simple tips. How to come out of the blocks. Breathing techniques. Easy ways to improve her times. Then Ruth Ann asked if she could run with Summer in the morning, build her own routine. Summer had never enjoyed working out with others, but she relented.

To Summer's surprise, Ruth Ann understood the solitude of a morning jog. She did not bother Summer, didn't want to chat, never asked her to explain anything. Ruth Ann ran without saying a word, but within a week Summer began to initiate light conversation.

They eventually took it to the track, where Summer helped Ruth Ann put the tips into practice. Then she helped Ruth Ann develop a full sprinting routine, based on the one she'd learned in college. This included extensive stretching before and after the sessions.

Summer couldn't remember who made the first move. It didn't matter.

Even as a teenager, Summer hadn't acted like she did around Ruth Ann. They found places and times to be together, risks she'd never tried with anyone. They went on like that for weeks before the reality of their situation hit, when Ruth Ann began to talk about her upcoming volleyball two-a-days. She was still in school. She was underage.

She.

Summer had never been attracted to women. Hell, she still enjoyed sleeping with Butch. But the intense connection Summer felt when Ruth Ann's lips were on her body was indescribable. Summer hadn't fallen in love with a girl, or a woman, or a student, or a lesbian, or a neighbor. She'd fallen in love with Ruth Ann Beck.

Summer never found out if the feeling was mutual. She'd never told Ruth Ann how strongly she felt. They'd never uttered the word love, though they found every excuse to be near each other. Summer made sure one of her senior classes was library aide, which afforded them many opportunities. They shifted their morning schedules so runs and sprints could be done before class. Lunch hours were spent together when possible.

The strongest indicator of love Summer ever got was Ruth Ann's decision to attend a nearby community college. Ruth Ann graduated second in her class and, while her parents weren't extremely well off, she easily could have gone to a major university. Instead, Ruth Ann wanted to stay close enough to drive home on the weekends. Though she told her parents she wanted the ability to visit them frequently, Ruth Ann told Summer the decision was to keep them together.

Things had been going well before Ruth Ann returned for her first winter break.

Ruth Ann had chosen to stay in the dormitories, despite being close enough to live at home. She told Summer she wanted to have a "real" college experience. Staying close enough to visit seemed like a fair compromise. But when Ruth Ann returned home in December with a boyfriend, Summer wanted to scream.

She wanted to throw that short, weak little shit through Ruth Ann's front window.

But she couldn't do any of that. Forgetting for a moment that her relationship with Ruth Ann was a taboo, Summer had no right to be angry. She was still living with Butch, and most considered him her common-law husband.

It was difficult to get a moment alone with Ruth Ann while she was home. But when they were finally able to talk, Ruth Ann said her relationship with the boy had nothing to do with how she felt about Summer. And, as expected, Ruth Ann compared it to Summer's relationship with Butch. It made sense, but logic had little to do with how Summer felt about Ruth Ann.

Much to Summer's delight, the boy had to return two days early to rejoin the school's basketball team. That allowed Summer, on the last day of Ruth Ann's stay, to finally let go of her most closely kept secret.

The adrenaline rush from putting those three words out into the universe made Summer's hands shake. They left Ruth Ann speechless. She gave a rushed goodbye hug to her parents and practically threw her bags into the bed of her father's rusty pickup.

SUMMER WALKED out of her house with a bowl of coleslaw. Butch was putting his first batch of hot dogs, burgers, and barbecue chicken into a tin pan. The annual Fourth of July feast was about to start, whether she was ready for it or not.

She needed to forgive him. Her heart would never stop aching over the loss of Ruth Ann, but Summer also knew she could never get that love back. And after all the terrible men she'd been with, only Butch had never wavered in his love and commitment for her. And if she was wrong, if he had cheated, Butch had the damn good sense not to tell her.

They met at the last remaining space on the tables. He paused to let her place the glass bowl on a crowded buffet table.

"Look, I will always be upset about what happened," Summer said. "But I can't go on like this forever. So, I forgive you. You need to stay sober, but I'm ready to move on."

Summer looked up and was greeted by Butch's smile. "I love you so much. I won't disappoint you again. Not if I can help it, anyway."

She leaned up and in and kissed Butch lightly on the lips while taking the food he was still holding. "I love you too."

Summer spent another minute getting the buffet exactly how she wanted it. She looked down at her watch and smiled. One minute until 2:30 p.m. Just in time.

She turned around to see her son coming through the side gate with a pack of friends in tow. Sammy was the quarterback and the group's leader. He'd inherited the combined athletic abilities of his parents, and expectations were high this season. Summer waved to the boys as they passed through the gate.

She fought the urge to change her expression as Paul ran up to join them. He, too, was smiling and obviously trying to avoid eye contact. But, like most men, he couldn't help himself.

Summer tried to hold her own smile when he looked at her, but she turned away after just a fraction of a second and began looking for the quickest way out of her yard. She'd expected to see remorse for what he'd done that morning. She'd found something much darker.

It made Summer want to run.

23

I woke to the sound of the shower running. I found my phone and checked the time: 5:30 a.m., an hour until we had to leave for Jorge's house. Veronica would learn to skip the shower and get the extra forty-five minutes of sleep.

I rolled toward the bathroom. A large mirror hung above a spacious sink area. In the reflection, I could see that Veronica hadn't closed the door to the shower room, allowing me to see inside.

I knew I shouldn't keep looking when I heard the shower stop. Peeking at Veronica naked without her knowing was wrong. But I couldn't look away. As she stepped out, I was surprised by her beauty. Nobody on the job had given her the title of *new hot girl*, and she was not classically beautiful like Sylvia had been. But her curves were truly that, not a product of being overweight, as evidenced by a flat stomach that hinted at the abs underneath.

After drying herself, Veronica pulled up her towel and looked out the door to see if I was still asleep. I closed my eyes until she was ready to wake me up.

"Hey, it's six o'clock," she shouted from her side of the room.

I opened my eyes slowly. She was fully dressed in her sloppy work clothes, her dark, wet hair pulled back into a ponytail, her transformation into pipeliner complete. I was about to get out of the bed when I realized I'd slept in nothing but my boxer-briefs. I'd made a stand and ditched the undershirts. I wasn't shy, but my voyeurism had caused a physical reaction she would not appreciate.

I rolled over to face her. "Why don't you run down and get us some free muffins and Danishes while I get ready?"

"Do I look like your personal assistant?"

"I figured you'd want to be out of the room while I got dressed, that's all."

"Well, you're right about that. I'll be back in ten minutes."

———

"Listo?" Jorge asked.

"Vamonos."

As Jorge and Paul finished a thirty-inch weld, Zak walked up to me and leaned in. "Hey Beck, y'all come holler at me when you're done."

I nodded as I heard Jorge yell for another rod.

"Sorry." I popped a rod into his glove. "Zak was talking to me."

"What'd he say?" Jorge's voice was muffled through his red bestickered pancake, a thin, round, face shield with a dark slot for viewing damaging UV blasts.

"We all need to go talk to him when we're done here."

Jorge nodded his head before striking an arc. "Did he sound pissed?"

I held up my right hand to shield my eyes before turning toward him. "No."

"X-ray has been out here the last couple of days. I hope we didn't bust a weld."

"I doubt that. You two are the best out here."

Jorge shook his head. "Hey man, you never know. If welders

start getting cocky, they start making mistakes. And after all the shit Jillian did, they're looking for reasons to run us off."

There are several ways to bust a weld. We'd already seen examples of the most common: insufficient penetration and slag. Insufficient penetration, or IP, happened when a welder didn't lay his first layer of metal deep enough into the bevel between pipe ends. Or, as the term suggests, they didn't penetrate the gap deep enough. Almost as a reminder, one of the machines on the job site featured a custom sticker depicting a welder above the suggestive phrase *Welders Penetrate Deeper!*

Another common way to bust a weld was leaving slag on the freshly laid metal in between passes, or trips around the circumference of the pipe. Slag is a byproduct of stick welding's chemical reaction—or, as Veronica and I knew it, the crap we buffed out of the weld using the grinder after every pass. If a helper didn't clean the weld well enough—and the welder didn't burn out any remaining slag with the tip of the rod during the next pass—it would get stuck in between the metal layers, leaving the weld weak and prone to bursting when oil was sent rushing through the pipe.

The people who can see insufficient penetration or slag in a weld were known as X-ray. They are inspectors who drive in pairs from site to site in small pickups with tall campers over the beds. Inside the campers are X-ray machines that show any defects in a weld.

The previous day, a team had walked up to a weld with a thin, inch-wide black strip. It was a film of the X-ray they'd taken of the weld. One of the men wrapped it around the pipe and made large brackets next to the weld with paint markers, then wrote SLAG in large letters. Someone had busted a weld, which meant he had to repair the defect.

Three repairs—whether from a busted weld, grind mark, or errant arc burn—and Zak had to run a welder off the job. That was rare. For more than a couple of welders to get fired mid-job bordered on disastrous.

That three-strike rule only amplified the weight of Sylvia's mysterious actions.

Veronica looked at me nervously as we walked toward Jorge and Paul, who were already standing next to Zak. "Do you think we're in trouble?"

"No. We're the best team out here. Don't worry."

They were cutting up as we approached. "Hey guys," Zak said. "Okay, a few things for y'all. First, you're kicking ass, and I really appreciate it. To show you how much I appreciate it, I'm going to send you all to Site Three starting tomorrow."

"What's out there?" Paul asked.

"It's real small. One launcher. Easy stuff. But we're counting on it being done quickly and correctly the first time. That's why it'll just be you two, with me pitching in when we need to. I've got a dozen other welders to finish up here and at Site One when all that bullshit gets figured out."

"Well we appreciate you," Jorge said. "I was worried we'd busted a weld or were working too slow."

"Nope. You all are my rock stars. But, speaking of Site One, there is one other thing." Zak pointed to Jorge and me. "Those Texas Rangers need to talk to you two again."

Zak turned his attention to Paul and Veronica. "You two come out here tomorrow morning. Jorge and Big Nasty will go to Site One. After they're done, we'll meet out here again and y'all can follow me out to Site Three."

Jorge started to speak but was drowned out by the whining of a grinder. He leaned in closer to Zak. "Sounds good. It's almost break time. What do you want us doing after that?"

"Sit on your nuts," Zak said before realizing that Veronica was standing next to him. "I mean, go sit in your trucks. I'm probably going to let everyone go at four anyway."

"Don't worry about it," Veronica said. "I've got bigger balls than these guys, anyway."

We all laughed at Zak, who was staring slack-jawed at Veronica.

Veronica was energized as we walked toward our respective rigs. "What do you think the Rangers want to talk to you about?"

Jorge and I looked at each other and shrugged our shoulders. We stood in silence for a few moments until Paul spoke. "Hey Ronnie, since we're not doing anything after break, would you go ask someone to help you find a sky hook?"

"What's a sky hook?"

"It's just what it sounds like. Find a labor hand to help you. I want to make sure we know where one is before we get here tomorrow."

Veronica nodded her head and started walking toward the parts trailer, her gait almost normal after a few days onsite.

VERONICA SLAMMED THE TRUCK DOOR. "Fuck you two assholes. I walked around on my sore feet for twenty goddamn minutes before someone finally told me."

Jorge and I could barely hear her over our laughter.

"Hey, looking for a sky hook is a rite of passage," Jorge said. "Beck did it last week. It means you're one of us now."

"But I'm not one of you. I don't want to be."

I took a deep breath to stop laughing. "We're sorry. We won't do it again."

"Good. Now, back to business. You two have some work to do tomorrow."

"Right," I said. "What all do you need to know?"

"Oh, you know, who was this Sylvia Davenport woman? Who killed her? Small stuff like that."

I let out an overdramatic sigh. "You know we're never going to get that out of two Texas Rangers. How about something small and specific, something we can realistically find out that will help you."

Veronica thought for a few moments. "If you two can tell me

the last place Sylvia Davenport worked, or maybe her age, that would help a lot."

I should've known both of those things, but I'd done a terrible job trying to get to know Sylvia. Sure, I'd gotten superficial answers—favorite color, music and movie preferences, eating habits—but I hadn't asked anything substantive. That was probably by design on her part. But it was also my fault. I had told myself I was trying to learn about someone I could potentially care about. But I was discovering that, though not consciously or with malice, I had only been trying to get into her pants.

"Okay," I said. "We can work with that."

"Good. If I don't have something for my bosses to run in a few days, something that's a legitimate scoop, they'll tell me to go home. Hell, since I've been basically MIA for a week, they might fire me."

"So?" Jorge said. "You've got a job. One that pays better, too."

"What did we just talk about?"

Jorge laughed. "Wait till you get your first paycheck on Friday. Then let's talk again."

Veronica was about to respond when someone knocked on my window. I turned my head and saw Zak, who motioned for me to roll down my window.

"Go home with ten. And remember, Jorge and Beck are going to Site One to talk to the police tomorrow." Zak looked at Veronica. "Do you have a way to get out here without these two?"

"Yep. Paul's going to be nice and pick me up at my hotel."

Zak nodded and began walking toward the next truck. After we pulled out of our spot, a line formed behind us. Jorge was flooded with calls asking where the welders should spend their free time and money that evening. They settled on Bennigan's in Borger.

Jorge looked back at Veronica. "I know Beck's not in, but how about you, Ronnie?"

"Sure. Why aren't you coming, Big Nasty," she said, putting an obnoxious emphasis on my nickname.

"*Big Nasty* doesn't ever go out and drink with us," Jorge said.

Veronica poked her head into the front half of the cabin. "You don't ever drink any beer in the room either. Are you an alcoholic?"

"No," I said. "I just like getting my rest, and I drank enough for a lifetime in college, thanks to this guy."

Jorge smiled. "Yeah, we did tear it up. But I always kept us out of trouble, didn't I?"

"Always."

Jorge had brought me out of my shell. At least, that's how it seemed from his perspective. The truth is I let him, but only after I'd decided to trust him as much as I'd once trusted my older sister.

Ruth Ann had given me my first drink. She'd come home late from a party one night and tried sneaking in through her bedroom window. Though she was as athletic as anyone in town, the beer had proven too much that night. She made enough noise to wake me. As it turns out, it wasn't only the beer that she'd consumed, but the can she was trying to hold as she attempted her less-than-stealthy ingress. She'd put her index finger to her lips for a sloppy *shhh* before breaking out into laughter. I was only thirteen, so I just stared at her. I'd never seen her drink or sneak out, so I had no idea what my brotherly duties were in that situation.

Ruth Ann read me like one of her friends' diaries. She convinced me she was okay and urged me to not tell our parents, for fear of angering them for no good reason. That relaxed me. She then offered me the rest of her beer, the Texas sibling's version of initiating a blood oath. From then on, I only drank in her company.

After she died, I hadn't touched a drop until I dubbed Jorge my surrogate older sibling. When we went our separate ways after graduation, I cut myself off again. I could've had some beers with him after I became his helper, but it rarely seemed necessary or appealing, except perhaps to dull the soreness. But that would be too temporary to justify the next day's cramping. The one exception had been during the strip club outing, where being a drunken fool was not only expected, but encouraged.

If I were to get drunk with him again, I'd have to stay over on his couch. That, or let Drunk Beck loose on Veronica.

24

EXCERPT FROM COLD SUMMER

The last person to see Summer in public was Simon Winkler, the afternoon cashier at Hinterbach's Sinclair station. She walked into the station at about 2:40 and bought a hard pack of Marlboro Lights. She did it with some regularity, according to Winkler.

She laughed while telling Winkler how she remembered at the last second to grab some cash before beginning the short trek to the green Brontosaurus, which only took about five minutes when she cut across Louisa Park.

"By that time, it was hot outside. I mean hot. She was wearing a short, sleeveless dress, but she was still sweating when she walked in," Winkler said. "She had exact change for me. Two dollars and eighty-nine cents. Of course, she was in there maybe once a week or so to tide her over between buying cartons in Kerrville, so she knew how much they cost.

"I remember she wiped her brow and said how

mad she'd've been if she'd've had to walk all the way back, get money, then come here again. And all for one lousy pack of cigarettes. I told her that since she was such a regular and everyone in town knew her, I'd've paid for them this time, long as she paid me back the next time she came in."

The conversation lasted about four minutes. Adding the five-minute walk back, Summer Foster was in her back yard, celebrating Independence Day with neighbors and friends, at roughly 2:49 p.m.

She would remain on that property for the rest of her life.

25

FRANKLIN JONES

July 4, 1999, 2:32 p.m.

Jones didn't have time for this, but he'd driven without
thought to the county courthouse. His BMW always
wanted to slip into its favorite spot. Jones had been power-
less, even though he was expected in San Antonio soon.

Since he was there, Jones decided to stay for at least a few
minutes. He reached into the center console and pulled out a
relatively cheap cigar, one he'd picked up on his last trip to the
city. He didn't smoke often, and when he did, he preferred the
Cubans in his humidor at home—another promotion gift. But a
drive was no time to fully appreciate and enjoy a Cuban, so he
kept less expensive singles in his car.

Jones unsheathed the cigar and rolled down his window
before cutting the tip, taking great care to make sure no tobacco
blew back into the car. Then he rolled it around in his mouth,
took his time to evenly light the tip, and settled in.

As he hung his left arm out of the car, Jones saw her. Summer
was walking toward the Sinclair station. He'd watched her make
cigarette runs at least once a week for months. She'd become a
dedicated smoker since Heller had killed that neighbor girl.

They'd been close, but Jones was glad the girl would no longer be competing for Summer's time.

He watched as she moved briskly toward the store, then turned his attention to an unsealed envelope in his passenger seat. On it was written *MY DEAREST SUMMER*. Jones picked it up and pulled out the letter he'd handwritten on his bank stationery.

My beloved,

Words cannot express how thankful I am to be back in your life. And by the time you're done reading this letter, I think you will be ready to move on from Butch Heller and accept my undying love.

During the two years since we've spoken, I have been made aware of Heller's continued affair with another woman. This woman, who has asked me to not reveal her identity, is a prostitute who frequents nearby drinking establishments. She first met Heller while working, and they had a sexual encounter in the back of his truck. He no doubt told you he was working late on a job or used some other excuse.

They had many more sexual encounters during a months-long affair, but she had to quit seeing all her clients when she became pregnant. Though nobody paid for a DNA test, she introduced the newborn girl to Heller, and it was obvious he was the father.

The baby, whom Heller had kept secret, soon fell ill. Her mother had no means to pay for medical care and Heller, not wanting to expose himself as the philanderer he is, was unwilling to pay for treatment. The baby died less than two months after her birth.

If you would like to meet this woman and hear her awful story in person, I can help arrange that. In the meantime, I sincerely hope you kick that animal out of your home for good and allow me to help you heal.

With all my love,
Franklin W. Jones III

JONES HAD WRITTEN the letter immediately after pretending to be with the Census Bureau and meeting Ethel "Candy" McDonough and her eight-year-old daughter, Verna. To maintain his cover, Jones asked how long they'd lived there. Candy said she'd inherited the house from her parents, as most people in the area did, and she'd lived there her whole life. To round out his fake interview, Jones asked if they were the only people who'd lived at the residence since Verna's birth.

That question sent Candy into a crying fit that bordered on hysteria. Verna eventually told Jones that she'd had a baby sister for a few months, but that the baby girl had died earlier that year. Candy finally steadied herself enough to shoo away Verna and tell Jones the rest.

Jones had nearly mailed the letter, but backtracked when he realized Summer may choose to bring the letter to the attention of the authorities and put their reunion in jeopardy. And, since the restraining order's expiration date was so close, he opted instead to tell her in person. If she reacted negatively and did not allow him to explain, he could still leave the letter with her.

Either way, Jones was about to get what he wanted.

He was only about halfway done with the cigar when she crossed Louisa Park on her way back to the party. He tossed it in the parking lot and started the car. He was already going to be late for his meeting. They were only going to wait so long and pissing them off would be a dangerous move.

JONES WAS a bit thrown to see the two FBI agents in street clothes. They were usually in suits, always gray or black, with dull-colored ties and cheap black shoes. Now they were both in khaki shorts and T-shirts. They were, however, wearing their familiar dark sunglasses.

Jones approached the men, who were sitting outside a coffee

shop in downtown San Antonio. "Agent J, Agent K, how are you this fine afternoon?"

"I can't believe people are still making that goddamn joke," said Agent J, a thirtysomething failing to pull off the just-rolled-out-of-bed look.

Agent K smiled. "Hey, if you want to compare me to Tommy Lee Jones, I'm okay with that. I'd be even more okay with it if you did it in front of my wife."

All three laughed as Jones pulled over a patio chair to the round, glass table.

"So, what's so important it couldn't wait until after the holiday?" Jones asked.

"You haven't checked in with us in over a month," Agent J said. "We figured scheduling a meeting on the Fourth of July would get your attention."

"Mission accomplished," Jones said. "But I haven't contacted you because I don't have anything to say. Just because I'm the president of the bank doesn't mean I can ask for all the documents you want. I inherited my secretary from my uncle, and if you think that old bird doesn't tell him everything that goes on in the bank, you're dumber than you look."

J bristled, but K started talking before his younger partner could respond. "We know that, obviously. But we've also got to get somewhere on this investigation. We have enough to arrest you for a whole lot of bad stuff, but we want the old man since he's the real criminal. Well, the real financial criminal, anyway."

Jones suppressed his urge to shout at the older agent. Did he think a dig like that would make Jones *more* likely to cooperate? It's hard enough to ask someone to bite the hand that's feeding him.

But agents J and K had shown Jones the federal documents they were waiting to file. All that was missing was the name. It could be his, they'd told Jones, or it could be his uncle's. The choice was his.

The crime—the big one, anyway—was embezzlement. Essentially, cash was being taken from his bank's vault and deposited into another bank under a version of Jones' name, Frank Jones III. If only ten percent more customers than usual came for cash withdrawals, his vault would be empty. The agents also had a hunch that the safe-deposit boxes had been raided for cash and valuables, though they had no proof.

Jones had no idea about the account or the embezzlement until the FBI had confronted him about a year ago. He couldn't take any money out of the fake account because it had been flagged for activity.

Jones hadn't tipped off his family. He wasn't sure what to do. So, he'd done nothing. And he damn sure wasn't going to get caught up in anything criminal until after he was clear to get Summer back.

"Do you have any better suggestions than last time?" Jones said. "Ordering a random accounting of the physical cash in our vault is a nonstarter, and I can't just hang out all day waiting to catch someone in the act."

"How about going in after-hours, doing the count yourself, and taking photos then?" K asked.

"I'd have to disarm the security system, which is logged in a central computer. And the police would notice a car in the parking lot after hours, so they may call it in. Then I'd be arrested for stealing the money anyway."

J cleared his throat. "I know that seems like a risk to you, but the alternative is that we arrest *you* for the embezzlement."

"Or, like we discussed before," K said, "you could confront your uncle while wearing a wire. Get him to let you in on the scam, give us the recording, and you're home free."

Jones knew that was his best option. But he'd be cut off. No money, no car, no suits, no cigars. And, most importantly, no Summer.

"Tell you what," Jones said. "Not this weekend, but next weekend, I'll plan on going into the vault with a camera. I'll come see you on Monday the nineteenth and show you what I have. Deal?"

They agreed and broke up the meeting. Jones now had two weeks to confront his uncle and figure out how to get as much of the old man's cash squirreled away as possible. Then he could ride off into the sunset with Summer.

But he had to get the girl first. Jones checked his Yacht-Master before getting back in the BMW. It was four p.m.—just enough time to get to Summer's house by five.

26

Walker's eyes were upon us as she and Agent Orange waited outside the tin building. Jorge pulled into the parking lot at Site One at seven sharp. Orange was spitting into a short Styrofoam cup. She was taking long draws of a silver Yeti.

"Wow, they're not messing around," Jorge said. "What did your girl say she needed from us?"

"The last place Jillian worked and her age. And she's not my girl."

Jorge opened his door. "But you know you want her to be."

"Shut up."

We slid out of Jorge's truck and shuffled toward the investigators. I was exceptionally tired after a fitful night of not sleeping, my brain not allowing for any rest. I kept thinking about getting arrested, wondering what handcuffs would feel like on my wrists. The alternative scenario was me trying to outwit two Texas Rangers to get the information Veronica wanted.

"Gentlemen, thank you for coming back to visit with us again," Walker said as we approached.

"You make it sound like we had a choice," Jorge said.

She smiled, taking Jorge's comment in the good nature it was intended. "You always have a choice. But, had you chosen not to come, we'd've chosen to get arrest warrants."

Jorge and I laughed as Orange dug out the tobacco from his bottom lip. "All right, let's get to it. Mr. Hernandez, you follow her." Orange looked at me. "You're mine, Bart."

I tried to remember Orange's real name as he opened the door. I'd started calling him that because something about his name reminded me of orange juice, but what was it? I was still drawing a blank as we sat down on opposite sides of a cheap desk.

"So, I'm Lieutenant Owen Johnson, in case you'd forgotten. And you, Mr. Bartholomew John Beck, have more explaining to do."

I felt my eyes widen as he placed a briefcase on the desk and opened it. "I'm still not sure what you're after. I haven't lied about anything, and I did not kill Sylvia."

He didn't respond as he laid files on the desk and put the briefcase on the floor beside his chair. He fidgeted with them for a few more agonizing moments before finally looking up at me. "We'll see about that. Let's start with you telling me about Tight Strips."

Tight Strips was the name of the strip club where I'd earned my nickname. It occurred to me that what happened there could be construed as an illegal sex transaction.

"That's a strip club in Oklahoma City. I was there a couple of months ago with a few of the other guys."

"And what happened while you were there?"

"I had a few drinks, got a few dances. It was fun. I don't see what it could have to do with Sylvia's death."

"Do you always wear glasses, Bart?"

I shook my head at the non sequitur. "Yes."

"When's the last time you had your eyes checked?"

"I... um... I don't know. Less than a year ago, I guess."

"Well, you should go get them checked again. Bad eyesight is the only way I can explain how you could have gotten a lap dance from a girl, found her dead less than three months later, and not know it was the same damn woman."

Agent Orange slapped a large photo onto the desk in front of me. It looked like a black-and-white still shot taken from closed-circuit TV. It was grainy, but you could plainly see a woman leading me by the hand toward the stairs that led to Tight Strips' VIP room. Her hair was dyed auburn, but it was Sylvia.

She hadn't given me the now infamous tug job, but Sylvia must've gotten to me later, after I was already drunk.

"Sir, I honestly don't remember all the dances I got that night. I had no idea she worked there, and I definitely didn't recognize her when I saw her on the job later."

"As a professional writer, I'm sure you've heard guys like me say this before, but people who investigate murders for a living don't believe in coincidences."

He ripped the photo off the table, replacing it with a photo of her body in the pipe.

"You got a lap dance from a stripper. Then you started working together. You tried getting close to her, to get her to take her clothes off without you paying. When she said no, you assaulted her. Then you found her dead two days later."

I shook my head and stammered again, trying to proclaim my innocence, but Orange was having none of it.

"You mean to tell me you were able to immediately identify Sylvia Davenport in this condition—" he pointed at the photo "—but you didn't recognize her as one of the strippers you bought dances from less than a month earlier?"

He continued talking, but my brain was too busy trying to catch up. I had obviously gotten a dance from Sylvia that night. But was I the only one? Jorge and Paul were there, too.

"Excuse me, Agent… I mean, mister… Shit. Lieutenant Johnson, another welder, Paul Henry, was there, too. And he's the one that brought her to the job as his helper. What has he said about all of this?"

"We haven't gotten him in here yet. We're starting with those of you who found her and were also at the club that night. Are you familiar with a Venn diagram?"

I fought back a smile. "Yes, I am. But it seems to me that Sylvia might've given Paul a lap dance that night, and during that time they decided she could make more money working with us. Does that sound possible?"

He leaned back and crossed his arms over his chest. "My working theory was that you, knowing that Paul needed an assistant, talked her into convincing Paul to hire her. I'm also looking into any other connections between you and Sylvia."

"There are no other connections. That was the first and only time I was ever at that place."

He leaned forward and began writing on a notepad. "Let's move on. When was the last time you interacted with the FBI?"

It seemed non sequiturs were part of Orange's interview-room routine. "I've talked with them for some of my books, but the last time was at least three years ago."

Orange tapped on his notepad with his pen, as though he was building up to something. "You see, I just don't believe anything that comes out of your mouth, Bart."

I shook my head. I was getting nowhere defending myself with this fucking guy.

"Look, I go by Beck, so that's how you're going to address me from now on. And if you don't believe me, I don't know what to tell you."

"You're not getting it, are you? See, when I tried to do a standard background check on this woman, I got a stiff arm from the feds. The FBI has her marked as part of a high-profile case. They all but told me to fuck off when I asked them what her role was."

I did my best not to react. Were the FBI behind Sylvia's crazy actions on our job site? "Sounds like you have a good lead that has nothing to do with me."

"Except you have a known connection with the FBI." Orange pointed at me. "Every time I turn over a rock in this case, something with your fingerprints comes crawling out."

"Except my actual fingerprints. You have no physical evidence, or you'd've arrested me already, instead of this bullshit interview trying to get a confession."

Orange leaned back in his chair. "Well, you've got me there. I was hoping you might be generous enough to just tell me what happened. If you do that and put me in a better mood, I might be able to get you less time, though the FBI won't take kindly to you murdering one of their CIs."

Orange was convinced I was guilty, and there was nothing I could do to change his mind. He was a seasoned investigator and knew I was lying about something. Fortunately for me, he was investigating the wrong case.

"This is obviously going nowhere," I said. "I did not kill Sylvia Davenport. I'm going to need a lawyer present at any future interviews."

"If that's how you want it. But I wouldn't leave Hutchinson County." He handed me his business card. "In case you decide to make it easy on yourself."

Agent Orange stood and motioned for me to leave the office. Jorge and Walker were laughing at an empty cubicle. He was obviously not under much suspicion.

After we got into Jorge's truck, I was anxious to find out how his interrogation had gone. "What did you find out?"

"That Miss Walker is divorced with a pre-teen daughter. She doesn't have much time to date, but she did give me her phone number."

"Dude, she knows you're married. And I was talking about the murder investigation. You know, the one where I'm a prime suspect."

Jorge started his truck. "I was trying to flirt my way into getting information. It didn't work though."

"Did she ask about me?"

"Yeah. She asked how I knew you, when we met, why I brought you on with me, that kind of stuff. She also asked me if you were home the night Sylvia died. What did the old man ask you?"

"He all but asked me why I killed Sylvia."

Jorge looked at me, the playful spark gone from his eyes. "Why do they think you killed her?"

I broke down my interview with Agent Orange and ended it by asking Jorge if he'd recognized Sylvia. He hadn't. We were typical men and didn't remember the faces of strippers we let grind on us. We also agreed that Sylvia had gone out of her way to avoid us outside of work, when she was in clothes that may have sparked more recognition. We had assumed she was either banging Paul on the side or hiding in her motel room. But if Veronica was right, she was sleeping with Jameson.

We parked at Allsup's. "What we really need to find out is why Paul brought her out here," I said.

"She probably found out he was a welder while giving him a dance, and she wanted a different way to make good money. It wouldn't be the first time a welder had taken a stripper out to be their helper."

"It wouldn't?"

"Nope. I'm not saying it happens all the time. But I've heard guys tell stories."

As if on cue, Paul parked his truck beside us. Jorge rolled down his window. "Your turn to talk to the cops?"

"Yep. Better than working, I guess. I left Ronnie with Zak."

Jorge smiled. "Hell yeah. But remember bro, snitches get stitches."

I opened my mouth but decided against asking Paul anything. I'm sure we'd all talk about it later at Site Three. And Veronica would appreciate being there to hear whatever he said.

As we pulled onto the highway leading toward Borger, Jorge called Zak to let him know we were heading his way. To our surprise, Zak told us he'd planned on us being off all day and to take off with pay. We hung up before he had a chance to change his mind.

"Well, what do you want to do?" Jorge asked.

I wanted to run. To get as far away as possible before I was arrested. But if I was already the focus of the investigation, leaving would only confirm their suspicions.

If these were going to be the last few days of freedom, I might as well enjoy them. "Fuck it. Let's go drink."

"Hell yeah, bro. All I have to do is talk my old lady into letting me go."

"Why? Just let her think you're at work."

"It's been a long time since you've lived in a small town," Jorge said. "Someone'll see my truck parked at the bar and tell her before we finish our first beer."

I nodded. His truck and the welding equipment in the back was easily identifiable. Jorge cranked up a local country station and sang about being more redneck than me as we drove to his house, where we found his wife smoking a cigarette on the front porch.

"Wait here," he said. "I'll be back in a second."

While Jorge walked over to sweet talk his wife, I found myself getting angry again. I tried hard every day to be positive, to be friendly. To be *nice*. I'd worked hard to cultivate a life that allowed me to work essentially stress-free. Like writing, this was supposed to be another easygoing lifestyle. But then some asshole had to kill this Sylvia Davenport and leave her rotting corpse for me to find.

I hadn't realized my teeth and fists were clenched until Jorge jumped back into the truck.

"All right, we're good," he said. "I have to be back for dinner at six, and I can't be too drunk to work on the house tonight. So, where do you want to go?"

"What bars are open at eight-thirty on a Monday?"

"The Hog and The Oasis are definitely open."

The Hog was what they called the Jolly Pig, but I'd never seen it. The Oasis was on Main Street across from the Morely

Theater. I'd driven past it, and it looked decent. "Let's try The Oasis."

Jorge answered by turning the music back up and revving his engine.

27

J orge dropped me off at five. I'd tried not to drink too much or too fast, but I was toeing the line between buzzed and drunk as I walked into the hotel room. The more I'd had to drink at The Oasis, the more convinced I was that solving the murder with Veronica was my only shot at avoiding a life sentence.

I put my laptop on the desk and opened it for the first time in weeks. I Googled *"Sylvia Davenport" + Austin TX* and clicked on the first link, which brought up a news article with the headline LOCAL WOMAN SPEAKS OUT ABOUT DAKOTA ACCESS PIPELINE PROTESTS.

A click brought me to a story that ran three years ago in the *Austin Chronicle*, the city's left-leaning weekly paper. The story was accompanied by a picture of Sylvia Davenport. I read slowly as my eyes struggled to focus.

Sylvia, who the article said had moved to Austin from California, was apparently an environmental activist with no day job listed. The story said she was well-known in those circles and sometimes acted as a de facto spokesperson for the movement against the Dakota Access Pipeline, a project planned by a Dallas energy company. It would start in North Dakota and run southeast through the Midwest, including a stretch underneath the Missouri River less than a mile from a Native American reservation.

Protests erupted when construction began at a site that may have contained Native graves and buried artifacts over three years ago. Guards near the site used pepper spray and guard dogs, causing injuries and a media firestorm. Sylvia Davenport claimed to have been there—a photo showed what looked like a dog bite on her calf—and she used the *Chronicle* to describe the scene and backstory.

The grinder and battery finally made some sense.

I was proud of how clearly I could think despite the six-pack and scattered shots I'd taken throughout the day. We'd gone from The Oasis to The Jolly Pig, which was, as the name suggested, a good time. Then Jorge had driven to Amarillo and spent a couple hours barhopping.

And now, with one web search, I'd figured out who Sylvia Davenport was and found an explanation for her destructive behavior.

But why our job? Why this pipeline? It wasn't the same energy company as the Dakota Access Pipeline, which had been delivering oil for two years. And we were only adding onto an existing pipeline, not laying anything new. And if she was still concerned with Native interests, our previous job in Oklahoma would've been a better place to start.

I Googled *"Sylvia Davenport"* + *Austin, TX* + *FBI*. Nothing useful popped up. I was left to fill in the blanks.

But it only took a few moments for my brain to do that. I should've been a detective. I was going to break this case before that asshole Agent Orange—after drinking all day—and leave him looking like a fool for thinking I had something to do with it.

And it was so damn obvious.

Sylvia had been sent by the FBI to get close to Jameson. I didn't know why, but that was the only reasonable explanation.

Veronica was sure they'd been sleeping together, so Jameson had to be Sylvia's target. Paul and Jorge had already known we would be testing to get onto this job when we were at Tight Strips. The FBI must've known that somehow and sent her to get friendly with the guys, many of whom were regulars during the two months we spent on the nearby job.

While discussing the life of a stripper that night with one of the girls—the one who'd earned my two hundred dollars—I'd learned the dancers were contract workers. Much like a freelance writer or a welder's helper, all the club needed were tax documents. Easy in, easy out. If Sylvia was a confidential informant for the feds, that would be a simple way to get her on the job. And her propensity for acting out against oil companies could explain how she was tangled up with the FBI.

Thoroughly satisfied with myself, I started to close my laptop. But I stopped short.

This time I Googled *Free Butch Heller* and scrolled through the results. I tried remembering which site I'd seen Veronica perusing. I remembered when I saw it: *ButchHellerIsInnocent.org*. I wanted to find and read the forum post claiming someone was with Heller when Summer was being killed. If I could figure out who it might be, maybe I could do something to squash the theory before it took hold. Was it true? Possibly. But the greater truth—my truth—had to remain the only credible theory of the crime.

I found a link to the post on the homepage.

POSTED AT 5:53 A.M. *Sept. 7, 2019, by Butch's Alibi*
BUTCH HELLER DIDN'T KILL SUMMER FOSTER

How do I know? Because I was talking with Butch that night while she was being killed. He was sitting outside my house drinking and telling me how much he loved her, lamenting about how he'd screwed everything up. Butch told me he and Summer had fought at her

Fourth of July party, and he didn't know if they could work it out this time.

He drove away from my house as the sun set that night, at about 8:35 p.m. The authorities say Summer Foster was likely killed during the fireworks show, which started a few minutes later and lasted 10 minutes. It takes nearly 20 minutes to drive from my house to hers, which means he would've gotten to her right after she died. He found her already dead, which is exactly what he's been telling everyone for twenty years.

I know what you're thinking. Why didn't I tell the cops this when they were investigating? Why didn't he? Butch and I have our reasons. He doesn't want me talking about it now, but I won't let him die because I didn't speak up. I'll be reaching out to his lawyers soon. Butch Heller will be exonerated.

I know what else you're thinking. Who really killed Summer Foster? I know that, too, but I'm still gathering proof to take to the lawyers. I only have a couple of days, but I'm close.

I clicked the back button and looked at the countdown displayed prominently at the top of *ButchHellerIsInnocent.org*. It looked like a digital clock, which read 07:06:48:32, the seconds counting down until midnight the following Tuesday. Whoever Butch's Alibi was, they were running out of time. There weren't any clues in the message, but there wasn't much substance, either. They may know Heller didn't do it. But there's no way they knew who did.

I closed my computer and my head spun. I needed to start eating and hydrating to avoid a massive hangover. Much of the morning would be spent riding out to Site Three, wherever that was, but I still didn't want to be puking in the truck. I decided the first step was a shower. Then I'd drink a cup of terrible hotel coffee and sober up enough to get dinner. I'd end the night with a Gatorade and a gallon of water before passing out.

I'd gotten down to my underwear when Veronica walked in the room. "Oh, hey. Sorry."

"Hey yourself," I said. "Come on in. I need to talk to you anyway."

She turned to face the door. "Aren't you going to finish getting dressed?"

"I'm not too worried about it." To my surprise, I wasn't.

"Have you been drinking?"

"Why yes, I have. How can you tell?" I was having too much fun screwing with Veronica. "Jorge and I wrapped up with the investigators early and decided to do some day drinking."

"Are you sober enough to tell me what you found out?"

"Yes, ma'am." I sat down on the bed. That shower would have to wait at least a few more minutes. "Our mysterious victim is one Sylvia Davenport, a previous employee of Tight Strips gentleman's club in Oklahoma City. I did not get her age."

Veronica blinked and looked as though she was ready to express her displeasure. It was time to give her the rest of the story.

"But they did tell me she was a confidential informant for the FBI."

Veronica sat down on the bed and crossed her legs. "Holy shit. How'd you get them to tell you that."

"Well, it turns out, I'm their prime suspect, so that asshole Agent Orange thought he was telling me stuff I already knew. She gave me a lap dance a few months ago, so he's sure I did it."

"What?"

"Yeah, it's fucking crazy, and I have no idea how I missed that fact. But they showed me a photo taken from surveillance video. So, naturally, they assume I'm connected with her in some substantial way. And, let's not forget that this woman was killed the same way as Summer Foster, who was my neighbor twenty years ago." I shook my head and laughed. "I'm gonna go to prison for a murder I didn't commit."

"Hence the day drinking," she said.

I nodded and stood. "I need a shower. Want to drive me to get food and hangover supplies after I get done?"

"Sure. But I get to pick the place. And you're paying."

TORTILLA CHIPS and tamales sopped up some of the alcohol, though I was still far from sober when we got back to the hotel room. Dinner had been more pleasant than I expected, and I began to feel like we'd turned a corner. I had finished explaining about Sylvia's sabotage and her history of protesting oil pipelines.

I got the feeling Veronica was finally appreciative of my efforts. Or maybe she felt sorry because I might be going to prison soon. Either way, she was warming to me.

"So, are you going to write a story about the murder now that you have some more information?" I asked.

We sat down on her bed. "Soon," she said. "I emailed my editor with what you gave me. She's going to run background checks to confirm everything."

"Did you tell her you're sleeping next to the Texas Rangers' top suspect?"

Veronica laughed. "I left that part out. For what it's worth, I don't think you killed Sylvia."

"Good to know. Who do you think did?"

"So far, the only people I know that she had much contact with were Jameson and Paul. If she came to work with this crew on purpose, and we keep using your Venn diagram, those two seem to be our only choices."

"Yep. I think targeting Paul would be a little too on the nose, though. It's got to be Jameson. Plus, we already know he's a creeper."

Veronica shook her head. "You're the one who said he's a coward, and I don't think Jamie is capable of killing anyone, either. Plus, what could he be doing that would interest the FBI?"

She was probably right about that. But she was wrong about Paul. "We must be missing something," I said.

Veronica put her hand on my knee. "We're not going to figure it out tonight. My boss said I have a week to wrap everything up. Once she confirms what we know, I'll have a ton of work to do. I don't even want to think about it right now."

Veronica hung her head and slumped her shoulders. "My neck is killing me. Do you know how to give a shoulder massage?"

I tried not to stare at her. The answer was no, I didn't have much experience rubbing the shoulders of attractive women. But I wasn't about to tell her that.

"Yes, ma'am."

Veronica made noises like I was doing the job right, so I began using more pressure. Meanwhile, my heart rate was rising along with my hopes.

"So, I've been meaning to ask you something," Veronica said.

"What's that?" I whispered into her ear.

"What was it like being so young and seeing something so terrible?"

My hands must've stopped because Veronica turned her head and apologized. "I shouldn't pry like that."

I resumed the massage. "No, don't be. I just haven't been asked that in a long, long time. People usually ask me what I've written lately, or about the process of writing the book."

"It must be hard to think about, even after all this time."

"It is."

I wasn't exactly lying to Veronica. The murder was hard for me to think about, insofar as I didn't want to remember what happened that night. I had talked about it a hundred times. To the arriving officer. To the first investigator, then his partner, then both. Then I had to go over it several times with the district attorney and other lawyers in his office as they built their case.

Then there was the trial, followed by writing the book. By the time I was a sophomore in college and had been on a summer book tour, I could hardly distinguish between my real memories and the rehearsed, edited version that I gave on the witness stand. That's what I used to write *Cold Summer*, which is why I read those passages every time I had to talk about the murder.

"How well did you know Heller and Summer before she died?" Veronica asked.

"Summer had been our neighbor all my life, so you could say I knew her well. She'd been helping train Ruth Ann in track, so they were close before she died. My sister, that is." Veronica winced when I applied too much pressure. "Butch was always kind of around, but we didn't talk much. Dad and I did help Butch rebuild his front porch. That was a few hours before he killed her, come to think of it."

"Why didn't you stay for the party?"

I thought for a moment before responding. I had to be careful, stick to the script. "I was still kind of depressed from my sister's death, as you can imagine."

"The only thing I never understood was what caused you to change your mind," Veronica said. "Why go back over there and join the party right when Summer was being killed?"

I'd never told anyone that part. I'd found a bottle of liquor stashed away in my sister's closet earlier that day. My parents hadn't touched her room in the six months since she'd been killed.

I wasn't as interested in preserving her space. Part of me wanted to be near her things, to remember her, so I'd go in there about once a week. I got nosier with each visit. That day, while my dad was mowing the lawn and my mother was out visiting a friend, I decided to look in the top of her closet. I found a locked jewelry box in the back corner.

I'd already located a small keyring in her desk drawer. The second key I tried worked, and inside the box I found a couple of love letters, a composition notebook, and a pint of pineapple rum. After my parents went to Summer's party, I opened the bottle and the notebook. By the time I was done with both, I was drunk and needed to go over to Summer's yard.

"I was sixteen," I finally said. "I suppose the thought of sneaking some beer and making out with a drunk girl was too much to ignore, even if I was grieving."

"If it weren't for bad luck, you wouldn't have any luck at all."

"I guess not."

Veronica pulled away and turned towards me. She leaned in slowly, putting her lips up to my right earlobe. "Let's see if we can change that."

28

EXCERPT FROM COLD SUMMER

Investigators had a hard time pinning down exactly when Heller left the Fourth of July party. Most agree he was still there at five p.m. Some are sure he was drinking beer and joking with a group of men and boys, including members of the Hinterbach Rams football team. Others point out that he was drinking a non-alcoholic beer and say he got into an argument with one or more of the people at the party.

Some say they heard people yelling in the trailer house. Others swear a brawl broke out in the middle of the celebration. Still more say Heller was throwing punches and kicks at another man as he went running out of Foster's front door. But all seem to remember a ruckus, though the timeframe couldn't be precisely identified by anyone.

Nobody remembers him driving away, though Det. Roland said none of the other partygoers remember Heller's presence when desserts were brought out at 7:30, about an hour before the sun was to set on the day—and life of the party's hostess.

29

BUTCH HELLER

July 4, 1999, 5 p.m.

The feel of a cold longneck in his hand meant all was right with the world. The longneck was an O'Doul's, which meant he could get the sensation of drinking beer—and some of the taste—without the alcohol and the heartburn that would come with upsetting Summer. Holding the bottle and jaw-jacking with his neighbors was enough to keep him content.

"So, how many of you young gentlemen have seen your girl-friend's whip cream bikini?" The question was directed at Sammy, Paul, and the other boys shoveling plates of brisket and blackened hot dogs into their mouths. They had all gone to one theater or another to see the movie *Varsity Blues* during the winter, and Sammy still made references to it almost daily.

The question got a big laugh from the crowd, including a few of the other fathers who'd played football in Hinterbach, all of whom looked around to make sure their wives weren't listening. The players mostly blushed, though a couple smiled like Cheshire cats trying not to tell the world they were finally getting laid.

Sammy was one. Paul Schuhmacher, Sammy's running

buddy who was expected to start at tight end, was another. Tall and aggressive, he had already been named preseason All-District by *Dave Campbell's Texas Football* magazine. So had Sammy at quarterback and Bernie Beck's kid at defensive lineman.

Heller shook his head and polished off his beer—or what he wished was a beer—then signaled to everyone else he was off to get another from the cooler. He walked to Summer and gave her a peck on the cheek.

"And how's everything going over here?" Heller asked.

"Fine. People aren't eating my potato salad like they were last year. I'm worried I'll have to throw some out."

"Nah. You know how people are. The longer they're here and the more they drink, the more they'll come back and eat whatever's on the table."

Summer returned to her fidgeting. "I hope so."

Heller leaned in closer and lowered his voice. "Hey, can I ask you something?"

"Sure."

"Did it hurt?"

Summer knew what was coming and rushed to get it over with. "Did what hurt?"

"When you fell out of the sky?"

Heller put his hand on her neck, which he was still getting used to seeing after her haircut. Summer shook her head, but also smiled. Heller had used that line when they first met. They'd been shopping at the H-E-B in Kerrville. It was also a hot July day, and they'd both been in the market for fresh fruit. That's what he told her, anyway. Heller was there for cheap TV dinners and snack cakes, but he ventured into the produce section as soon as he spotted her. The cheesy pickup line was the first thing he could think to say to such a beautiful woman.

Summer turned around. "You are so lame." She kissed him, another quick peck. "But sometimes you're very sweet."

"Thanks, honey." He reached into the cooler. "Okay, I've got to go drain the main vein."

"And back to lame."

Heller laughed as he jogged to the back porch and up the rickety wooden stairs that would probably end up being his next project.

After flushing the toilet, Heller looked in the mirror. He'd already sweated through his Charlie Daniels Band T-shirt. Another side effect of his sobriety was renewed attention to his own hygiene. When he was drunk, Heller didn't care how he looked or smelled. But now that his senses weren't constantly dulled, he found himself showering twice a day when he worked outside.

Heller pulled off the shirt and heard his cheap sunglasses—which he'd left sitting on top of his thinning brown hair—hit the linoleum before tossing the shirt onto the side of the tub. He then took a towel and dried off his hair and torso, focusing on his armpits. He applied some Old Spice deodorant before picking up the T-shirt and going into the bedroom to find a new one.

Though he didn't have access to a full wardrobe yet, Heller had snuck in a few items and hidden them in the top corner of the closet. He found a sleeveless white T-shirt, perfect for the middle of the summer—and showing off his arms.

He slipped on the shirt as he walked toward the back door to rejoin the party. He reached for the door but reversed course. He'd left his sunglasses, a pair of convenience-store specials meant to look like Ray-Bans, on the bathroom floor. Heller was scanning the floor for the black frames when he heard the door slam shut. Two hushed voices started arguing.

"You need to stop it," Summer said in what Heller assumed was her librarian's voice. "People are going to notice you staring at me."

"Stop being paranoid," a male voice said. "You're the one who's acting weird, standing over there all by yourself and not talking to anyone."

"Look, I think you should go. After what happened earlier today, I can't believe you even showed up."

"It would be weird if I didn't. Besides, you know I wouldn't miss a chance to see your sexy legs."

Heller heard the unmistakable sound of an open palm making firm contact with a man's cheekbone. He stepped out of the bathroom and saw Paul Schuhmacher holding his face and Summer pointing a finger toward the back door.

"You need to get the hell out of here now," Summer yelled.

Heller sprinted toward the teenager. "What the hell is going on here?" Heller yelled as he stepped in between the two. "What happened earlier today?"

Paul began laughing. "I fucked your old lady, that's what happened."

Heller looked him up and down. Paul Schuhmacher was cocksure and had his chest puffed out. Heller turned around to face Summer.

"What is he talking about? Why would he say that?"

Summer didn't say anything, but her face turned bright red. Her gaze dropped to the shag carpeting.

"Why would he say that?" Heller asked again, this time nearly yelling.

"Because it's true, old man. I bent her over that dresser in her room and showed her how a real man fucks." The boy smiled. "A woman like her deserves something better than your shriveled old ass. She fucking *begged* me for it."

Heller clenched his fists and his teeth before turning back to Summer. "Did you? I mean, you couldn't have. He's a kid. He's Sammy's friend for God's sake. Please tell me you didn't—"

"Look, it just happened, okay," Summer yelled before an awful sob came pouring out. She doubled over like someone had kicked her in the stomach.

Heller felt dizzy. When the ringing in his ears subsided, he heard Paul laughing from over his shoulder.

"You're so pathetic," Paul said. "Out there living in your football glory days and going to alcoholics' meetings every other day because you're too weak to control yourself. How did you ever expect to satisfy her?"

Heller debated kicking the kid's ass. He was only a teenager, so it would technically be a crime. And what would it do? It wouldn't erase the fact Summer had cheated, nor would it further his agenda of mending his relationship with her—if he still wanted that.

Then again, beating the ever-living shit out of Paul would be goddamn satisfying. He may be bigger and younger than Heller, but there's no chance he'd been in as many fights. And Heller could scrap. He'd grown up in bars and pool halls around the state, so he'd helped his dad when necessary. The fights continued into adulthood, followed by a brief respite thanks to Summer's influence.

Though Heller badly wanted to bruise the bastard's liver, he unclenched his fists for Summer's sake and pointed his index finger at Paul.

"Look, you need to get out of here right now before I do something we both regret."

"You don't really think you could take me in a fight, do you?"

"You feel like finding out?" Heller inched closer. "Leave. Now."

Paul smirked but took a step back. "Okay, fine. Fucking her was getting boring, anyway. Hell, she acted like she didn't even want it the second time."

"Get. The. Fuck. Out." When Paul didn't move, Heller took two steps in his direction. Paul stumbled back toward the front door. Heller kept advancing, and Paul turned around before throwing open the door and slowly descend the steps, pausing to look back when he'd reached the ground with a shit-eating grin.

Heller stopped at the doorjamb and watched Paul stroll down the street toward his house.

Summer started yelling, so Heller walked back in the trailer. He found her sitting on the far end of the couch, knees tucked to her chin. The sight of her made him angry, so he closed his eyes. "How long has this been going on?"

"I don't know."

"Goddammit, tell me how long you've been fucking that boy. You owe me that."

She sighed. "A little while after you moved out."

Heller took a deep breath, his eyes still shut. "How could you? I understand you being lonely, but you *kicked* me out, remember? And with a boy? One of your own students? I mean, what the fuck?"

Summer didn't respond. Heller couldn't hold it in any longer. He turned around and punched the nearest wall. His ring finger and pinky caught a stud, and he screamed in a mixture of pain, anger, and humiliation. Heller let out one more howl and allowed his breathing to slow before resuming his interrogation.

"At least tell me this is the first time."

Summer nodded. Heller searched her eyes for the truth. He thought about the times he'd watch her flirt with the boys and fathers who came over for her parties, all the times he was proud that the rest of the town wanted her.

He didn't believe her.

Heller turned toward the door. He heard Summer calling after him but couldn't make out the words, which were eventually drowned out by the sound of gravel flying from the driveway into the faded aluminum siding.

He needed a fucking drink.

None of the liquor stores were open. But there was one place he could go that always had some whiskey.

30

"You fucked her, didn't you?" Jorge asked as soon as Veronica had jumped out of his truck.

"Shut up."

"Dude, I can practically smell it on you two. There's no use lying to me. You're terrible at it."

I wanted to lie. I wanted to say we'd made love all night, that we hadn't slept and almost called in sick so we could keep going.

Instead, as usual, I relented and told him the truth. "No, we didn't. I thought we were going to. We had a moment and kissed. But then she got all weird and pushed me away. She literally kicked me out of her bed."

"No shit? How was she this morning?"

That was the confusing part. After I'd hit the floor, Veronica opened her mouth like she wanted to explain. But then we stared at each other for a few awkward seconds before she turned her back and shut off her bedside lamp.

"She's a little nicer toward me now, I guess."

Jorge looked confused. "I meant, what did she say when you asked her about the kiss?"

"We haven't talked about it. I mean, what am I going to say? *Hey, that's not cool, leaving me with blue balls like that.*"

Jorge laughed. "No. But you could ask her why she freaked out on you."

"True. I guess I'm just embarrassed."

Jorge nodded. It'd taken nearly thirty-five minutes to get out to Site Three, and that was after driving to Site Two and having a twenty-minute tailgate meeting. The road to Site Three was less defined than any we'd driven before. It was washed out in several areas—if it were to rain, even a four-by-four wouldn't guarantee a successful exfiltration—and required climbing and descending nearly half a dozen steep hills.

We'd missed the morning break, and members of the skeleton crew at our new, tiny site were starting to emerge from their trucks. There were two riggers, neither of whom looked like they'd been on many jobs, and two young men standing beside twenty-pound fire extinguishers.

The site itself was also less defined than the other two. Rather than a large flat area for dozens of vehicles and other machinery to operate, Site Three was a small strip at the top of a hill. An old launcher was fenced off, while about fifty foot of pipe had been exposed leading from the launcher down the hill, which was only about thirty feet wide. It was on this hill that Jorge, Paul, Veronica, and I would put the finishing touches on a pig receiver —which is the mirror image of a launcher, meant to catch the filthy swine after its trip down the line.

Because much of the room was needed for the track hoe, Jorge and Paul parked their welding rigs at the bottom of the hill. That meant Veronica and I had to schlep the extension cords, leads, rods, tools—and goddamn railroad ties—up the hill before work could begin. Yet another disadvantage to being on the top of a hill was the wind, which blew into us unencumbered for miles.

The introvert in me would enjoy the relative solitude of this new job site. And my ears would love having to deal with just two welding machines growling at us from the bottom of a hill rather than half a dozen in a fifty-yard radius.

But the work itself would be noticeably harder. By the time we were set up to start welding, Veronica had figured that out, too.

"This sucks," she said. "I'm so ready to be done with this shit and get back to my cool, windless office."

I spit out the dirt that had gathered in my mouth. "On the bright side, we're going to get in shape."

Veronica looked around to make sure nobody was in listening range. "So, do you really think you're about to get arrested? If the Rangers ask for you again, I won't be able to hold off on running what I already know, including that you're the one they're looking at for the murder."

"I don't know. I mean, I didn't do it, so if the criminal justice system works, they won't arrest me."

"We both know that's not true."

I caught a strange tone in her voice. Something left over from the night before? "Wow, thanks for the reassurance."

"You know what I mean. Investigators and DAs screw up all the time."

I couldn't deny that, though I preferred not to think about it. "I hope you'll be able to write something before that happens, showing that I'm *not* the most likely suspect."

"I'll need two things for that. First, I need to go see Jamie one more time."

"Get him to admit to knowing Sylvia better than he lets on," I said. "Good thinking."

Veronica nodded and looked around, avoiding eye contact. Things were going to stay awkward until we talked about it.

"So, about last night—"

"Let's not and say we did," Veronica said. "You were drunk, I was a little homesick, and I took advantage of the fact that you're a lonely guy. I'm sorry about that, but I don't feel anything for you."

RICK TREON

"I don't have a crush on you. But thank you for at least acknowledging that something happened."

"It would probably be best if we pretend it didn't. It was a mistake. Simple as that."

I WAS LYING on my bed and thumbing through Facebook when Veronica walked into our room reeking of beer. She immediately flipped open her laptop and began hammering away.

"What did you find out?" The words stumbled out of my mouth. I had done a terrible job of trying to sound nonchalant.

"You're not going to like it."

"What do you mean? I don't care who Jameson is or why he killed that woman. I just care that it was him and not me."

She continued to type. "It wasn't Jamie."

"How do you know?" I popped up from the bed to look over her shoulder when she didn't respond.

"I think I know who did it. But you're not going to like hearing it." She typed a name into one of those background check websites, one for which I assumed the *Ledger* had an account.

Paul Henry Schuhmacher.

"You should've told me Paul was Grant Schuhmacher's son," she said. "It would've saved me a lot of time."

"I don't see how that's relevant." I struggled to stay calm. "I'm telling you, he's not a murderer. Did you even look into *Jamie*, or do you like him too much?"

Veronica didn't respond to my insinuation that she wanted to sleep with our cowardly foreman. "My bosses had already run Jameson's name and we didn't find anything suspicious, though he had one arrest for public intoxication in Tulsa a few years ago. But the *Ledger* couldn't find anything on a Paul Henry. At least not one with a photo that matched. So, I went over to talk to Jameson today because he has access to employee documents.

194

That's where I saw Paul's full name. Paul Henry Schuhmacher, with three h's—more than unique enough to narrow down."

I clenched my teeth. "You lied to me about why you went there."

"No, I didn't. You assumed."

I replayed our conversations. She was right. I had convinced myself Jameson was the bad guy and hadn't even asked why she was going over there after work.

We looked back at her computer screen, now populated with information about Paul. Two large vertical photos dominated the left side, one stacked on top of the other. The top was a driver's license portrait that looked like the man I'd been working with. The other was a mugshot of a younger, more menacing Paul Schuhmacher.

"Did you not know about his arrest in Lubbock fifteen years ago?" Veronica asked.

I shook my head.

"A Tech girl came out just after his senior season there and said he raped her. And not frat-boy shit either. Her account was brutal. He was arrested on a sexual assault charge in early 2004. It was big state news because he is the son of the then-State Senator. How could you have missed that? I thought he was your friend?"

I did the math in my head. "It was still in college and not exactly following the news. That was before smartphones and push alerts. And we were teammates, but we ran in different circles."

"And nobody from Hinterbach told you? A small town like that?"

"I didn't keep in contact with anyone from there after I graduated high school, and my parents moved away a month after they got me settled in college. After Ruth Ann died, none of us wanted to be there anymore."

Veronica stared at me. I couldn't tell if she believed me or not. Her eyes dropped to her laptop. "It looks like he was convicted of second-degree sexual assault later in 2004 and sentenced to eight years in prison." She used her finger to follow the lines of text on the right side of the screen. "He bounced around a little bit early on but served most of his sentence at the Allan B. Polunsky Unit in Livingston." Veronica looked up at me. "That's where they house the worst of the worst."

We both contemplated this. Though I hadn't been close with Paul in decades, I refused to jump to conclusions yet. "You know, none of that means he killed Sylvia."

"No. But there is one more thing. It's nothing concrete, but everyone at the *Ledger* knows that the FBI has been after Grant Schuhmacher for years. We can't ever confirm it, though."

Paul's father, who was the beloved mayor of Hinterbach when I was there, did have a meteoric rise to his current status. He was relatively young when he was elected to the State Senate, and only stayed one-and-a-half terms before running for his seat in the House.

Even as mayor he always had a lot of money for campaigning. And he was known for favoring certain Hinterbach citizens. There was even a rumor he manipulated the school board.

When we played there, the board wanted to implement mandatory drug testing for all athletes. The resolution was defeated every year until Paul graduated.

Veronica typed Sylvia's name and brought up her background. "She'd been arrested a few times for protesting. But see this last one?" She pointed at the screen again. "This is a federal charge of mailing threatening communications to a government employee. She was arrested and charged a year and a half ago, but never went to trial. That must be when she started working with the FBI."

"Shit," I whispered.

"Yeah. I think your batshit theory about Sylvia is right. She was working as a confidential informant for the feds. You just had the wrong target. She was trying to get incriminating information out of Paul, the disowned son of an allegedly crooked United States congressman, and pass it along."

That explained Paul's motive. He obviously had the means and opportunity. But there were a few unanswered questions.

Veronica beat me to them. "But if we're right, why did he leave the body where it would be found? And why in the hell would he stick around until that happened?"

My stomach turned to stone. The fight. The screwdriver.

"He wanted to make sure he did a good enough job framing me."

We sat in silence, each staring at respective spots on the eggshell walls.

"Well, I need two more sources before I can finish my story," Veronica said.

"The Texas Rangers, who won't talk to you."

"And Paul Henry Schuhmacher."

31

EXCERPT FROM COLD SUMMER

Grant Schuhmacher was among the dozens of partygoers at Summer's house that evening.

Schuhmacher graduated from Hinterbach High and, through his influence as town mayor, played an active role in shaping the school district's academic and athletic policies. And, by all accounts, he and Summer had a strong working relationship. He would recommend new works of literature for the library, and she would help coordinate community events for the space, as well as summer activities for her students.

"I made it a point to stop by every year," Schuhmacher said. "I always got there in time for her world-famous pecan pie and apple cobbler. She served them a la mode, and it was my job to bring the vanilla ice cream."

"But the main reason was herding folks at the party to the park across the street for the fireworks," he continued. "Things never got too wild at her house. But it seemed to help having me remind folks that the park was the best place to watch. Our residents worked hard on the fireworks show, and I always made sure it got the biggest attendance possible."

Though Louisa Park was a short walk from Summer's back yard, there was no direct line of sight. Not only were vehicles lining the curb, but trees and other vegetation blended in with the wooden fence that separated the buffet area from the street. It also would've been difficult to hear the goings-on in the backyard. One of the teens had brought a boombox with them, and the blaring music mixed with screaming toddlers and the laughter of drunk fathers and sons.

In keeping with tradition, Mayor Schuhmacher was the last one to leave Summer Foster's back yard.

Nobody, except for her killer, saw her alive after he crossed the street.

32

SUMMER FOSTER

July 4, 1999, 6:30 p.m.

Summer sat frozen on her couch. What were her options? She was going to end up on the news like that teacher in the Pacific Northwest. Was it better to out herself? Or should she let Butch get drunk and tell everyone in town, one by one, until the police or school district launched an investigation?

No. She felt better in control. But to whom could she confess?

Perhaps she should write a note and go buy a gun. If only Butch weren't such a pussy and had one in their house. But after her purchase, should she make her suicide public or private? How would Sammy react if she killed herself? Would he be better off with her dead or in jail?

Her brain was still spiraling, but Summer knew none of those options would play out immediately. Butch would take some time to get properly hammered. And there were the dozens of neighbors outside, most of whom were finishing their dinner and would be expecting dessert soon. Summer looked at the clock hanging on the living room wall, which was leaning off-center after Butch's outburst, a slice of cleaner wallpaper peeking out. It was just after six-thirty. If she didn't get her pecan pie in the oven, she would fall behind schedule.

And yet, she couldn't take her eyes off the large, wooden timepiece that had been there since she was a child. She studied the roman numerals and admired how rustic it looked. She once again watched the second hand for eight minutes before finally unfolding her legs and standing to put the clock back in place.

Summer set timers for the pie and apple cobbler, which had to come out first, then returned to her seat on the couch. She stood to remove the cobbler, then once again for the pecan pie. She knew she'd have to stay standing and return to her life, whatever that meant now.

She'd just set the pie on the cooling rack when the second-to-last person she wanted to see walked through the back door.

"Summer Foster, I believe you look lovelier every time I see you. And I love what you've done with your hair." Grant Schuhmacher was holding a plastic gallon of cheap vanilla ice cream, its yellow contents matching the impurity of the man cradling it under his armpit.

Hinterbach's mayor, who flirted in a southern gentlemanly way, had lived around the corner for as long as she could remember. And for that entire time, he'd been married to Gina, who was still an English teacher at Hinterbach High. Paul was born when they were both in their late twenties.

"Hi, Grant. I'm running a little bit behind."

"No problem at all." Grant walked toward the freezer. "Sorry for barging in, but I didn't want the ice cream to melt."

"It's fine. I appreciate you bringing it."

Grant opened the olive-green freezer door. "It wouldn't be the Fourth of July without it. Say, I didn't see Butch outside."

"Oh, yeah." Summer turned away from Grant so he couldn't see her face turn red. "I sent him to get more ice and chips to hold people off until these cool down enough to serve."

"Good thinking."

Summer waited a few moments, hoping Grant would go

back outside to hobnob until she was ready to put back on a smile. Instead, he began walking toward her couch.

"Come, let's sit while we wait for the pies and that rascal boyfriend of yours," he said.

She didn't say anything. But dealing with one person was better than facing the crowd outside, so Summer staggered over and sat as far on the opposite end as she could. Grant swiveled gracefully to face her, crossing his right leg over his left.

He was overdressed as always, wearing a light beige linen suit with a baby blue, short-sleeved collared shirt underneath. His hair was cropped close, his usual Independence Day look, with the slightest hint of silver at the temples. His square jaw had a late-evening stubble, and a small tuft of chest hair was peeking out through the opening of his shirt, which was down a summer-casual two buttons. On many other days, Summer had thought of Grant Schuhmacher as a handsome man. But on that day, she saw something different.

And older version of Paul.

"Paul's been telling me about the books you recommended the juniors read before classes start back up," Grant said. "That *Lord of the Flies*, well he loves that one. Of course, he knows which group he would fit into."

Summer nodded. It was a joke to him, but she saw flashes of it that morning.

"Now, that other one, he's not so sure about it," he continued. "And I must say, after reading a little bit of it, I'm not so sure about it either."

Summer sat up a bit straighter and cleared her throat. "*Fahrenheit 451* is a classic."

She was thankful for a momentary distraction from her own thoughts. Summer had already defended the Ray Bradbury novella to teachers and the administration ad nauseam.

"Most of the nearby school districts teach that book much earlier than we do. Not only does it instill the values of free speech and critical thinking, it also builds a lifelong love of literature and helps show how a society that doesn't learn from its past is doomed to repeat its mistakes, like the Nazis burning books."

Grant nodded thoughtfully. "I see those points. I guess it's all the science-fictiony stuff that gets us. I'm partial to westerns myself. *Lonesome Dove*, now there's an American classic, though I suppose it's too adult for us to teach. And those *Hank the Cowdog* books, Paul sure did love those."

"Those are both fine choices. That's the great thing about libraries: There's a book in there for everyone."

A few more awkward moments passed before Grant spoke again. "Butch sure has been gone a while. Did he run up to the Sinclair? Or did you send him all the way to H-E-B?"

"I'm not sure where he decided to go. I just gave him a list."

"You never can tell with him, can you? I am glad you seem to be straightening him out, though. He told me he would start helping Paul get ready for this season, kind of like you did for the Beck girl, may she rest in peace. But he's been a no-show so far."

Summer retreated into herself, and her head swirled again with thoughts of Ruth Ann. Of Paul Schuhmacher. Of Butch.

She must've done a poor job hiding it. Grant's rugged smile faded, and he slid toward Summer's end of the couch.

"Hey, is everything okay?"

Summer tried to hold it together, but fight or flight began to take over. She remembered Miss Kitty being tag-teamed that morning outside her house. Summer began inching her back deeper into the couch and pulled her knees up to her chin again.

"Stop it," she whispered. "Just stop."

Grant did as he was told and held up his right palm. "Okay, okay. Tell me what's going on. Let me help you."

Summer wanted to say that his fucking son is what happened. That his son was an animal that needed to be put down.

"My son did what?" Grant asked.

Summer's right hand shot up to her mouth. Had she said all that?

"I don't understand," Grant continued. "Why would you say that about Paul?"

Summer closed her eyes and felt tears stream down her cheeks. She'd apparently made her choice.

"He… he raped me."

Grant let his hand fall and pushed himself back to his end of the couch. "What did you say?"

Summer sniffed and wiped away the rest of her tears. If she was going to do this, she might as well do it right.

"I said your son, Paul, raped me. Earlier today."

"I don't understand."

"He forced me to have sex. In my bedroom."

"I know the definition of rape, dammit," Grant said. "What I mean is, how could that happen?"

Summer took a deep breath and exhaled slowly. "Paul and I began sleeping together when school let out for summer."

Grant opened his mouth but didn't say anything. He looked to his right for a few moments before turning back to face Summer. "You know, not to be confrontational or accusatory, but technically *you* are in the wrong."

"I understand that. But earlier today, I told him to leave. Butch was going to be home soon, and I had to get started preparing for all of this." Summer pointed toward her back door. "But instead of leaving, he forced himself on me."

Grant stared expressionlessly at Summer before pursing his lips. "If what you say is true—and you'll understand if I don't automatically believe your accusations which, quite frankly, I find to be outrageous—where does that leave us?"

"What do you mean?"

"Well, on the one hand, there's you, having sex with a student, which is a state felony, I believe." Grant held up his hands, miming Lady Justice's scale. "On the other hand, we have Paul, who you—the confessed criminal—have accused of not stopping your *illegal* sexual activity when you said no. You see the dilemma, right?"

"Are you trying to say that those two things are equal? What I did wasn't violent. Hell, if he'd've come to you and said he nailed the hot librarian, you'd be giving him a high five right now."

"I resent that implication. But nonetheless, we have two wrongs. They may not make a right, but I think we both have something to gain by letting sleeping dogs lie."

Summer closed her eyes and shook her head. Grant Schuhmacher was a cliché politician through and through. She wondered which he was protecting more: his son's reputation or his own.

She looked back up at him. "The apple really doesn't fall far from the goddamn tree. You've talked me into sweeping this under the rug—for now. But you should know that your brainiac son went and bragged to Butch. I'll let you handle shutting him up."

Summer smiled when Grant's eyes widened. She stood and picked up the pie. He was still sitting on the couch when she reached the back door.

"Well, Mr. Mayor, are you going to get the ice cream for me?"

THE LAST HOUR had been the best of her day. Few things are as cathartic as a confession. And, though Summer hadn't let Grant in on all her secrets, she'd done enough to get her a little high. Not quite the runner's high she loved, but enough that the smile on her face was genuine.

"Okay everyone, time to make our way over to the park for the fireworks," Grant said.

Summer waved to her guests as they tossed the paper plates and plastic cutlery into the black fifty-gallon trash cans on either side of the buffet line. Several of the drunk fathers asked if she was going to join them. She told them she'd be there in a few minutes, but she wanted to clean a little while she still had daylight.

She smiled, watching the horde march toward the lawn chairs or blankets they'd set up. No matter the questionable shit she'd done, Summer was a pillar of the Hinterbach community. She could live with a few secrets to maintain that status.

Though she was in a good mood, Summer could no longer put off her need for a cigarette. Out of courtesy, she tried not to smoke when she was hosting, even outside. There were a few people in every crowd who didn't smoke, and there were kids present. She didn't particularly like smoking either, but in the late seventies—and probably today, though she couldn't officially know since her job was to punish such misbehavior—middle- and high-school girls who didn't were considered outcasts.

Summer contemplated her life as she breathed in the filtered joy. She watched as a tow truck hauling a car pulled into the courthouse parking lot. The car was a silver luxury sports coupe, and it sparkled—except for the large dent in the passenger-side fender.

It was far too nice to belong to all but a few of Hinterbach's residents, and she knew what they drove. Plus, the mechanic shop was closed. Perhaps the truck driver lived here and was stopping on his way to Kerrville.

Summer turned back to the mess in her yard. Should she start with putting trash in the cans, or should she gather up her serving dishes and put them inside? The bugs were already getting bad, and they would swarm to the food if she didn't get it inside soon.

Summer started tossing serving spoons into the bowls.

Then she heard his voice.

33

I didn't like Jorge's flirty nature now that we were adults. He always seemed one step away from cheating on his wife, and it often created conflict where none had existed. But as I pictured Paul slicing and bludgeoning the woman I used to call Jillian, I realized Jorge's shady ways could be the key to keeping me out of prison.

While Veronica continued researching and writing with her white earbuds in, I called my best friend.

"Hey man, what are you doing?" Jorge asked.

"I'm with Veronica, and I need your help."

"Bro, if you don't know where to put it by now, I don't think I can help you."

My expression hardened, despite the fact Jorge couldn't see me. "Jorge, I need you to shut the fuck up and listen to me for once."

"Oh." I heard Jorge walk to a quieter room. "Okay, what's up?"

"Do you still have Walker's cellphone number?"

"Who?" Jorge apparently collected so many phone numbers he couldn't keep track.

"The Texas Ranger."

"Oh. Yeah, I saved it in my phone as something else. Why?"
I waved at Veronica to get her attention, then gave her a thumbs up. "Awesome. I need to talk to her, but I only have Agent Orange's landline."

"Agent who?"

"The other guy. Anyway, text me Walker's number."
The receiver crackled as he sighed into his phone. "She told me not to tell anyone I have it. She said it was for my personal use only and to call the other guy if we needed to talk to them."

"I know. But she's nicer and might take me seriously."

"All right, all right." Jorge was whispering, and I could picture him checking the hall to make sure his wife wasn't listening outside the door. "I'll give it to you in the morning."

Jorge was normally not so dense. I tried to avoid feeling paranoid, but a small part of me wondered why he was being so difficult. "Goddammit, I need you to text it to me right now."

"What's so important you need to call her after ten?"

Under normal circumstances, I would have told Jorge everything. But one of two bad things could happen if I did. Jorge might call Paul and put us all in danger. Or Jorge still wouldn't give me Walker's number, which would mean he was complicit.

But if I appealed to our friendship, and the threat to my freedom, he might finally give in.

"Veronica and her editors found out some stuff that could help Walker in the investigation," I said. "I need to make sure they know about it before they arrest me. And Veronica could use a quote for the story she's writing right now."

"Oh wow, that's great. So, who did it?"

I hated lying to Jorge, but he would have to forgive me later. "Tell you what: let me talk to Walker, see if we agree on who it is, then I'll call you back. Deal?"

"Fine, but you better call me back, fucker. You always say you will but never do."

I was terrible about calling people back. My ways wouldn't

change that night, either. I didn't like talking on the phone in the first place, and I truly didn't have the time. "I will, I promise."

A minute later, I tapped on Jorge's text and added *Pablo Escobar* to my contacts, then corrected the information. Fight-or-flight kicked in and I had to take a deep breath before calling. "Hello, is this Caroline Walker?"

"Uh, yes, this is she. With whom am I speaking?"

"It's Bartholomew Beck."

"Hold on," she whispered. I could hear her say something, though it was muffled, as though she was holding her hand over her phone. "How did you get my number?"

It only took Walker a moment to answer her own question. "Jorge gave it to you, didn't he?"

"Yes, but I told him it was an emergency. And it is, I swear."

"Look, without giving you too many details, I can tell you that you're no longer a suspect in the death of Sylvia Davenport."

"So, you've figured out Paul Schuhmacher did it."

I heard footsteps, bootheels on tile. She wasn't at home. "How do you know?" she said, no longer whispering.

"You know my background. I'm capable of gathering facts. And since your boss seemed to think I was suspect number one, I decided to prove my innocence before he arrested me."

"First, he's my partner on this, not my boss. Second, leave the investigating to us. You could get hurt."

"I'll remember that next time I'm accused of murder."

I was angry with Walker. But I had to calm down so we could work together. "I'm sorry," I continued. "By the way, where are you? Are you with Agent Orange right now?"

Walker snorted. "Yes, and I need to get back to what we were doing."

"Y'all are about to make an arrest, aren't you?"

"I can't tell you that. But, *if* we were, it would require an arrest warrant, which would mean getting our criminal complaint and related affidavits in order. And that stuff takes time, so I need to go. But do me a favor and keep your head down until we make this hypothetical arrest."

I barely had time to end the call before Veronica bombarded me with questions. I recounted our conversation, with extra emphasis on Walker's warning to keep quiet.

"Did you both agree that your conversation was off the record?"

I considered what she was saying. Veronica wanted me to give her information for her story. "No. But I'm not a journalist."

"But you're a true-crime writer, and she knows that. Legally, you're in the clear."

I shook my head. "Can you even use anything Walker and I talked about?"

"Did you lie to me?"

I did not want her to use me as her source. Though I was no longer a suspect, making enemies in law enforcement was not in my best interest. But I couldn't explain why to Veronica, whose one-track mind was fully on the story I needed her to keep chasing.

"No, I didn't lie. But you better keep my name out of it."

34

EXCERPT FROM COLD SUMMER

In the time that passed between Heller's arrest and his trial, restaurants and coffee shops in Hinterbach were filled with conversations about the man in jail, the woman buried in the cemetery, and the kind of evil that transpired that night.

Nobody in town claimed to have proof she was cheating on Heller. But perhaps an act of infidelity was never necessary. The knowledge that she was coveted by every man she passed on the street may have been enough. Perhaps there was something insidious about Hinterbach, and whatever evils lie beneath its quiet surface had come to a head that night.

35

FRANKLIN JONES

July 4, 1999, 8:30 p.m.

Jones muttered to himself all the way from the tow truck to Summer's house. His plan had been derailed by a summer rain shower and some dumbass who couldn't drive when the pavement got wet. That dumbass' wreck happened just after the crest of a hill, and Jones didn't have time to stop. He slid sideways and crashed into the station wagon.

Jones wasn't hurt, though the same could not be said of his BMW. He would have to get the passenger fender and dashboard replaced, and the rest of the interior would have to be redone after the bottle of red wine broke in the backseat.

He might not have made it to Summer's house at all if it weren't for his new mobile phone. Jones hadn't planned on cashing in his favor with Patty so soon—and he had to shell out even more cash to his barber's fiancé for the tow and the detour to Hinterbach—But it was worth it to see Summer and torpedo her relationship with Butch Fucking Heller.

Jones was stealthy on his approach to her trailer. His original plan was to make a splash, perhaps reconnect with some of the neighbors, particularly Mayor Schuhmacher, a patron of his bank. But any interaction now would mean having to explain what happened to his car. The next obvious questions would be: Why had he driven to San Antonio on a holiday?

He didn't want to come up with a reasonable explanation. As he approached Summer's backyard undetected, Jones gave himself an attaboy and breathed a sigh of relief before speaking. "I love what you've done with your hair."

Summer stopped cleaning but didn't turn around. "What the fuck are you doing here?"

Jones had planned for this kind of pushback. He stopped and put his hands in his pockets, hoping to disarm her and checking to ensure the note was still there. "Hello Summer. Don't worry, I come in peace."

She turned around. "In peace? The fact that you even have to say that means you know you shouldn't be here. Now get the hell away from me."

"I deserve that. But you should know the restraining order expired at midnight." He took a step forward. "May I please come closer? I came to apologize and reintroduce myself."

"Reintroduce yourself? I know who you are. You're a controlling asshole who can't stand to not get your way. A rich kid who only knows about money and thinks it can buy affection. I don't care if you have dropped, what, five pounds? Or if you think you can behave now. You're the same asshole I never loved and never will."

His preparation didn't blunt the pain from hearing Summer's contempt. But he *had* changed. He *could* control his anger now. He *was* more considerate of others' needs and *would* spend the rest of his life being sweet to Summer.

To do that, Jones knew he would need to prove himself. Standing by and retreating at her first pushback would not accomplish that, so he stepped toward her again. "Summer, sweetheart, it's okay. You can relax. I'm relaxed."

She picked up a long barbecue fork and pointed it at him.

"You need to stop right there. If you don't leave, I will scream, then go inside and call the police."

"Please don't." Jones held up his left hand. "I know what I did. But I went through anger management. I learned a lot, like taking ownership of my decisions. I needed it, and I will *never* be that person again."

Jones walked a bit faster toward Summer. She froze for a moment before sucking in a breath. He could tell she was about to scream, so he sprinted the last few steps and covered her mouth while taking away the fork.

"It's okay," Jones whispered. "All you have to do is relax and hear me out. If you don't like what I have to say, I'll leave, and you can go watch the fireworks."

Summer's breathing slowed, and she stopped struggling. She nodded her head, so Jones took his hand off her mouth.

"I didn't see Butch in the park, but I take it you two are still together?" he asked.

Summer nodded.

"Well, I have something to tell you that will make you change your mind about him. It all started with him having sex with a woman in his truck outside of a bar. That woman was a hook—"

Summer stomped on Jones' left foot and lunged sideways. She was strong and nearly escaped his grasp. But he was stronger. He held onto her wrist with his right hand and yanked Summer to him, her back slapping into his chest. His left hand found its way to her mouth again.

"Why do you always make things more difficult for me? I wish you would be more considerate of my feelings and allow me to express myself. Can you do that?"

Tears dripped on his index finger and the web of his thumb. Summer nodded again.

"Thank you." Jones kept his hand over her mouth. "As I was saying, Butch had sex with a prostitute in his truck outside of a bar. About nine months later—I apologize for not having exact dates for you—that prostitute had Butch's child."

Summer relaxed her body and tried to turn and face Jones. He let her, though he kept his grip on her wrist and moved his right hand to her hip to maintain control.

"Even if that were true," she said, "how the hell would you know something like that?"

"I think you know the connections I have around here. But rest assured, I checked it out myself. I've met the woman and I've seen the child. Well, I heard the mother talk about her. Sorry. I don't ever want to lie to you. Not like Butch has."

Summer stared into Jones' eyes, and he smiled. This was how he'd imagined their reunion going.

"Let's say I believe you, which I don't," Summer said. "But even if I did, your reason for telling me is transparent and gross. You want me to get mad at Butch so you can worm your way back into my life. Well, I've got news for you. I lied earlier. Butch and I are not together. He left earlier today, and I don't know if he's ever coming back."

Jones felt lightheaded for a moment, a feeling of joy pricking at his skin and eyes.

"Wipe that shit-eating grin off your face," Summer said. "Just because Butch is gone doesn't mean I'm going to get back together with you."

Summer tried to push away from Jones, but he held fast.

"Don't you get it?" she continued. "I don't like you. You make my skin crawl. I'm going to have to shower for an hour after you leave to wash the gross off of me."

Jones shut his eyes and tightened his grip.

"I wish you hadn't said that."

He grabbed a fistful of hair. His right hand slipped around her waist and Jones lifted her a foot off the ground. He looked around. The back door was at least twenty feet away, but he could take her around to the other side of the shed.

He took two steps before hearing a male voice behind him.

"Hey, what are you doing?"

Jones set Summer down and lowered his hand from her

mouth. "Don't scream or make any quick moves," he whispered in her ear.

Jones turned his head and saw a burly figure walking toward him. It was probably a teenage boy, though he had the beginnings of a full beard and looked like he could lift Jones' BMW. He was short, though, which Jones could use to his advantage if things got physical.

"Hey there, sport," Jones said. "I was just giving my old friend here a hug."

"We both know that's not true," the boy said. "I remember you. You're that rich guy who beat her up a few years back."

Jones froze, realizing who the kid was. He was the neighbor boy with the weird name. Garfunkel or Sebastian. Something like that. The boy knew him and could make trouble if Jones didn't play it right.

He felt Summer take a deep breath and turn toward the boy. "Hi Bartholomew. Yes, this is Frank, and he was dropping by to say hi. But he was about to leave. Isn't that right, Frank?"

"Yes, that's right," Jones said through the teeth of his clenched smile. "I mostly came by to drop this off."

Jones took out the letter he'd written and pressed it into her palm. "Please read it. It's the rest of the story I was telling you earlier."

Summer took a step back and nodded. "Well, thank you for stopping by. I'm sorry you missed dessert."

Jones stuffed his hands back in his pockets and brushed past the kid, who smelled like pineapple rum. He snuck back to the tow truck, where Patty's fiancé was still waiting. Jones had paid him seven-hundred dollars to wait in the courthouse parking lot for as long as it took.

The sun was setting, so Jones quickened his pace to beat the darkness. As he reached the truck, Jones turned around to look at Summer with the last rays of sunshine. She and the boy were cleaning the tables. The note was hanging out of her dress's tiny pocket. He needed to give her a day or two to read it. By the time his car was ready to drive back, she'd welcome him in. She'd thank him for the care he'd shown by doing such thorough research on Butch.

"Hey, are you ready?" the driver shouted through the passenger window.

Jones opened the door and climbed in. "Yeah, there's nothing else I can do today."

"Everything go okay?"

Jones shut the door and closed his eyes, comforted by visions of Summer, sitting in their room in his house after he took her out of the cesspool that was Hinterbach. "Yeah, I'm good. I'll get her soon enough."

36

J orge frowned at me as I climbed into his truck. "You didn't call me back last night."

We sat in silence for a moment before it was broken by the sound of Veronica slamming the back-passenger door. Chipper as always, she started talking before feeling the tension.

"I know," I said. "Listen, one more thing has to happen, then I can tell you everything. And it should happen soon."

"Whatever." I knew Jorge's tones. He was annoyed with me, which didn't happen often.

"Look, I'm not trying to shut you out. We just can't tell anyone anything right now."

Jorge chose silence as his response. I laid my head back against the seat and closed my eyes, though I knew I wasn't going to get my morning nap.

When Jorge parked at Site Three, we all noticed the absence of a white pickup.

"Did Paul call and tell you he was running late?" Veronica asked Jorge.

"Nope. Try calling him."

Veronica and I looked at each other. All of us had traded numbers. "He's your friend," she said.

I thought about pointing out that she was his helper. But without explaining why I didn't want to call him, she was right. I was the most logical person to make the call.

I put my cell on speakerphone, but all we heard was Paul's voicemail message—a female robot voice reciting Paul's number —before hanging up.

"I wonder if he called in sick," Jorge said. "Let me call Zak and see what's up."

I looked at Veronica in the rearview mirror as we listened. We were wondering the same thing: Had he already been arrested?

"What's up?" we heard Zak ask.

"We're out here at Site Three, but Paul isn't here," Jorge said. "Did he call you?"

"Shit. No. You try to call him?"

"Yeah, but it went straight to voicemail."

"Okay," Zak said. "Let me try. I'll holler back in a minute."

Jorge reached below his feet and pulled a breakfast burrito out of a paper Allsup's bag. Veronica and I had stayed in the truck during his morning stop, not wanting to poke the bear.

Jorge tossed one my way. "You're welcome."

I held his olive branch with both hands. I considered Jorge my brother, and I couldn't lie to him any longer. I was about to start talking when his phone rang.

"Did you get ahold of him?" Jorge asked Zak.

"Nope. You guys hang tight. Jordan and I'll head your way."

Jorge tapped the big red receiver and looked out the windshield. "You not talking to me hurts. But I get it, man."

I opened my mouth, but Veronica spoke first. "It's not his fault. I told him he couldn't tell anyone until... that thing happens. Speaking of which, do you want to check on that, Beck?"

It took a moment for her question to register. When it did, I nearly hopped out of my seat. "Right. Yeah, hold on." I looked back at Veronica. "Do you want to come with me?"

"No, it's okay. I'll have Jorge tell me some embarrassing stories about you while I wait."

It took a bit more muscle than usual to open my door. The Texas Panhandle wind machine was turned up to eleven. We weren't parked on top of the hill, but it was still howling.

I checked the top right corner of my phone's screen. No service. I walked up the hill, a labor that only resulted in one bar. I made a mental note to get a better plan now that I was making decent money.

"Hello, Caroline?" I was yelling, cupping the bottom half of the phone into my face to block the wind. We told each other we were breaking up before she finally understood who'd called her.

"Goddammit. You need to stop and let us do our job."

"I wanted to make sure you'd arrested Paul and ask if you need any help from me."

I knew by her extended pause that I wouldn't get the answer I wanted. "We only got our arrest warrant finalized a few minutes ago. We haven't arrested anybody. Why did you think we'd arrested him?"

I turned toward the road leading up to Site Three, expecting to see his truck bearing down on us. "He didn't show up to work today. You said you *haven't* arrested him?"

"No. Have you tried calling him?"

"Do you think I'd be calling you if we hadn't?" I tried taking a deep breath to calm myself, but it was difficult in the wind. "Sorry. What should I do if he shows up?"

"Act normal. But call or text me as soon as you can without being noticed." Though she couldn't see me, it was like Walker could sense the worry on my face. "Listen, I'm sure we'll find him before you have to do anything like that. But the sooner I get off the phone with you, the sooner that happens."

I TRIED TO STOP IT, but I wasn't quick enough. The wind hit my face shield just right, flipping it over my head and turning it into a sail. My hardhat flew off and smacked Jordan on the shoulder.

He jumped and turned around. "Man, this is stupid. They need to call a wind-out."

We were on top of the hill, and the gusts threatened to knock Veronica off her feet. It was getting worse the longer we worked.

"Quit being a baby," Jorge said, barely audible through his pancake.

"What's he talking about?" Veronica asked. She was a helper with no welder, so Jordan and I were using her as a helper's assistant. That wasn't a real job title, but she didn't know that, and we didn't feel like walking up and down the hill.

I shrugged in response. I hadn't heard of stopping work on account of wind. But if it were a real thing, I wouldn't mind it, even if we got a short check. My mind was not on work, and I kept looking on the horizon to see if Paul was on his way to tie up loose ends.

"A wind-out," Washington said. "It's like a rainout. If it gets too windy, these guys will leave shit trapped in the weld, no matter how much we grind and buff on it."

"That's what the wind boards are for," Zak said. "Pay attention and we'll be fine."

The wind boards were four-foot plywood squares with thirty-inch semicircles cut into the bottom. Jordan and I had been holding them onto the pipe to block as much of the wind as possible while Jorge and Zak welded.

"Speaking of these wind boards," Jordan said, "Ronnie, time for you to bust your wind-board cherry."

Veronica put her hands on her hips. "The wind is about to blow me away as it is. It'll carry me ten miles if I'm holding that thing."

Jordan laughed. "Hey, you'll have to do it sooner or later. And my arms are getting tired."

"Somehow I doubt that," she said.

Jordan stopped smiling and stared at her. "What, because I'm a big black guy, you assume I'm strong and athletic? Racist much?"

The color drained from Veronica's face as she started power-walking to Jordan. "Oh my God, Jordan, I am so sorry. I absolutely didn't mean to imply that bec—"

We howled in laughter as Jordan and I popped new rods into our welders' gloves.

"You should see the look on your face," Jordan said. "You talk all kinds of shit out here, so I thought I'd get you back."

As quickly as it had turned pale, Veronica's face burned red and she pointed at Jordan. "That's not fucking funny. Quit laughing."

Jordan held up his hands. "Okay, okay. I was serious though, come here and hold this thing."

Veronica took the wind board from Jordan and took up a position behind Zak and him.

The gust hit me hard, but it nearly blew Veronica over. Her board slipped below the pipe, where Jorge was about to finish his half of the weld. We all heard a single spark, but none of us dared to react.

As our boss, Zak should've been pissed and stopped the weld so we could cut it out. But as much as had gone wrong, he was probably a short hair away from getting run off the job, too.

He looked at me and nodded over his shoulder. I had the best angle to check on the Site Three inspector, whose job it was to find errors like arc marks. Though this one was normally not a "window watcher"—the term for a welding inspector who sits in his truck all day and monitors the job through his windshield—the wind was enough to keep him in the cab of his pickup.

"He's still cabbed up," I said. "No way he saw it."

Jorge nodded and the welders resumed their work. This would be the third time Jorge had left an arc mark since I started working with him, so I knew the first step in hiding it. I knelt beside Jorge and spun off the wheel I'd been using, replacing it with the tiger pad.

"I am so, so sorry," Veronica whispered. "Tell him it was my fault. If I get fired, it's no big deal."

"That's not how it works, but I appreciate you saying that," Jorge said. "What you can do, though, is go get a water bottle, take a drink, then add some of the beer salt in my center console. Make sure you screw the lid back on."

"What?"

"Go get a water bottle," Jorge said, his voiced raised a few decibels to counteract the wind, "take a drink, then—"

"I heard you," Veronica whispered, "but I don't understand why you want me to do that."

Jorge peeked over his shoulder to make sure the inspector was still in his truck. "You'll see. Now hurry up so you can have it ready as soon as we're done with the weld."

By the time Veronica reached the truck, Jorge was ready for the tiger pad. He worked light swirls beside the weld, then put a little more pressure on the arc mark. It was a decent blend job, though polishing the rust off near the mark only drew more attention to it. As he dug deep enough into the pipe to take off the extra metal left by the accidental contact, Veronica returned with the bottle. Zak had left the area to preserve plausible deniability.

"Knife," Jorge said, holding out his hand.

I took mine out of a leather holster on my belt. He flipped open the blade and poked three holes in the bottle's lid before handing back the knife.

"Spatter pad."

Jordan and I wrapped a black rectangle of floppy rubber around the weld. Spatter pads are used to keep sparks and beads of misguided metal away from sensitive areas like valve ends. We also put them over welds when it rained, keeping the metal from cooling and cracking.

"Watch this," I whispered to Veronica.

Jorge shook the bottle and squeezed, spraying homemade saline over the area he'd cleaned. Rust formed almost instantly, blending in with the rest of the pipe and virtually erasing all evidence of his work.

"Holy shit," she said. "That's like a magic trick."

Jorge stood and smiled at his new piece of art as Zak approached.

"This is a good stopping point, and it's almost lunchtime." He looked at Jorge. "Let's go tell him we're done working in this shit."

They were only over at the inspector's window for a few seconds before turning to us. Jorge made a sound that resembled an owl's hoot and gave us the umpire's signal for a home run. To us, that meant it was time to roll up our extension cords and leads, toss the rest of the crap in the bed of the truck, and get out of Dodge before someone changed their mind.

37

I checked my phone every few minutes on the ride back to the
hotel. I was so distracted by the lack of a missed call or text
that I hit my shoulder on the door jamb walking into the room.

"A watched pot never boils," Veronica said.

"Thanks, Confucius."

She sat on the bed and opened her laptop. "All I'm saying is,
they'll find him. That's what they do."

I threw the deadbolt on the door. "So, we just sit and wait
and hope a killer doesn't come after us?"

"If he didn't show up for work, he's on the run," Veronica
said.

I nodded, hoping the act of moving my head up and down
might help convince my paranoid mind. "So, I told you Walker
confirmed that Paul is the person they have the arrest warrant
for, right?"

"Yep." Veronica was typing like she was on a deadline.

"You're going to file the story before the arrest?" I asked.

"If you'll let me get it done in time. After the arrest, they'll
put out a news release, and I lose the scoop."

That was a bad idea. I put my hand in front of her screen. "If
you do that, he'll know who you are."

"You think he reads the *Ledger*?" She grabbed my wrist and moved it.

I didn't like her plan, but short of tossing her computer across the room, I didn't see a way to stop her. "I'm going to take a shower."

"Wait." She lowered her laptop screen but didn't close it. "Let me go first. The hot water in this place sucks and I don't want you to use it all."

"Can you spare the time?"

She considered my question, then picked up her phone. "I'll set an alarm on my phone for five minutes."

Veronica darted toward the dresser, grabbed clothes, then marched to the bathroom. When she'd closed the door, my eyes shifted to her computer. It hadn't gone to sleep yet. I made my move when I heard running water.

Murder on the High Plains

By Veronica Stein vstein@lonestarledger.org

BORGER — The Texas Rangers, working in conjunction with other local authorities, were engaged in a manhunt Monday on the High Plains of Texas, searching for the son of a U.S. Congressman they believe killed a woman and hid her bludgeoned body in an oil pipeline near the small town of Fritch.

Paul Schuhmacher, 43, was working as a welder at the job site and his alleged victim, Sylvia Jane Davenport, 28, was there as his welder's helper.

Schuhmacher, who was convicted of sexual assault in 2004 and served eight years in state prison, met Davenport at a strip club in Oklahoma and brought her onto the job site in the Texas Panhandle.

The rest of her story was in pieces, full of highlighted notes written in all caps. My name didn't appear in the text. I let out a deep breath and was about to close the computer when I noticed another document open behind her *Ledger* story.

The shower was still running, so I pulled it to the front.

THE ULTIMATE ALIBI: HOW THE MAN WHO KILLED SUMMER FOSTER HID IN PLAIN SIGHT FOR TWENTY YEARS

It can take decades to fully understand the effects of a single action. Few events get that treatment, but those that do are called watershed moments—points in time separating the world that existed before from the reality left in its wake. The term is overused, but for many in the Texas Hill Country, the murder of Summer Foster on July 4, 1999, was one such moment.

But what happens when the new courses of a town, a publisher, an author, and a murderer, were all caused by a lie?

What happens when the world finds out Butch Heller didn't kill Summer Foster?

I slapped the laptop screen shut. She'd been lying to me. Veronica was working on her story about Summer's murder. Weren't journalists supposed to be honest?

"Did you read the whole thing?"

Veronica was standing naked in front of the sink, staring at me underneath wet hair and holding my razor in her hand. The shower was still running. Had she set me up by leaving her laptop open, or was she planning to steal my razor to use for her legs?

"Yeah," I said. "It's good. Good scoop. Your bosses should be happy."

She took two steps toward me. "Cut the bullshit."

We both turned our heads when the alarm on Veronica's cell-phone went off. She'd set it on the toilet, so she stepped back into the shower to stop the shrill noise and turn off the shower.

"Fine," I said loudly enough for her to hear. "I thought we had an agreement."

She walked back out, still naked and dripping. "I don't make agreements with pieces of shit like you."

"Excuse me?" Part of my anger gave way to confusion. I had been nothing but nice to Veronica. And I'd given her a great story. All I'd asked in return was for her not to pursue a story that I knew to be inaccurate—which was also a nice thing to do for her, I thought.

"You heard me," she said. "You're a piece of shit who doesn't deserve my trust or respect."

"Hold on a minute, I think you've gotten some bad information. I don't know who you think I am, or what you think you know about me. But whatever it is, it's not true."

Veronica's mouth smiled softly, but her eyes burned with a different emotion. I couldn't tell if it was excitement or anger.

She tossed my razor into the sink and stalked toward me.

38

EXCERPT FROM COLD SUMMER

W hen police interrogated him the night of his arrest—after he'd spent enough time sobering up in his second home, the city drunk tank—Heller insisted he found Summer already dead in her yard after returning to Hinterbach.

Heller's lawyer later argued that he was too inebriated to have the coordination needed to hit Summer with any accuracy. Heller's blood-alcohol level tested at 0.1 percent, and that was after the murder, arrest, and processing at the county jail. The lawyer said no man that drunk could have controlled a woman who was so strong and athletic.

However, District Attorney Gamble called an expert witness to dispute the claim, a doctor who regularly consulted with the San Antonio office of the FBI. Dr. Clyde Talbot told the jury he'd studied video of HPD's initial interrogation of Heller. After viewing the tape, Dr. Talbot said he was certainly drunk, but not enough to have kept him from functioning well enough to kill Summer Foster—a fact Gamble told the jury in his closing.

Like much of the evidence, it was a case of he-said, he-said. But that didn't seem to bother the jurors, who offered a guilty verdict after less than two hours of deliberation.

39

BUTCH HELLER

July 4, 1999, 8:37 p.m.

Heller sat in the driver's seat of his Pontiac, sipping on a bottle of cheap Canadian whiskey. He was still stewing, not yet ready to drive back to Summer's house and confront her, but too angry and drunk to stay and talk with Candy.

The bottle had come from her cabinet. He didn't tell Candy why he was upset, and she didn't ask. Silently drinking away their misery, whatever it was, had been their favorite pastime before his sobriety.

Heller nearly dropped the bottle when the passenger door opened. Verna tumbled in and sat cross-legged on the seat.

"Hi Butch," she said. "Why are you out here?"

Though she was only nine, Heller had never seen such a mature girl. Verna often spoke with the presence and authority of a CEO and had a vocabulary that might make real titans of industry jealous. Despite her outward appearance and profession, Candy was a hell of a mother.

"Well V, I guess I'm embarrassed," Heller said.

"Embarrassed of what?"

Heller took a long drink. "The woman I love doesn't love me

back."

"Mom loves you, though."

"I know. But it's not the same. You'll understand—"

"When I'm older," they said together.

Heller smiled. "I bet you get sick of people saying that to you."

"You have no idea."

Heller screwed the lid back onto the bottle. "How've you been? You still like school?"

She shifted in her seat. "It's okay. They're going to let me read *A Connecticut Yankee in King Arthur's Court* for my Accelerated Reader points this year. It'll count for the whole year. They're the suckers, though. I'll get it done in a month."

Heller only wished he was as smart as that little girl. "Sounds like a good idea to me."

They sat in silence for a few more moments, not looking at one another. He was about to walk her back inside when Verna spoke.

"So, you missed the six-month anniversary of Jeannie dying. Mom wasn't happy with you."

Heller could feel her eyes on him, but he didn't meet her gaze. "I know, V. I was too sad to come."

"I figured. We were real sad, too. Mom put flowers on her grave, but I went out later to pick them up, just like you said."

"Good girl." He opened the bottle again and took a drink.

"You could go out to her grave right now. I would go with you."

Heller finally looked at Verna. Her eyes were wet. He sometimes forgot how young she was. Though Verna was not his daughter, he was as close to a father figure as she was ever going to get.

Verna needed to mourn her sister with him. Even a drunken asshole like Heller could see that.

"Okay," he said. "Let's go. You want to drive or walk?"

"You've been, quote, drinking. We better walk."

Verna uncrossed her legs and hopped out. She walked quickly and shouted at Heller to hurry up.

"I'll catch up with you in a minute," he said.

Heller did not want to catch up with Verna. He hated the idea of being near his buried daughter. Candy and Verna still called her by the name they'd picked out, but Heller couldn't. By not remembering her by her name, Heller hoped he could also forget the memory of that night. Parts of it, anyway. He couldn't forget Ruth Ann Beck's death. Even when he was close, Summer would remind him. And if it wasn't her, someone would. Ruth Ann's death had been a major event in these parts.

The baby's death, however, had been easily contained.

To start with, there was never a birth certificate or any record of Candy's pregnancy. They'd never been to the doctor, and she had no family to tell, other than Verna. Heller had given Candy money to get through her pregnancy and had stolen prenatal vitamins and other necessities from a local pharmacy. It had truly been a secret pregnancy. The birth had been no different, with Heller giving her the prescription pain pills instead of an epidural and delivering the baby in Candy's bathtub.

But Heller hated having a secret family, and Candy hated having a baby. She was a wonderful mother to Verna, but the girl trying to rush Heller toward her sister's grave had been born out of love.

Candy had a boyfriend years ago. He died in a construction accident, but not before V's birth. The boyfriend had known Candy was a prostitute, and she knew he ran around on her. But it worked for them, and they'd once lived in a happy home.

After his baby was born, Heller had desperately wanted the same feeling with Summer.

On the night Ruth Ann Beck died, Heller had decided to merge his two worlds and create a beautiful new reality. The alcohol—the same cheap stuff he was drinking as he walked behind Verna down County Road K—had clarified things. Heller would take the baby and introduce her to Summer. It would be hard at first, but Summer wouldn't throw too big a fit with the baby there. Heller would explain how much he loved them both, and how badly he wanted them—along with Sammy—to be a family.

Candy was fine with the idea, though she would miss the self-enforced child support Heller had been paying. She never bought a car seat. Verna's had been pawned long ago and Heller had no reason to take the baby anywhere. Candy only left when Heller was there, or she left Verna to babysit. Heller did his part by bringing mountains of non-perishable groceries, diapers, and other baby essentials, purchased from stores at least one county over.

Without a car seat, Heller had instead taken the seat Verna used to feed her baby sister—a jumbo, a Dumbo, something like that—and secured it in the back of the cab of his truck with a seat belt.

Heller was still not sure why his first reaction after the collision had been to check on the other driver. It should have been to check on his own daughter. What Heller saw when he finally checked the back seat of his pickup made him drop to his knees.

He had still been sobbing next to the dent in his fender when Verna tapped him on the shoulder.

She had been playing outside and ran up to the truck when she heard the crash. She did the little kid thing and asked rapid-fire questions. Heller hadn't been able to answer through his sobbing until Verna asked if she could help.

Though Candy's nearest neighbor was at least two miles away, the trucks were in the middle of a highway. Somebody would come along soon enough, and Heller knew he could be arrested for two counts of manslaughter. What happened next was terrible. But, in the moment, it seemed like his best option.

Heller got a spade out of the toolbox in his truck. He told Verna he was going to walk out into the field across the highway and dig a hole. He asked the girl, who was only eight years old at the time, to carry her baby sister out to him.

AFTER IT WAS DONE, Heller had told Verna she could never tell anyone. Not even her mother. He reserved that hell for himself. He said Verna could never come back out to where they'd buried her sister, either. But knowing Candy would at some point, Heller told Verna that she had to look over every day to make sure nobody had left anything there.

"See, no flowers," Verna said as Heller approached the shallow grave, which now had some grass and other plants growing on top. It had caved a bit, and he wondered if the dent would attract attention.

"Very good, V. I am glad you're taking good care of her." Heller polished off the bottle, then carefully screwed on the lid and slipped it into the back pocket of his jeans.

"Yeah. I miss her sometimes."

Verna sniffled.

That sound, so soft he barely heard it, was somehow too much. Heller lowered his face into his palms and began weeping.

It began as a normal cry. But Heller couldn't stop the momentum before it turned into an uncontrollable sob. He fell to his knees, re-living the pain. He began screaming her name, repeating *Jeannie, Jeannie,* at least a dozen times.

Heller felt weak and dropped onto all fours. He opened his eyes and stared through the ground to his daughter. He saw the life they never had together. He yearned for the joy of seeing Jeannie take her first steps, walking from him into Summer's open arms. He missed the family dinners he'd never have with Jeannie and Summer, discussing how Sammy was doing in college. He could smell Jeannie's perfume as he hugged her on graduation day and feel her tears of joy as they danced at her wedding reception.

The visions faded when Verna reached down and put her hand next to his. Heller took it and squeezed.

40

Veronica flipped open her computer.

"Do you want to put on some clothes?" I asked. She ignored my comment and scrolled through the document. I looked over her bare shoulder and realized it wasn't a news story. It was a manuscript.

"There never was a Summer Foster story for the *Ledger*," I said. "You're writing a book. Fiction, obviously."

"Oh, I'm writing a news story, too. I have to get Butch out of prison. Then there will be a major audience for the book."

I stared at her. I hoped she would wink, or laugh, or do anything that indicated this whole thing was a practical joke. I got nothing. "I still don't understand what the hell is going on. Why are you trying so hard to convince people that Heller didn't kill Summer?"

"Because I know he didn't."

It had been years since I'd felt this panicked. I tried to hide it by looking angry, furrowing my brow and forming fists I wouldn't use. "I beg to fucking differ," I yelled. "Are you dense, or do you keep forgetting that—"

"Look, we both know you didn't see Butch kill her."

I turned around and walked toward the sink. I didn't vomit,

choosing instead to continue the angry routine. I tried punching the wall beside the mirror but missed and shattered my reflection.

Veronica laughed as I turned on the faucet to wash the blood off my knuckles. "And that lie is based on what?" I asked. "That idiot on the Free Butch Heller website who claims he was with him that night?"

"Yes, actually."

I dried my hands on a white towel. "Give me a fucking break. Some crackpot obsessed with a twenty-year-old murder posted some absolute bullshit on a message board." I looked down at the ruined towel. "You, your bosses, and your publisher are going to get sued. Maybe by me."

"First, you should know that I run that website."

I spun around. "Do your editors know that?"

"No, but it doesn't matter. At least not for our current conversation."

Veronica paused, giving me a moment to piece things together. "Okay, so you have access to the identities of the people who post on your website. You know who claims to be Heller's alibi for that night."

Veronica shook her head. "That's not how it works. I do know who it is, but not because I have their web information." Veronica looked back down at her screen. "Okay, here it is. I'm going to read you something."

"Are you sure you don't want to put some clothes on?"

"You know, I've thought about you nonstop for all these years, but I never pictured you as such a prude."

Veronica cleared her throat. "As he was bludgeoning Summer Foster to death, the man who would be set up for her murder was a thirty-minute drive away, holding the hand of a little girl who had just turned nine years old. Her name was Verna McDonough."

VERONICA EMERGED from the bathroom wearing a T-shirt and shorts. "You happy now?"

I nodded. She'd been scrolling in her document trying to find the correct paragraph to read for her big reveal when I told her I was going to leave and ruin her theatrics if she didn't put on some clothes.

"Why don't you search the document for a few words from whatever chapter you're looking for?" I asked. "It would save you time."

"I've spent years writing this. It's not like I can remember it word for word."

I could remember my manuscripts, but I kept that to myself. I needed her to get to the damn point.

"All right, here it is." She cleared her throat again. "After the little girl graduated from college, she decided to use a different name for her chosen career, a nom de plume to hide her identity. The girl liked it so much that she legally changed her last name a few years later.

"She didn't have to choose a new first name, just ditch the nickname her prostitute mother had always used. The girl's new surname was both an homage to the Texas German community in which she grew up and a metaphor for how solidly she was committed to her life's goal—freeing the man she still saw as a father figure. The German translation is, quote, rock."

Veronica looked up at me expectantly. Did she expect me to speak German just because I grew up in Hinterbach?

"Idiot," she whispered before continuing to read. "The girl knew having a pen name would be important when she found a job that allowed her to report on Heller. Though she believed in journalism's ideals and what it means for American democracy, she'd known for some time that she would have to use that job to advance her own agenda. Though she was not aware of any known ties between Heller and her mother, having a byline with the last name McDonough was a chance she couldn't take.

"But she saw no problem having the byline Veronica Stein above such reports."

IT WASN'T TECHNICALLY a blackout because I didn't lose consciousness. I had been standing behind Veronica and reading along, but I'm not sure what happened after I read her name. The next thing I remembered was sitting on my bed, reciting back to Veronica the secret she'd shared.

"*You* were with Heller that night," I said. "You do know he's innocent."

I still had one more secret, and I prayed she hadn't figured that out, too. "Do you have any evidence against Franklin Jones?"

"I do," she said. "But, once again, it's not evidence that's relevant to our current conversation."

Veronica didn't wait for me to seek clarification. "Tell you what, I'm going to find that section and let you read."

I slapped her laptop shut. "For fuck's sake, Veronica—or Verna, or whatever your goddamn name is—just tell me what you need to tell me."

Veronica huffed, but quickly relented. "I know at the time you were busy making news and not reading it, but not long after Butch was arrested there was a big story about a Kerrville banker being arrested on fraud charges?"

I closed my eyes. It took me a moment, but I did recall something. "Yeah. He was retired but got caught stealing cash from his own bank and depositing it somewhere else."

"Right," Veronica said. "That man was related to Jones, who was the bank's president. The old man they arrested was its chairman."

"Okay."

"Jones wasn't arrested at the same time because he gave up his uncle in exchange for immunity."

"And I assume you have proof of that?"

"No, I make stuff up like you."

I was past the point of putting up with her shit. "Will you get to the fucking point already?"

"After giving up his family, Jones went into hiding. But he was still obsessed with Summer. He would send for blonde prostitutes to live out his fantasies."

"And your mother was a prostitute, so she knew Jones."

"Almost," she said. "Jones did this for a long time. Hell, he probably still has blonde girls driven over to his mansion. My mother did know about that job opportunity, but she was a redhead and refused to dye her hair and piss off her regulars. But the man in charge of rounding up the girls did come over from time to time. I followed him outside one day during my senior year of high school and told him I was willing to dye my hair and play the part."

I tried to swallow, but my throat was too dry. She was with Heller that night. She'd spoken to Franklin Jones.

I knew what was coming next. But I needed her to say it.

"What did he tell you about that night?"

Veronica smiled. "You know what, I'm running late. I figured I'd need to get away from you to finish the story, so I told Jameson I was going to stop by his place. He probably thinks I'm coming over to Netflix and chill."

She packed up her computer and grabbed my keys off the nightstand. "So you don't follow me. Just stay here and let it happen. I'm sure the stories will be posted in the morning."

I should've stood up to confront her. Instead, I used every bit of strength I still had to stay upright on the bed. "Can you please answer my question?" I whispered.

She dropped the keys into her computer bag and leaned down to my ear.

"He told me the truth."

41

EXCERPT FROM COLD SUMMER

With no confession or other witnesses, the only account of Summer Foster's murder is the one provided by me, Bartholomew John Beck.

42

SUMMER FOSTER

July 4, 1999, 8:47 p.m.

Summer wasn't sure what else to say to the Beck boy. She thanked him as soon as Frank was out of earshot, then wondered if she should scold him for drinking. Summer had caught a familiar scent in the air, the one she'd loved on Ruth Ann after a shot of pineapple rum.

Part of Summer wanted to reminisce about the loss she and the young man shared. She opened her mouth, but snapped it shut after realizing she wasn't ready for that, even after all this time.

Fortunately for Summer, he spoke first and offered to help clean up. Bernard and his wife knew how to raise kids. Summer lit a cigarette and they began throwing away paper plates, red cups, and plastic cutlery. It was pleasantly silent as they waited for the show.

"You know, I've never been a big fan of fireworks," Beck said. "I don't care about all the colors, and I'm not a pyro like my friends."

Summer blew out a long drag. "I'm kind of the same. Especially this year."

"Why's that?"

"I don't know," she lied. "I guess I'm not in the mood to celebrate."

They worked for another minute or two without talking, but Summer decided she should at least see where he was on his summer reading list. His interest in books had been obvious since he was a freshman.

"Have you read anything new lately?" Summer asked.

Beck leaned over to pick up a paper plate that had missed its target. "I finished something a few minutes ago, actually."

"Oh yeah? Fiction or nonfiction?"

"Nonfiction. Sort of a memoir, I think."

Summer stopped working and turned to face him. She was interested, especially since she didn't carry memoirs in the library, only biographies. "Those can be amazing, but teenagers usually don't read memoirs. Who was it about?"

"It was about this ambitious woman whose plans were put on hold by a bad relationship."

Summer couldn't recall a memoir like that, though Beck had given her a description so vague it could've applied to anyone. Hell, it could've been about her, back when she wanted to run in the Olympics but got pregnant instead.

"I'm not sure which one that is. I know you're on summer vacation, but why don't you give me a little book report on it while we work. I'll tell Mrs. McBride to give you some extra credit next semester."

"Sure, Ms. Foster." He leaned against the edge of one of the picnic tables. "So, this girl has, like, everything going for her. She's smart, she's good at sports, her parents and little brother love her, and the boys are all crazy about her. You know, the typical All-American girl."

Summer nodded. "But then something bad happens."

"Right," Beck said. "Well, first she starts having some problems with her father. He was this big jock in high school, the same high school she's going to, but he was never good enough to play football or basketball in college. But the girl, she could be great, and he wants her to be a college athlete so he can live that dream through her, you know?"

"I do." Summer returned to cleaning. "That's called living vicariously through someone else."

"Right. So, he's trying to live vicariously through her, and he's getting real rough on her. She finally tells him she's as good as she's ever going to get with his help, hoping he'll lay off. Instead, he goes out and finds her a personal coach."

"I see, so this girl's father is rich. That's an important detail. You need to put facts like that in your reports earlier."

"No, the family's not rich," Beck said. "I mean, I guess they're not poor. But the dad doesn't hire a coach, he gets a neighbor to help the girl out. The neighbor was real good when she was in high school, too."

Summer tossed the plate in her hand, but then turned around to look at Beck. He wasn't near the tables anymore. He was standing in the middle of the yard looking at her. There was a chance he was still giving her an account of a book he'd read, but Summer didn't think so.

"Bartholomew, what did you read?"

He smiled and took a step toward her. She could see a bit of his older sister, mostly in the eyes and nose. And his legs. Beck walked around on a pair of tree trunks, though his calves were almost furry below his long basketball shorts.

"I told you, it's a true account of a young woman's life. Don't worry, I'm about to get to the good part."

Summer jumped when she heard the first bomb explode over Hinterbach.

"So, the girl starts training with the neighbor woman and her times start improving. And the girl realizes she'd made a new friend. Pretty soon, their training gets more intense, and the neighbor woman starts becoming friendlier and touchier with the girl. The girl likes it, and the neighbor lady asks her one day if she'd ever kissed a girl."

"That's a lie." Summer covered her mouth as soon as she'd said the words, wishing to God she could take it back.

Beck stepped closer. "How could it be. It's in this nonfiction book. That means it's all true, right?"

Summer decided it was time to play the adult card on Beck. Despite his physical appearance, he was still only sixteen and had been taught to respect his elders. "Now you listen here, Bartholomew Beck, you need to stop this right now before I tell your parents."

Beck continued his advance, getting within a few feet of Summer. "So, the girl didn't answer. She just looked up into the neighbor lady's beautiful blue eyes, then reached up and kissed her. They start having sex, and the girl falls head-over-heels in love with the woman. And they spend a lot of time together running, so the girl gets real good at track. Her grades are also good, so she gets a partial scholarship to the University of Texas. But the girl doesn't tell anyone, because she's so in love with the neighbor lady that she decides to stay and go to the local community college."

Summer was crying. *Ruth Ann had loved her.*

But those tears soon turned cold on her cheeks. Nobody goes through a monologue like his without planning something terrible. Beck had found his sister's diary, gotten drunk on her liquor, and cornered Summer.

She flinched as the fireworks got louder. The show was closing in on its finale. She only had to hold him off for a minute or two.

"You don't have to finish this," Summer said. "I don't want to hear it any more than you want to say it. Tell me what you want me to do, and I'll do it."

Beck froze for a moment, then sprinted toward her. She took off to her left, but soon realized she'd chosen the wrong direction. She was at the shed within seconds. Before she could correct her course, Beck had grabbed her shoulders.

She kicked and threw punches, some of which landed, but it

was like trying to fight a bear. Beck wrapped her up and jerked her toward him, screaming something unintelligible in her face. He tried to throw her down, but Summer resisted successfully. She felt his breathing slow. He just needed to get the anger out of his system.

She sighed.

Then the world tilted.

Summer was aware of herself—of her body, of her shallow breath—but only in the loosest sense of the word. Feeling had been replaced by numbness. She tried opening her eyes, but only saw glimpses of fading light and amorphous shapes, though she felt darkness leaning over her.

Summer wanted to tell the boy to call 911. Her mouth wouldn't move.

43

I didn't set out to kill her. I was a drunk sixteen-year-old searching for reason and justice in a life that rarely provides either.

The composition notebook I found in the top of Ruth Ann's closet contained a detailed account of her love affair with Summer. It included beautiful details. Stories about staring into each other's eyes, exploring each other's bodies, discussing each other's secrets and fears. I cried when my sister described the moment she fell in love. I threw the diary across her room when she wrote about how fortunate she was to have checked the mail alone the day her scholarship offer to UT arrived. She immediately walked to the banks of Freddy's Creek and tossed the package, then told our parents an assistant coach called that afternoon to say she wasn't going to get an offer.

If she'd been alive and I'd read that diary, there's a chance I could've forgiven Summer for sleeping with my sister—I remember feeling jealous while reading those parts—and denying her a chance at a better education. But she was dead. And it was Summer's fault. My beloved sister chose that community college to stay close to Summer. If it weren't for their affair, my sister wouldn't have been driving past County Road K on that horrible night.

If not for Summer Foster, my sister would be alive.

But as mad as I was, my goal was never murder. I had gone there looking for a confrontation, but I only wanted to yell. I wanted to tell Summer that I knew what she'd done. I wanted her to fear the consequences of me telling my parents or her boss. I wanted her to feel my pain, even if it was only for a few moments.

After I'd accomplished that goal, my altered state and excess testosterone got the best of me. I grabbed her and shook, yelling an uncontrollable string of nonsense about fairness and fate and how it should've been her that died on that lonely road. Then I tried to throw her down, but she stopped me.

I spent many years wishing her resistance had snapped me out of my hysteria. But as soon as I felt her body relax, I threw her down, expecting to knock the wind out of her and leave her bruised.

Then I heard the sickening sound of her skull giving way to the corner of the picnic table.

I wish I could claim convenient amnesia from there. I can't. I looked around to make sure nobody had seen me, then drug her to the shed and found the bluntest object I could find. Her death had been an accident, but I wanted to make it look like someone had done it on purpose. Part of me still thinks I saw the faintest hint of life as the hammer came down where her skull had met the table, but the right side of her head was already dented and seeping blood, and the nearest hospital was too far away to save her.

If she was still alive, I truly believe I kept her from suffering more.

And the coverup? Finding a hammer and bashing her head in more, then driving a screwdriver into her eye to make it look like her attacker was a crazed lunatic? The framing of an innocent man, who as I sat on my bed was days away from being executed? The profits I made off *Cold Summer* that cemented Heller's reputation as a violent killer?

He did not kill Summer, but Butch Heller was not an innocent man. I read that note in Summer's pocket, the one detailing how he let his own daughter die because he refused to own up to his infidelity. I processed those words as I hid in a thicket of nearby trees and watched Heller stumble to Summer's body and have one last conversation with her.

I also considered framing Franklin Jones. Since I'd chased him off just a few minutes beforehand, that was my first thought after realizing she was dead. But I never would've gotten away with it. He could've hired real lawyers, whereas Heller was left with a public defender. Jones was also a pillar of the Hill Country community. Heller was a known low life, the perfect patsy.

I heeded Heller's plea to call the police as he staggered through Summer's gate. The decision to say I'd seen him kill her was almost unconscious, like the only plausible response I could give when the operator requested the nature of my emergency.

In the ensuing decades, many have speculated that Heller was innocent of killing Summer, but nobody had accused me. I'd been allowed to move on, living a life of being nice and giving a voice to others who had been destroyed by monsters like me. But after someone had finally confronted me with the truth, I realized that no amount of making up for this secret would ever be enough.

Confession was my only route to absolution.

NOT ONLY HAD Veronica taken my keys, but she'd driven my car to Jameson's hotel. We needed to talk before she finished her story. Not to keep her from publishing the fact I killed Summer Foster, but to give her my full accounting. Anything less and I might as well keep lying.

Fortunately, Jordan agreed to give me a ride to Fritch if I let him take a couple of Veronica's beers. His excuse to leave was a new pack of cigarettes, so he had no time to waste and was already out of the motel parking lot before I got to Jameson's door. I wished Jorge were with me, but I did not want to put him or his family in danger.

I listened during the long pause after my knock. Hushed voices and rustling sheets.

Jameson, shirtless and wearing a pair of boxer briefs, barely cracked open the door. "Big Nasty, what are you doing here?"

"I need to talk to Veronica."

He put his finger to his lips and lowered his voice. "She's not here."

"Come on, I know she's in there. She told me she was coming here, and I heard her talking before you opened the door."

"Look, I'm telling you, she's not in here."

I acted like I was turning to go. Jameson was starting to shut the door when I spun around and bull-rushed him. I busted through to find a woman burrowing under a dingy bedsheet.

Veronica had stooped to sleeping with Jameson to get more information for her stories. She was about to upend my life and help send me to prison, but not before having some fun. Anger bubbled to the surface. I was about to rip off the sheets and start screaming when I noticed FR clothing leading to the bed. Then I saw a United States Marine Corps tattoo slipping out from under the sheet.

"Sorry, Melissa," was all I could manage before Jameson ushered me out of the room.

"Don't you fucking tell anybody," he said once we were out in the parking lot.

"I didn't see anything—as long as you're straight with me. Did Veronica stop by here a little while ago?"

"No, I swear. She told me she was coming over but never showed up. So I called Melissa."

Jameson shut the door and I pulled out my phone. Veronica didn't answer. I left a voicemail, then sent a text.

Stopped by Jameson's. Said he hasn't seen you. Where are you?

Why would Veronica lie about where she was going? Then again, all she did was lie to me. I was still holding my phone when she called back.

"Hey, we still need to talk about all of this," I said. "Come pick me up."

"Veronica's not available at the moment."

Paul. After nearly dropping the phone, I looked around, half expecting Agent Orange or Walker to pull up and ask to trace the call. No such luck.

"Where's Veronica?"

"You mean *Verna*?"

How did he know that? Were they working together somehow? "You know who I'm talking about. It sounds like we've all got some things to discuss. If you come pick me up, I'm sure we can work it all out."

"We're headed out to Site Three right now."

That made no sense. Paul did not have a key to the gate. "How are you going to get in?"

"Jorge taught me his little trick. Plus, if I can't get the gate open, I have a master key in the bed that'll open any lock. Either way, I'll leave it ready for you to come in after me. You're right— we do have some stuff to talk about."

"I can't come after you. Veronica took my car."

His laugh made my skin crawl. "Looks like I won our bet. She said you'd recognize your own ride in the parking lot, but I told her you wouldn't."

I jerked my head around, searching until I saw my black sedan tucked between two dually pickups.

"The key fob's in the cupholder." Paul ended the call without giving me a chance to respond.

Veronica had driven here to finish getting employee information from Jameson. Paul had taken her.

His joke about the master key was a reference to either the torch or a cutting disc, both of which would make quick work of any padlock. But Paul couldn't be in his rig, which was undoubtedly being monitored by Walker and Agent Orange. So what was he driving?

I had no time to figure it out in the parking lot. I'd see for myself in less than an hour.

44

Paul had used a torch. In the middle of the day along a busy highway, the man I once considered a friend had parked, turned on the valves to the oxygen and acetylene, attached a torch, and cut into one of the padlocks on a rancher's gate. Anyone could've seen him.

What else was he willing to do?

I thought about this as I inched my sedan along the rough terrain. I would have to ditch the car at least a hundred yards away, where the road got nearly vertical and even Jorge's pickup had slowed to a crawl.

I pulled the car as far off the trail as possible and hiked. I was thankful the wind from earlier had blown in a cold front, leaving dark gray clouds hanging low on the horizon. When I summited the tallest hill, my vision reached far enough to see Jorge's truck on top of Site Three. Was Jorge with him? I thought about calling Jorge to make sure he was safe at home, but my phone was useless.

I was still about fifty yards out when Paul jumped out of the driver's side. He waved to me, then carefully stepped down the hill before climbing into the cab of a track hoe. Its top half swiveled, and the arm reached out as far as it could, its fingers clawing at the virgin prairie. It swiveled again, quickly dumped out the contents before going back in for one more healthy dollop.

Paul emerged from the machine and pointed up to the truck. "I'm going to bring the truck down here," he said casually, as though we were back from our lunch break and about start a weld. "Come meet me."

I did as he asked because, despite my best efforts, I hadn't come up with a plan on my walk. The only reason to dig that hole was to hide Veronica's body. And probably mine. I looked around a final time, hoping inspiration would hit and I would form an escape plan. Running was not an option. We were several miles from civilization and Paul was much faster than me. There was also nowhere to hide. We were exposed, though ironically the remoteness of our location made this one of the best spots to kill a person. Or two.

He parked next to the soon-to-be grave and jumped out. "Hop in the bed and put the cutting disc on Jorge's other grinder, the old one without the safety."

My hands were shaking as Paul's plan came into focus.

I had just reached the tailgate when the pickup rocked like a boat hitting choppy water. I looked around the cab and saw Paul carrying Veronica over his shoulder. Her hands were zip-tied behind her back. Her feet were similarly restrained, with a healthy amount of duct tape closing her knees together. I heard muffled screams and assumed her mouth was also taped shut.

I wasn't sure how much Paul knew about me or Veronica, so I played dumb.

"What the hell are you doing?"

"Well, I'm obviously going to kill her." He dumped Veronica on the ground like a bag of flour. "And you're going to help."

"Why?"

"I'm going to kill her for the same reason I was going to kill you. She knows I killed Sylvia."

I thought about the best way to look shocked by this news. I took too long.

"Look, you can assume I know everything," Paul said. "About you, about Veronica, about your conversations with the Texas Rangers. All of it."

"If that's true, why am I not tied up like her?"

Paul walked past me and dropped the tailgate. "Like I said, you're going to help me."

I grabbed Paul's arm as he tried to walk back to Veronica. "I'm not going to help you kill anyone."

"I know you prefer killing alone. So do I. But right now, we don't have a choice."

You prefer killing alone. Veronica had told Paul about Summer. "When did she tell you?"

Paul jerked his arm out of my grip. "After I grabbed her, she wanted to bargain with me. She told me getting revenge on you was the real reason she was here, not to cover Sylvia's murder. I got her to unlock her laptop so I could snoop around. As you know, she was doing both."

I looked over at her. Veronica's body was facing away from us, but her head craned our direction as she listened. "When did you know we were onto you?"

"She apparently asked Jameson to see the paperwork I filled out to get hired on, including the photocopy of my driver's license they made. That sounded real suspicious to Jameson, but he let her do it anyway because she fucked him."

Veronica shouted through the duct tape in protest. He looked at her. "Hey, I'm just telling him what he told me."

Paul turned back to me. "So, Jameson tells me that she was looking through my stuff. I figured that if she's doing that, I better find out why. So, I looked her up online. If a reporter is here, trying to get my real name and learn more about me, I figure she must at least suspect I killed Sylvia."

Paul walked over to Veronica and kicked her in the ribs. She rolled toward the hole. "And two days ago, those Texas Rangers came to my trailer and asked me questions. The girl wrote down the VIN from my truck as they left."

"So why not run? Get as far away from us and the police as you can?"

Paul kicked her again, forcing her to the edge. "I'm going to do that. But it takes a little bit of time when you're under surveillance. Plus, I need to get rid of Veronica."

I looked up at Jorge's rig. "And you needed to use this because they're watching your truck."

"Bingo."

"What excuse did you give him?"

He kicked Veronica again. "I didn't. He posted about the wind-out on Snapchat as soon as he got home, so I knew he'd eventually end up at The Oasis. I drove there and waited for him to go inside." Paul shook his head. "Maybe someday he'll learn not to leave his keys in the center console."

"And Jameson had already tipped you off that Veronica was planning on coming over to his hotel room."

Paul gave Veronica one last kick, sending her disappearing into the ground. "Yep. I was cutting it close, too. But she pulled up in your car about a minute after I got there. The best part is I didn't even have to go and get her. She recognized the truck and walked right up to my window."

That didn't make sense. "Why didn't Veronica run as soon as she saw you?"

"I told her I didn't do it and I deserved a chance to tell my side of the story." He looked down into his makeshift grave. "I knew you'd be too tempted to make your story better. And you were more than happy to let me start telling you my life's story, weren't you?"

I jumped up into the truck bed, allowing me to see Veronica. She was in the fetal position, her chest heaving.

I dug around in the toolbox, picked up the machete, then took a few steps toward the tailgate. "Sounds like I'm caught up.

Now let us go. You still have a chance to leave and get away with this."

"Hey," Paul shouted. "Put that down and get the grinder ready like I asked. We've got work to do."

I gripped the machete tighter and pointed it at him. "Why would I do anything you say? You're going to kill me no matter what I do."

"Look, we both have something to gain by having Veronica dead. And if you help, I know you won't tell anyone you've seen me. Then I'll disappear."

"And if that doesn't work for me?"

Paul pulled a black pistol from behind his back and held it at his side.

45

The gun was Jorge's. He hadn't told me he kept one in a compartment hidden underneath his truck's stereo, probably because he knew I'd be uncomfortable. Not because I was anti-gun—although I was more likely to hurt myself or my friends than successfully defend myself—but because they were forbidden on the job. And for all my shortcomings and past sins, I was a rule-follower.

Paul told me the pistol was a last resort. Instead, we would use Jorge's grinder—the one that didn't require depressing a button when pulling the trigger, allowing for easier use—and bleach it afterward. Then the grinder and discs would be ditched somewhere in another field, probably a couple states away. Between the distance, the bleach, and the fact that Jorge and I were no longer suspects, there's no chance law enforcement would find them.

"I'll scatter the body parts, too," Paul said as we changed into old FRs next to black body-sized trash bags. "We'll take her apart inside the hole, but not bury her here. They'd find her in twenty minutes. But the blood will soak into the ground and be buried deep. I hope their dogs won't smell it, but if they do, they'll be digging for at least a day. That'll be a nice distraction."

I turned around to take off my jeans, using my body to shield my hands while I checked my phone. Still no signal. Paul continued explaining the plan as I changed into a pair of work jeans so tight in the thighs I could barely pull them up.

"I know of a dozen open job sites in Oklahoma and Kansas. I can go out to them in the middle of the night and put an arm here, a leg there, bury them in trenches with pipe already laid in them. The cops'll never think to look there. But even if they do, the pipeline will be filled back in soon."

The plan would work. But if I were to participate, I had a request. "So, I'm not putting the body parts in my car. Even if we split them up into more of these trash bags, I am not risking blood leaking out into my trunk. And there's no reason to make Jorge a suspect, so I don't want to use his truck."

"Remind me to never let you plan a murder. Before this job started, I had some friends bring me a dually owned by one of my dad's companies." Paul zipped up and began putting on a shirt, covering a chest and stomach that matched his arms. "After we cut her up and pack her in the trash bags, we'll bury everything here for a little bit. I'll come back in my dually, dig her up, and drive her out of here in that."

Paul was more calculating than I could've imagined. He'd been planning this since testing for the job. He'd known he'd kill Sylvia from the moment he met her at the strip club.

"So, your girl told me what happened twenty years ago," he said. "But she didn't tell me why you killed poor Miss Foster."

I didn't want to answer. But if I was going to get Veronica and myself out of there alive, I knew I had to keep Paul happy. In my experience, the best way to do that was to get people talking about how smart they are. "I want to hear how you figured out Sylvia was working for the FBI."

"That was easy." Paul slipped on a pair of gloves. "She was terrible at lap dances. Plus, she was too interested in me that night. Then when she asked me if she could come work with me,

I knew she wasn't really a stripper. Now hurry up and get your shirt on."

I was stalling, which Paul had picked up on. But I was also enjoying the cool weather, goosebumps feeling like millions of tiny rewards for busting my ass in the heat all summer. If this was going to be my last day of freedom, I was going to enjoy the little things.

"So why agree to bring her out with us? You could've never returned her calls and left her shit out of luck."

"If there's one thing I learned in prison, it's that if someone is gunning for you, they're going to keep coming until you confront them head-on."

Prison. How did Paul know Sylvia wasn't trying to get close to him for something that happened while he was there? "I still don't understand how you knew she was with the FBI and looking for information on your dad."

Paul jumped into the hole and kicked Veronica again. "Just by listening to her talk. Sylvia was way too smart to be mixed up with anyone I had a beef with when I was locked up. She used words I'd never heard, and I got pretty literate by reading books in the pen."

He pulled his gloves off and tossed them up to me. "Go get me that new pair in the backseat," he said. "I wouldn't want to use a pair with Jorge's DNA all over them, just in case. Speaking of books, you got some brass balls, going all-in on framing Butch. That's some elaborate shit."

"Yeah, well, he killed my sister." I turned to walk to the pickup. "So, you were saying you knew she was too smart to be connected to anyone you had a problem with in prison."

"Yeah. When I ruled out anyone from that part of my life, there was only one other reason anyone would want to work on a fucking oil pipeline just to get close to me. The FBI has been trying to get enough evidence to arrest my dad since before I left for college."

I tossed him the gloves. It felt like Paul had accepted the fact I was in on this with him. Time to see if I was right.

"So, are we going to do this?"

Paul checked an imaginary watch. "As soon as you get that grinder ready."

Since Paul had the experience cutting with the grinder, he would be the one to use it on Veronica, who began screaming again through the duct tape.

"Hold on," I said. "Aren't you going to kill her first?"

"Why use more than one tool? Just makes it easier to get caught. I'll start with cutting her throat like I did Sylvia, only this time I'm not using that piece of shit baby grinder of hers, so I can keep going until her head comes off."

"Won't the disc break?"

"Well, you just found four in the toolbox. And I'm going to wear your face shield for protection. Which reminds me, I need you to bring me your face shield, too."

During my first job site orientation, Jorge and I had to watch five hours of safety videos as required by the Occupational Safety and Health Administration. When my eyes wandered during a particularly boring part of the instruction, a poster on the back wall caught my attention. It showed a close-up of a man's face. Coming out of his right cheek was half of a disc, the text underneath the photo warning us not to use a grinder without a face shield.

"Good idea."

I finished reassembling the grinder, plugged it into the extension cord connected to the welding machine, and laid it on the tailgate next to the machete. I dug in the cab and emerged wearing the hardhat and shield, started Jorge's machine to power the grinder, and gathered the tools. I took off the hardhat and tossed it down to Paul, then knelt beside the hole, which was just over five feet deep. He put on the hardhat and turned to Veronica, who began screaming through the duct tape and writhing in the dirt.

Paul flipped the face shield down and, without looking back at me, reached out his hand.

46

I thought the machete would be more effective. When Paul made the mistake of blindly holding out his arm, expecting me to be a good helper and hand him the murder weapon, I reached behind my back and pulled the blade from my waistband.

But the machete was dull and my swing too timid. The blade hit Paul's forearm bone with a sickening thud, but I'd expected it to slice through like something out of an Indiana Jones movie.

I reached back to take another swing. As I tried to guillotine Paul's wrist, I felt a strong grip on my ankle, followed by the pain of small rocks and prairie brush digging into my back. Paul pulled at my left leg to drag me down. I used my free hand and reached for something to slow my descent, but all I could hook was the extension cord. The grinder and I went tumbling.

Paul kicked me in the side of the head and grabbed my right wrist to take away the machete. Though I was stronger, he had leverage and the use of two hands. He pried the handle out of my grip as he kicked me repeatedly in the gut. I rolled with the momentum and pain, and my elbow grazed the cutting disc. I grabbed the grinder with one hand, positioned my thumb and index finger, and rolled back toward Paul, blindly swinging as I pulled the trigger.

Paul dodged the arc of my arm—except for his ankle, which took a second to slow the advance of the disc. Paul's shriek rose above the exhaust of the welding machine and startled me. He still brought the machete down, but it wasn't hard for me to dodge. Paul dropped the blade when it hit the ground and used both hands to tug at the grinder, which was now attached to his ankle as the cutting disc dug into his bone. I pulled the trigger again, but the disc was lodged too firmly. The disc didn't spin, but the grinder did and we both lost our grip as it whipped around his foot.

Paul remained doubled over, holding his lame leg. I scrambled toward the machete and secured it before standing and facing Paul. He'd stopped screaming and broke the disc at its center, removing the grinder but leaving part of the disc sticking out of his blood-soaked jeans.

Paul reached behind his back and pulled the pistol from his waistband.

"Enough of this shit," he yelled. "I should've killed you before we even started this fucking job."

I raised the machete and prepared to bull rush him, but something wasn't right. "Why would you want to do that?"

"You think you and Butch are even, don't you? You think putting him on Death Row is the right punishment for the accident that killed your sister. But what about taking Summer away from him? You two aren't even close to even. But you will be."

Paul aimed the pistol at me. I closed my eyes.

47

The moment you wait for certain death is not like the movies would have us believe. I didn't see a montage of my life. I saw no visions of a future I wouldn't live. My brain was still in the present, trying to process what Paul had just said. He'd wanted to kill me from the moment we reconnected at the strip club. And for what? Retribution on Butch Heller's behalf?

I was still searching for the missing piece of information when I heard the click.

The gun hadn't fired. I opened my eyes to find Paul panicking. He must've thought Jorge kept one in the chamber. I charged at Paul, let out what I'm sure was a ridiculous-sounding primal scream, and began hacking at his arm. When he dropped the gun, I changed my target and brought the machete down on his neck.

Paul fell after the second swing. He quit making noise after the fourth.

I dropped the blade and let my right arm dangle in exhaustion. I tried through labored breaths to ask if Veronica was okay, but then realized she still had silver tape over her mouth. I peeled it away as gently as I could, though she still whimpered.

"How bad are you hurt?" I asked.

"No broken bones as far as I can tell. Except a few ribs."

I knelt beside her and struggled to rip the duct tape from around her knees. Paul had gone around her legs at least three times, and I wasn't making much progress. I felt in my pockets for a knife I knew wasn't there. "Listen, I'm going to go get that machete," I told Veronica, "but it's just to cut you loose, okay?"

She nodded. The machete did the job, and I motioned to the zip ties around her feet. She nodded again, and I used the tip of the blade to cut the black plastic. She rolled over so I could cut the ties around her hands, too.

"You had me fooled," she said after standing. "I really thought you were going to help him kill me."

I'd considered it. What person in my situation wouldn't have? But when I saw the machete was still out of Jorge's toolbox, I knew I had a fighting chance.

"Hey," Veronica said, "could you drop that thing, please?"

"Oh, sorry," I dropped the blade beside my feet. "But yeah, I had to be convincing enough for Paul to let his guard down."

Her gaze shifted past me to his body. I turned to follow it.

"What should we do with him?" I asked.

I stared at Paul's neck. I'd gotten about halfway through, and his head was lying crooked. He died facing us, his eyes open. Even in his last moment Paul looked angry.

"We shouldn't hide the body," Veronica said. "Then those Texas Rangers will keep looking and keep digging into everything." She motioned around the hole we were in. "No pun intended."

"Like I always say, honesty is the best policy."

Veronica stared at me until I realized what I'd said.

"Since then, I mean."

Veronica started crossing her arms but stopped and reached for her ribs.

"I'll never convince you that I'm a good person, will I? Even though I saved your life."

"I'll consider it a start."

I had to take what I could get and move on. "So, we're agreed: we tell Walker and let the chips fall where they may."

I helped her out of the pit, and we started walking to Jorge's truck. She took a few steps on her own. I walked up next to her and put her arm over my shoulder when it became obvious the pain wouldn't allow her to hike alone.

I knew it was selfish, but I had to see if Veronica could help make sense of what just happened. "Were you able to hear what Paul said right before he tried to shoot me? That stuff about me and Butch Heller not being even?"

She nodded. "He told me all about that, bragging about how he could tell me everything since I was about to be dead. He was a narcissistic asshole to the bitter end." She winced and we stopped walking. "I probably should've put it together yesterday when I read that Paul did his time at the Polunsky Unit. That's also where they hold Death Row inmates. Hell, I've been there half a dozen times to see Butch."

I'd been there a few times, too, nervous each time I would somehow see Heller. "But Butch was segregated on Death Row."

"Paul was a cocky, violent prick. He got in fights and was eventually sent to Ad-Seg. Normal inmates have their own solitary cells separate from Death Row, but Paul Schuhmacher was never considered a normal inmate. At that point his dad was either a state senator or congressman, so Paul only got the best of the best. And at the Polunsky Unit, that meant his solitary was on Death Row, per the warden."

"So, when Paul realized he was on the same block as Heller, he reached out through the guards."

Veronica shook her head. "Butch reached out to Paul. Butch really did find religion on the inside, and he wanted to help straighten Paul out. They had some kind of falling out right before the murder. Paul didn't give me any details on that, but he said they bribed the guards and got notes to each other for years out there. Paul told me Butch became more of a father figure than his own dad." Her pain seemed to disappear for a moment and a smile emerged on her dusty face. "Butch had a way of doing that."

I motioned up the hill, and we resumed our climb. As we walked, I tried filling in the rest of the blanks. I couldn't. "I get that Heller told Paul that I killed Summer, and Paul wanted to kill me for it. But I still don't understand how Heller found out I killed Summer."

Veronica groaned as her bare foot slipped in a patch of loose dirt. "That was me. After I figured it out, I visited Butch. I was nineteen. It was about a month before he was supposed to be executed the first time. Butch told me later he called Paul from Huntsville right before it was about to happen. Well, he called Paul's father—he had that number memorized—and he conferenced Paul in. That must be when Butch told Paul you killed Summer."

As soon as Veronica said it, I remembered reading about the call in her story. "Paul's planning wasn't for Sylvia," I said. "He was always going to kill me."

Veronica was tearing up from the pain and fell to her knees on the side of the hill. I sat down beside her and asked if she wanted me to go ahead and try calling for help.

"No, stay with me. Just in case he's not dead."

I stood and peered into the hole. I could see the gash in his neck, even from that far away. "You've seen too many horror movies. But I'll stay."

Veronica squeezed my arm. "Yes, the truck was for you. But he knew he'd have to figure out Sylvia's game first. Paul said when he realized she was working with the FBI, he knew he couldn't risk having someone like you who was, quote, semi-famous, end up missing or dead. But when you and Sylvia had your public falling out, he realized he could get rid of both of you by killing her and framing you for it."

Veronica drew in a deep breath and stood. We resumed our slog up to Jorge's rig.

"I know you have every reason to hate me," I said as we took our last steps up the hill. "But will you visit me in prison? Other than Jorge and my parents, I probably don't have anyone else who will."

Veronica sniffled and wiped away a tear. "You're right. I do have every reason to hate you. You killed a woman and sent someone I love to prison for it."

I looked away, embarrassed.

"But," she continued, "you saved my life. That doesn't make up for the lives you've taken. But I don't think I can do it anymore. I don't think I can file those stories or finish my book."

Hope filled my lungs. But by the time I exhaled, I knew I couldn't let that happen.

Veronica reached into the back seat of the pickup and flipped open her laptop screen. She typed in the password and was navigating her files when I walked over and grabbed her right hand.

"No, don't delete anything," I said. "I'm ready for whatever's coming. I need you to do what's right. And that's writing the truth."

She looked up at me and resumed tapping on her computer's trackpad.

"And since I know you need a confession for your story to work, here it is." I nodded down and gave her a moment to open the file.

"On the night of July Fourth, 1999, I, Bartholomew John Beck, killed Summer Foster in the yard of her home in Hinterbach, Texas, during the town's fireworks show. I grabbed her and threw her into one of her picnic tables. Killing her was an accident. But after I knew she was dead, I dragged her over to her own tool shed, got out a small sledgehammer, and beat the side of her head to cover up the crime. Then I found a screwdriver and stabbed her in the eye before walking across the street to my house, where I called 911 and told them I'd seen Butch Heller beat her to death."

When she finished typing, Veronica looked up and asked one more question for her story.

"What was up with the screwdriver? She was already dead, right?"

"Yeah. I'd gotten drunk and read my sister's diary right before going over there. There was a lot of stuff in there, stuff I'm not going to tell you, but she wrote about how much she loved Summer's eyes. For some reason that stuck in my head." It still did. All these years later and I still watched to see what people's eyes were telling me. "Summer died with her eyes open, so when I was trying to make it look like someone else had killed her, that seemed like the right thing to do."

"Can I put that—"

"Of course." I pulled out my good-for-nothing phone. "You can put everything you saw and heard in the story."

"And the book?"

I nodded and started walking toward my car in search of a cell signal.

Walker picked up on the third ring.

"Where are you?" she asked.

"I'm with Veronica Stein and—"

"With who? Never mind. It doesn't matter. We've found an abandoned truck we think belongs to Paul Schuhmacher."

"At a bar in Borger."

Walker paused. "How did you know?"

"He told me where he left it."

"You made contact with him but didn't tell me?" She was yelling so loudly I moved the phone away from my ear.

"I called you, remember? This is me telling you."

"Where is he? Where are you?" Walker sounded frantic.

"I'll drop you a pin. But I have to tell you something first."

48

EXCERPT FROM COLD SUMMER

Summer's funeral was attended by more than a thousand people, even though Sammy was her only living relative. Nearly every student attended, along with their parents. Many townsfolk had grown up with either Summer or her parents, so they attended, too. All but one member of the Hinterbach Police Department, left alone to handle phone calls, was there. The same was true of the Nimitz County Sheriff's Office, who had to leave behind a 911 dispatcher.

The large turnout had been expected, so the service took place at the Hinterbach Memorial Cemetery rather than inside a church. The casket was closed, but a procession shook hands with Sammy and touched the ornate coffin, which donated by a group of local businesses spearheaded by Falkner Backerei and Kaffee.

Summer hadn't attended any of Hinterbach's churches since her parents passed, so four men of the cloth—the same four who would later hold the town meeting—took turns reading passages from their Bibles and offered comforting words. Mayor Schuhmacher and several other prominent members of the community spoke, too.

Perhaps the one person conspicuously missing from the service was Franklin Jones, who hadn't been seen in public since her murder. When asked later if that was a reason to reconsider him as a suspect, Det. Roland referred local media to the FBI's San Antonio field office.

A spokeswoman declined to comment about Jones, citing an ongoing investigation.

49

FRANKLIN JONES

July 4, 1999, 8:52 p.m.

P atty's fiancé, Darren, was not one for conversation. They rode together in silence as Jones contemplated his path forward. That car wreck had derailed his plans. As a result, his new first impression with Summer had not been his best. Jones knew she was not going to be convinced of his commitment without a more aggressive approach.

Jones could be a tough negotiator when necessary. He would get his way.

The first step would be spending more time with Summer. She'd need that time to discover the improved Franklin Jones. But she would not consent to this time together. Not initially.

He would've gotten that process started immediately if not for that damn neighbor kid. But it would happen soon enough. Jones would force Summer to go with him to his estate outside of Kerrville. He did not relish the need to take her, no more than he'd enjoyed having to discipline her two years ago. But, like so many others, Summer did not know what was best for her. She was lucky he was there, ready to set her straight.

The first step in this reunification would be to get his car running and looking its best. That's what Darren was for. Procuring Summer wouldn't be easy, and Jones may need his help with that, too.

Jones looked over at Darren. "I really appreciate this. How quickly do you think you can get it fixed? Body, interior, everything."

"How much money do you have?"

Greed is an amazing thing, simple and universal. Once a person learns that, the things he can accomplish are only limited by the amount of money he can access.

"Enough to get it by the end of the week or sooner," Jones said. "How many employees do you have in your shop?"

Darren looked skeptical. But, as Jones had assumed, the promise of more money from his new rich friend compelled Darren to keep talking. "Eight, including my secretary and the girl who does our accounts payable and receivable."

"Are any of those folks capable of running your shop for a few days if you're gone?"

Darren smirked. "I wouldn't trust any of them for more than a couple hours."

Jones had figured as much. Darren was perfect. "What if I gave you enough capital to hire a couple of qualified folks to run things for you?"

"What are you getting at, Mr. Jones?"

"I'd like to see if I could hire you to do some personal errands for me from time to time."

Darren turned his head toward Jones. "Personal errands?"

Jones pointed out the windshield. "You don't want to hit a deer. We can talk about it after you get me my car back. It'll be easy money, though. And if you aren't willing, somebody's going to be getting my money."

Darren nodded but didn't pry any further. Jones smiled. Darren didn't know it yet, but he would be helping Jones secure Summer's love.

Content he'd done enough with Darren, there was one other

plan he needed to set into motion—as soon as he found some privacy. Though he could probably purchase some temporary hearing loss from Darren, Jones didn't want to risk scaring off his new Guy Friday. Hearing Jones' side of a conversation with agents J and K might be too intense.

Because of the measures he would have to take in his personal life, Jones needed to change strategies with the FBI. Though he didn't find his new intentions for Summer immoral, he knew they would be considered criminal. Fortunately, Agent J and Agent K were getting a bit desperate to put Jones' extended family in prison.

Jones would serve his uncles up to the feds, but only in return for favorable treatment if his name was brought up in a criminal inquiry. If they were willing to strong-arm a man as important as Jones, those two were already predisposed to toeing the line between the law and what is right.

And if that wasn't enough, Jones had an ace up his sleeve— Hinterbach Mayor Grant Schuhmacher.

By the time Jones returned to the Hill Country after college, Grant was running a budding real estate firm. He owned about ten percent of the commercial real estate in Hinterbach in addition to several rental properties around town.

When Jones was named the VP of his bank, Grant came calling. He wanted to move his cash and loans and get the buddy discount. Jones didn't see the advantage. He told Grant no at first and didn't feel any remorse. Then Grant came back and revealed his other sources of cash flow, the ones that used his real estate transactions to launder money. The problem, Grant said, was that his legitimate enterprise was too small to hide the entire river of money available through his underworld contacts.

Grant said if he could get a large cash infusion to buy up as much land as possible, Jones could charge as much interest as he wanted, earning a nice profit for the bank and a hefty personal commission.

Of course, the point of a successful money laundering operation is to leave no proof. But when Grant Schuhmacher became mayor and confessed his larger political ambitions, Jones knew it would be smart to collect blackmail material and skim an even larger percentage of the washed money.

It was finally time to use it. He would serve up his old friend Grant to his new friends in the FBI, then hole up with Summer and live off the cash.

50

The crime scene around Sylvia's body was nothing compared to the mess that descended upon Site Three. The biggest difference was the presence of the FBI, which had no doubt been brought in after Walker and Agent Orange's inquiry into Sylvia. There was also a substantially larger contingent of DPS troopers. I counted eight SUVs and pickups, with plenty more on the way, judging by the cloud of dust stretching to the horizon.

Walker and Agent Orange were the first to climb the hill toward Veronica and me. I pointed to where they could find Paul.

"Why don't you and the CID guys go down to the body?" Walker asked Orange. "I'll get their statements."

Orange turned around and whistled, though the sound wasn't traveling far in the wind. We could, however, hear him cursing as he held down his hat and began walking toward the throng of investigators collected below.

"First, do either of you need medical attention?" Walker asked.

"She does." I pointed to Veronica, who was sitting in the passenger seat of Jorge's pickup.

"No, I'm fine," Veronica said. "I've got some bumps and scrapes, but I'm okay."

I looked at Walker. "Her ribs are broken."

"We'll have someone drive you to an ambulance as soon as we're done getting your statement. Obviously, they couldn't make it all the way out on this road. But we've got a couple not too far away."

Walker pulled out a notepad and looked at me. "I'll have to interview you two separately. We'll start with Miss Stein so we can get her to that ambulance."

I sat down on the tailgate and recalled the afternoon's events. I wanted to make sure I could tell the story as accurately as possible this time.

After three minutes that felt like three seconds, Veronica limped past me on her way to the cluster of police, followed by Walker.

After hearing my account, Walker assured me the state would consider what I did justifiable homicide, especially with Veronica as a witness. Agent Orange, who had walked up to us halfway through, seemed less caring, though he did give me a "no hard feelings" and shook my hand.

They stayed behind to deal with Paul and told me to find my way to an ambulance.

"Will I have to pay for the ambulance ride? Because the last time I rode in one, I got a three-thousand-dollar bill in the mail."

"I don't know the answer to that," Walker said. "But, if you're worried about it, just tell a uniform we told him to give you a ride to your hotel room."

"What about my car?"

"I'm afraid that's considered part of the crime scene," she said. "Someone will be in touch when you can get it."

"It's parked like a hundred yards away. How is it part of the crime scene?"

"We're casting a wide net. Why? Is there something out there you don't want us to see?"

I laughed. "Just unpurchased copies of mediocre books. But seriously, I don't want to be marooned at my hotel forever. I won't have my car—" I turned and pointed to Jorge's truck "— and this is my best friend's primary vehicle."

"I know it's a pain in the ass. But that's an unfortunate part of being involved in something like this. But I'm sure you already knew that."

I did. I wasn't looking forward to the rest, either.

———

IT'D BEEN forty-eight hours after she disappeared into the orgy of police and Veronica wasn't answering my calls, texts, or emails. I was mostly nervous about my own future, but a part of me also hoped she was emotionally solid. I was not sleeping well, and she'd nearly been killed after hearing that she would be cut to pieces.

I'd been cooped up in the room for most of that time. My car and Jorge's truck were still being processed by the DPS, and Walker had no idea when mine would be released. Jorge had picked me up once to go eat and left me with bags of groceries, but his other vehicle was in almost continuous use by his wife.

Along with the groceries, Jorge had brought me some of his wife's generic Ambien, which I'd been keeping on my bedside table with a glass of water. It was only 8:15 p.m., but I popped three of the pills and turned on a podcast, letting the soothing voice usher in the Sandman.

———

DOUBLING THE DOSE WORKED, and my sleep had lasted fourteen hours. I found my phone and saw I hadn't missed any texts or phone calls. I checked my email without much hope, but among the newsletters and unsolicited messages was a reply from Veronica.

I tried to open the email, but cobwebs left from the sleeping pills and my fat fingers caused me to delete it. I cursed loudly and slammed the phone on the bed. I knew it wasn't permanently gone, but I would have to wake up a bit before trying again. Plus, emailing was the most passive way to communicate. Whatever she'd sent did not need to be dealt with urgently, so I found a can of Diet Coke and ran a hot shower.

When I sat down at the desk, I felt ready to receive whatever terrible news was waiting. The feeling didn't last long.

After finding the message, I noticed it had been sent a few minutes after midnight. It was a reply to my email, and the body consisted of two links, both to *Lone Star Ledger* stories. They'd been online for more than eight hours. Why wasn't I already in an interview room somewhere answering questions about Summer Foster's murder?

I clicked on the second URL: *https://www.lonestarledger.org/news/9-13-19/questions-answered-before-execution-butch-heller.htm*

Questions answered before execution: Butch Heller, convicted of brutal 1999 Central Texas murder, slated for death at 9 p.m.

By Veronica Stein vstein@lonestarledger.org

Since his arrest on a murder charge in July 1999, Butch Heller had never wavered on two points. He continued to maintain his innocence in the brutal slaying of Summer Foster, the crime for which he has been on Death Row for nearly two decades. Heller also said earlier this year that he still loves Foster, whose life was taken as the small Central Texas town of Hinterbach watched its annual Fourth of July fireworks show.

He changed his position on one of those issues earlier this week.

After the Texas Department of Criminal Justice denied his request

for a final interview before his execution—scheduled for 9 p.m. today—
Heller sent a letter to a Lone Star Ledger reporter. The seven-page,
handwritten document covered a wide range of topics, but it ended
with a confession—and a promise.

"I wish I could see you," Heller wrote. "I wish I could see anybody
outside of these walls. But I ruined that a long time ago. I got drunk
and killed her. I sometimes wonder how our lives would've turned out
if I hadn't."

A photo of the letter's final page broke up the text, and the
"confession" was digitally highlighted. I clicked on the little
microscope icon in the corner so I could read as much of it as
possible. The handwriting was almost as bad as mine. It was
possible Veronica had written the letter herself, but my gut said
it was Heller. I clicked on the x and returned to the story.

Heller continued to lament on the life he might've led were it not for
the events of July 4, 1999 (read more about the murder here) before
ending the letter by previewing his final moments.

"I don't think I'm going to say anything before they inject me.
They're going to ask me if I want to say any last words, and I'm just
going to shake my head, then drift off. I've said everything I need to say
in this letter. Thank you for reading, and for coming to visit. It has
meant the world to me."

Before confessing to beating Summer Foster to death, Heller
answered a few other questions that had surrounded the case.

Authorities have claimed Heller believed Foster—the woman with
whom he lived for the greater part of two years before the murder—was
having an affair. They pointed to that as his motive for killing Foster,
but they were never able to prove it.

But in his letter, the only copy of which was sent exclusively to the
Ledger, Heller confirms the long-held theory.

"One of my biggest regrets in life, other than the obvious one, is
blowing up at Summer after she told me about sleeping with that

neighbor boy. She told me in the middle of her party, and that's why I left to go drink. If I'd stayed there and talked it out with her, I probably wouldn't have gotten arrested."

I wondered who this neighbor boy was. Someone I went to school with? What counts as a neighbor? What's a boy to someone as old as Heller? My sister might not have been the only high schooler she'd slept with before I killed her. The notion that I did the world a favor by ridding it of a serial predator passed through my thoughts.

No. Few people deserve what I did to Summer.

The other central figure in the investigation and trial of Butch Heller is Bartholomew John Beck, Foster's former neighbor who witnessed the murder as a 16-year-old. He recounted the slaying to the police that night and was District Attorney Martin Gamble's key witness during the trial. Beck later wrote a true crime book about the case. Writing as John Beck, Cold Summer: The true story of a murder that rocked the Texas Hill Country *debuted at No. 47 on the* New York Times *bestseller list for hardcover nonfiction and remained near that spot for two weeks. It was similarly ranked when the book came out in paperback.*

When he heard the letter read via telephone, Beck first said he was not the "neighbor boy" Heller mentioned. Beck then said he was pleased Heller had found peace with what he did, and he hoped his execution could help bring closure to those affected by the case.

"Butch Heller changed a lot of lives that day," Beck said. "Summer Foster was a pillar of the Hinterbach community in the 1990s, and she is still missed by many of the people whose lives she enriched. We can only hope they find some peace when this case comes to its final resolution."

Gamble and Heller's defense attorney, Jackson McGrady of Austin, declined to comment for this story. (Read McGrady's comments on the 20th anniversary of the murder here*)*

One question never answered by Heller—either during police and media interviews in the 20 years since killing Foster, or in the letter sent to the Ledger—*is why he left a Phillips head screwdriver sticking out of her eye. Police and other authorities never provided an explanation, except to say that it was a crime of passion.*

It appears the answer to that question will die, along with Heller, at 9 p.m.

The last two paragraphs were a message to me. Veronica wasn't going to tell anyone, though I'd gathered that by the fact that she'd digitally printed Heller's confession and provided photographic evidence. There would be no authorities knocking on my hotel room door. The ghosts of Summer Foster and Butch Heller might finally leave me alone.

As relief floated from my gut to my head, I clicked the other link: *https://www.lonestarledger.org/news/9-13-19/murder-high-plains.htm*

Murder on the High Plains: The son of a U.S. congressman killed a confidential FBI informant. Then he turned his sights on me.

By Veronica Stein vstein@lonestarledger.org

BORGER — Paul Schuhmacher stood over me, cold eyes staring through the clear plastic of an industrial face shield, waiting like a surgeon for someone to hand him the instrument of my death.

I'm not ashamed to admit that I urinated on myself. I'd been working with Schuhmacher, the son of a prominent Texas politician, for about a week. He was "my" welder, and I was "his" helper on an oil pipeline between this small town and Fritch, both of which are north of Amarillo in the Texas Panhandle.

But during that week, I came to realize the son of U.S. Rep. Grant Schuhmacher, R-Hinterbach, was a violent killer.

> *The man about to hand Schuhmacher a grinder, fitted with a blade designed for cutting through steel, was Bartholomew John Beck—the true-crime author whose name is most closely associated with a brutal Central Texas murder in 1999. Beck had told me about the recent slaying of Sylvia Davenport, whose body he discovered stuffed inside a piece of steel pipe near Fritch. I drove north from Austin expecting to get the scoop on a small-town murder.*
>
> *I had no idea I would become the killer's next target.*
>
> *Because you are reading this story, you know that Schuhmacher was unsuccessful. What follows is the true story of Davenport's murder, the search for her killer, and how Beck saved my life.*

The rest of Veronica's story was broken up into sections, much like her longform anniversary story had been, though there were no intricate graphics or other multimedia elements. I read the rest of the article, which was as accurate as I could expect from someone trying to hide the fact that her savior had gotten away with homicide two decades ago.

It even included a no-comment comment from Grant Schuhmacher's office:

> *Congressman Schuhmacher was devastated at the news of his son's death. He will cooperate with the authorities in any way necessary as the investigation unfolds. The congressman requests the public and media respect his privacy as he mourns this tragedy.*

After digesting both articles, I had a few questions for Veronica. I started by leaving her a voicemail, then tried hard not to sound frustrated in the text I sent.

> *Hey, read your email. I have some questions and things I want to talk about. Call me when you can, please.*

I put down the phone and wondered how long I would have to wait.

The answer came less than ten seconds later.

"Thanks for finally calling back." I immediately regretted my passive-aggressive greeting.

"Sorry, but I wanted to make sure you read the stories before we spoke."

"That makes sense, I guess."

"We obviously have a lot to talk about, but I'll let you ask your questions first."

"I appreciate that," I said. "How long have you had that letter from Butch? I'm assuming he really did write the letter."

I heard her chuckle. "Wow, paranoid much? Yes, he wrote the letter. It was waiting in my mailbox when I got back. It had only been there a day. By the way, you're not—"

"No. I'm not the neighbor boy who was sleeping with her, though that would've made a better story. And no, I don't know who he is. I never even heard any rumors."

"I didn't think you were," Veronica said. "That's why I made sure to put in your denial."

"Thanks for that."

"What other questions did you have?" she asked.

"We both know Heller wasn't confessing to killing Summer in that letter, though you did a great job framing it that way."

Butch, despite taking two innocent lives, seemed to have turned into an honest man since losing Summer. I had to believe he was done lying and manipulating people. I had to believe a man could change—truly reform and redeem himself—after doing something despicable.

That's how I knew Heller was confessing to something else.

"I don't know why you made it seem like he'd confessed to killing Summer instead of our sisters, though. I thought we'd agreed that you were going to write the truth. What changed your mind?"

I couldn't see her, but I knew tears were leaking from the corners of her eyes. "A combination of things. I spent a lot of time hating you, hating the thought of you walking around out there in the world while Butch couldn't. But then I got to know you and realized you weren't the conniving, deceitful monster I'd imagined. You're a genuinely good person who saved my life and is willing to finally tell the truth."

I heard that sniffle of hers and had to hold in my own tears.

"But even after all of that, I was still going to follow through with the original plan," she continued. I waited for more, but I only got silence.

"And then you read the letter," I said.

"Yes. There was obviously a lot in that letter that I didn't write about or show my editors. But the bottom line is that Butch is ready to die. He wants it, and he asked me to let him find peace."

We both observed an undeclared moment of silence, even though Heller wouldn't be dead for nearly twelve more hours. I had no more questions for Veronica, though plenty for myself.

I'd spent two days coming to grips with the fact I would spend the rest of my life in jail, with intermittent furloughs to appear in court during what was sure to be a nationally televised spectacle. My parents—who were already concerned because I was mostly drifting through life—were going to be mortified.

Veronica interrupted my navel-gazing. "Now I have some things I need to tell you."

"Right. Sorry."

"First, I'm going to cover Butch's execution tonight for the *Ledger* and the AP."

"Oh Jesus. Are you going to be able to do that?"

She sighed. "Yeah, I think so. Don't forget, I've been lying as long as you have."

"True."

"The execution is late, which means the AP in Dallas is going to need the story to be filed as soon as it's done. It needs to be written ahead of time."

I smiled and shook my head. She may have gotten in it for dubious reasons, but Veronica was a dedicated reporter. "You called to get a quote from me. A real one this time."

"I figured you'd want to since this story will be published in most papers across the country. Except the major Texas dailies, the *Times*, and the *Post*. They're all sending their own reporters."

"Can I email or text it to you a little later?"

"Email it to me in the next hour or so if you can. With traffic and getting into the media viewing area, I'll have to take off about five hours before the execution."

"Not a problem. Anything else?"

"We're in a good place, don't you think?"

"I do." I didn't know if I believed myself, but how else was a person supposed to answer that question?

"Good. I have an idea. This whole story we're involved in is crazy when you think about it. Paul killing Sylvia and trying to frame you by staging her body. Her connection to the FBI and trying to sabotage the job. Your journey into, then out of, then back into the national spotlight."

I agreed but didn't say anything. I already knew where this was going.

"And, as you saw on my computer, I've already started a manuscript. I'll have to get rid of the parts about you killing Summer, but I bet I can keep—"

I jumped out of my seat. "Wait. You didn't delete that?" I could feel heat traveling from my chest to my face. "Didn't you give your computer to the DPS crime lab as part of the investigation?"

I looked at my door and saw flashes of a SWAT team breaking it down.

"I deleted it off the computer, then off my cloud account when I got cell service. But I had a copy on a thumb drive at home."

My breathing slowed some, but I continued staring at the door. "So, you want me to hook you up with my old agent and publisher, right?"

"Not exactly. I want you to help me finish it."

Veronica continued to surprise me. "That's an interesting offer," I said. "Can I think about it?"

"Of course. I wasn't trying to pressure you into anything."

I sat down and leaned back in my chair. "Okay. Thank you."

"Well, that's what I wanted to talk about. I'll be looking for an email with your quote for my stories."

I ended the call and started to calm down. Then I heard a knock on the door.

51

EXCERPT FROM COLD SUMMER

No witnesses spoke on behalf of Butch Heller at his sentencing hearing, during which the same jury that found him guilty of murder would decide between the death penalty or life imprisonment. But he and his court-appointed attorney, who had been two years ahead of Summer Foster in high school, listened to a parade of friends and community members describe Summer as the beacon of Hinterbach. Every speaker called for his death.

When the judge asked if he had anything to say, Heller finally broke his silence.

"Your honor, members of the jury, I'd like to thank you for taking time out of your lives for me," Heller said. "I know you didn't have a choice, but that doesn't mean your efforts aren't appreciated, even by me. But I'm going to take up a few more minutes. I need to get this on the record.

"I am guilty of a lot of things. I'm a

drunk. Not always a fall-down, belligerent drunk, but a drunk, nonetheless. I've stolen things. I'm a liar. Most of what you've heard about me is probably true. Except for one thing: I did not kill Summer Foster."

The jury took less than an hour to hand down the death sentence. His attorney stopped advocating for Heller the moment the verdict came in, though he had been contacted by some big-shot Austin lawyer and agreed to help in the transition. Heller's appeal was filed a month later, and thus began a legal process that continues as of the publication of this book.

52

BUTCH HELLER

July 4, 1999, 8:54 p.m.

As he navigated the final mile to Summer's house, Heller was learning how drunk a man can get after losing his alcohol tolerance. He'd done okay during the first few hours, but after Verna talked him into visiting Jeannie's grave, Heller lost all will power.

The whiskey started hitting Heller as he passed the small WELCOME TO HINTERBACH sign on Highway 16. He watched the last of the fireworks fizzle in the sky but shifting his eyes to the horizon made him lose focus. He swerved to miss one of the cars parked on the curb and slowed to a crawl.

He sped up again when he saw Summer's house, hurrying to give her his confession. It had taken a conversation with pure innocence to make Heller realize that he could still find happiness.

The car didn't slow as fast as he wanted. Heller knew he wouldn't be able to pull in behind the line of cars parked outside her yard. He stomped harder on the brake pedal and pulled off to the left, cursing as he felt the Pontiac lurch over the curb. He kept steering across the sidewalk and put the car in park before its long nose hit the fence.

He opened the car door and stumbled out. "Summer, are you here? Summer? We need to talk."

Heller found his way to the gate and nearly fell as he pushed his way through. He closed his eyes, begging his body to cooperate. She would not take what Heller had to say seriously if he couldn't stand up straight and deliver his message with conviction and sincerity.

He rose and took a deep breath, then tried to glide toward the tables that weren't clean yet.

"Summer, baby, are you out here?"

As his eyes adjusted to the darkness, Heller could barely see the outline of someone lying near the shed. At first, he thought she fell. He rushed toward her and knelt beside her head. He was about to caress her face and comfort her, but he pulled his hand back when he felt the sticky film on her skin.

"Jesus." Heller grabbed her shoulders and began gently shaking her upper body. "Summer, can you hear me?" That's when he noticed the screwdriver sticking out of her right eye, the end of the handle tapping the grass beside her face.

Heller slumped over the body. He thought he would start weeping—and he did feel tears pricking at his eyes—but he chose a different reaction.

"Honey, I know you can't hear me down here. But maybe you're already up in heaven and can hear me there, so I'm going to say this just in case."

Heller looked up to the sky. "I love you. I have since the first time we met, and I will keep loving you until the day I find you up there. I shouldn't have gotten so mad at you earlier. You had every right to cheat on me because I've cheated on you."

He paused for a moment. As ridiculous as it was, Heller still needed to gather his courage.

"I counted on the way over here, and I've slept with four other women since we started seeing each other. Three of them were one-night stands, all of them after having a few too many. I was also drunk the first time with Candy. And God's-honest truth, I never thought I'd see her again. She gave it up for free the first time. But when she told me she was a pro, I started paying her. We continued for months. I wasn't seeing her when she told me about the baby, though. I swear."

The tears finally fell from Heller's eyes and he could no longer speak over the crying. But he had to. Summer deserved to hear the whole confession.

"I hope you know that I wanted to tell you. I thought about it every day, but I was too weak. Any time you wondered where I was, from about a year ago until the wreck, I was helping Candy through the pregnancy or helping with the baby—" Heller shook his head at his continued cowardice, then drew a deep breath "—with *Jeannie* after she was born."

He reached down and grabbed Summer's hand—which was not nearly as cold as he expected a dead person to be—and interlocked their fingers.

"I know we had our talk about the wreck that killed Ruth Ann Beck. But I'm a degenerate liar and still couldn't tell you everything. I had Jeannie in the car with me that night. I was going to bring her to meet you. I was hoping you'd see her beautiful little face and fall in love with her. I wanted us to be a family. But then the wreck happened, and I was the only one who got to walk away, even though I was the only one who should've died."

Heller began crying so hard he couldn't hear or see anything. But now that he'd had his conversation with Summer and could feel the accompanying catharsis, Heller remembered he was holding the hand of a woman who hadn't died of natural causes. He would go to jail and never get out if anyone saw him like this.

Heller jumped to his feet and thought he might pass out, but he weaved toward the gate and made it to the street.

He wasn't sure what made him come to, but Heller could hear a woman's frantic voice. He couldn't make out words yet, but her face told him enough.

"I need to call the police," Heller said. He repeated the phrase two more times before his head was clear.

"You stay right here," she said. "Don't you dare move."

"What's going on? Why won't you let me call the police? I need to call the police."

"Oh, the police are on their way. They'll be here in one minute, so don't you dare move."

Heller tried standing, but he was met with resistance. He looked at the hand that was pushing down on his left shoulder, then followed the arm up to Jeremiah Schmidt.

"I didn't... I didn't..." the rest of his denial was stuck in his throat. Would it matter if he could eventually spit it out? Would anyone believe him? The answers were no and no. He was guilty.

Heller slumped back against the door, unwilling to fight. He heard the sirens approaching and closed his eyes, hoping they would let him sleep it off on a cot in a cell instead of the drunk tank.

53

Fucking housekeeping. I shook from adrenaline for ten minutes after I heard that knock, though I appreciated the fresh towels and toiletries she'd brought for me.

After walking to a convenience store to pick up some junk food to ease the stress, then trying and failing to distract myself with hotel cable, I decided to surf the internet for hours on end.

Then the hour finally came. I hit the refresh button again and got nothing. Veronica had responded to my email with her Associated Press login so I could see her story as soon as it hit the wire. I'd logged onto *newsroom.ap.org* at 9:05 and searched for *Butch Heller* with the filter set for *Newest First*. I found a rewrite of her *Ledger* preview story, but not her execution story.

9:20. I refreshed again.

They obviously hadn't used the headline Veronica suggested. The summary indicated she'd followed the AP rules and written an inverted pyramid. I'd gotten used to her flowery writing, and this wasn't it. She was probably glad they didn't give her a byline.

. . .

Texas Executes Man convicted in Fourth of July slaying

AP--US--Texas Execution,1st Ld-Writethru

Sept. 13, 2019, 9:18 PM (GMT 02:18) – 583 words

Associated Press

HUNTSVILLE, Texas (AP) — A 63-year-old Texas inmate was executed Thursday evening for the Fourth of July murder of a high school librarian two decades ago.

Butch Heller received a lethal injection for the fatal beating of Summer Foster on July 4, 1999, outside of her home in Hinterbach, a small Central Texas town. Foster, the Hinterbach High School librarian, had been Heller's live-in girlfriend for at least two years before the slaying that attracted national attention and sparked the bestselling true crime novel, Cold Summer.

In a report filed earlier Thursday by the Lone Star Ledger, *an online nonprofit news organization based in Austin, Heller said he wouldn't be giving any last words prior to his execution. True to his word, Heller shook his head when asked if he'd like to speak, then closed his eyes for the last time.*

Bartholomew John Beck, the author of Cold Summer *who witnessed the murder when he was 16 and testified in Heller's trial, said Thursday afternoon he hoped the Hinterbach community could find closure in Heller's execution.*

"Butch Heller caused a lot of pain for a lot of people, including me," Beck said. "What he did may never be forgiven by those who were close to Summer Foster, but perhaps knowing he was punished to the fullest extent of the law will help bring them some measure of peace."

Heller's defense attorney, Jackson McGrady of Austin, was not present at the execution and declined comment earlier Thursday. In past interviews, Jackson has said he didn't feel authorities properly investigated other suspects.

Heller had been slated for execution once before but received a stay from the United States Supreme Court less than an hour before he was to receive a lethal injection.

VERONICA'S STORY went on to include some backstory, though I suspected the editors chopped up her prose.

Evaluating this story and being upset at the AP editors had my adrenaline pumping. I hadn't cared this much about writing in a long time. Was it because another writer had finally shown interest in working with me? Was it because I cared about that person? What did Heller's execution, and the official end of the Heller case, have to do with how I felt?

I picked up my phone and started a text to Veronica.

Read your AP story. Hack editors, but you did a great job. Thought about what you said earlier. I think

A text from Jorge came in. I stopped typing to read his message.

Hey man, gonna get my truck back on Monday. There's a test in OKC on Wednesday for a job. $18/hr and $125 per diem, all seven days. You in?

EPILOGUE

Franklin Jones
September, two years later

J ones hated how loudly Darren slammed the front door.
Every day. It was simple carelessness and constantly jolted
Jones out of his memories.

"Got everything on your list," Darren said. "I'll put it all on
the island in the kitchen."

"What about the book?" Jones asked.

"I said I got everything, didn't I?"

Jones didn't like being talked back to. But Darren knew too
much to fire, and Jones couldn't hire Darren to kill himself.
"Bring it to me. I need to see it."

Jones was in his study, where he spent most evenings either
reading or ruminating on the past. He hadn't left his property in
more than twenty-one years, so Jones knew how to keep himself
stimulated without losing his sanity.

Being a hermit was more habit than necessity at this point.
The statute of limitations for any of his financial crimes had
expired more than a decade ago. While there is no such limit for
prosecuting murder cases—not that he'd ever committed such

an evil act—Jones knew he remained a suspect in Summer's death. But even that had become a moot point two years ago with Butch Heller's execution. He'd confessed in the days leading up to the state-sanctioned murder, a practice that had been stopped by the Legislature less than a year later.

Jones was free to leave if he wanted. But to what end? After Summer's death, there was simply no reason. Darren was there at least once a day, and Patty visited once a week to make a special meal. She also gave Jones a haircut once a month. He used to have Darren bring girls on the weekends, but that had all but stopped the last few years.

Jones might want one in a few hours, though, depending on how stimulating the book was.

Darren slapped the hardcover on Jones' desk. "*The Ultimate Alibi*," Darren said. "What's it about?"

"My past—and our future."

Darren didn't react to Jones' cryptic response. Jones paid him handsomely to do his bidding and keep his mouth shut, so Darren had stopped asking questions decades ago.

Before opening the book, Jones turned it over and read about its authors on the back of the dust jacket.

He started with the girl. He'd already seen her photo in the e-book, but Jones still got a thrill from holding her portrait in print. Though she'd changed her name, Jones had recognized her almost instantly as the young woman who'd shown up at his house more than a dozen years ago, the hooker who asked questions about the night Summer died. She probably didn't remember the encounter, but Jones also remembered her as the little girl standing beside Ethel McDonough in her house at the end of County Road K.

Veronica Stein is a longtime investigative journalist who went undercover with an oil pipeline crew to cover the brutal murder of a young woman. The Ultimate Alibi is the true story of that murder, Stein's own brush with death at the hands of the violent son of a U.S.

congressman, and how those events connect to an infamous murder more than two decades earlier.

Next up was the boy who ruined Jones' life.

John Beck has been an author since the age of 18. After writing the true-crime bestseller Cold Summer, *documenting the 1999 murder of Summer Foster in the small Central Texas town of Hinterbach, Beck wrote four true crime books before co-writing* The Ultimate Alibi *with investigative journalist Veronica Stein. His first mystery novel is set for release this spring.*

Jones had searched for his name in the electronic version earlier that day. Since he was free from any prosecution and no longer a suspect in Summer's murder, he'd provided a statement for the book—through a lawyer, of course.

"I had absolutely nothing to do with the tragic death of Summer Foster. I loved her, from our days on the track team at Hinterbach High School to the day she died. She was an angel on earth long before she was taken to heaven. My only regret in life is that I was not there that night to protect her, to take her away from that place and out of the path of the monster who took her life."

The rest of the book was likely a terrific blend of fact and fiction, a real page-turner. It had just debuted at number one on the *New York Times, USA Today* and *Amazon Washington Post* bestseller lists for hardcover nonfiction.

The lives of Beck and Stein were a whirlwind right now. They were busy with media interviews and book events. And both were soon-to-be millionaires with literary reputations to protect.

He summoned Darren. "Leave word for Congressman Schuhmacher. We have something urgent to discuss."

Jones smiled. The time was finally right to get even with Bartholomew Fucking Beck.

ACKNOWLEDGMENTS

You wouldn't be reading this novel without the amazing folks at Fawkes Press. Publisher Jodi Thompson understood my vision from the beginning and was more enthusiastic after a second read. Her support for this story and these characters—and for me as an author—has been outstanding.

Fawkes Press Editor TwylaBeth Lambert grew up in the Texas Panhandle and was intimately familiar with the setting. I couldn't have asked for this story to be in better hands. Leaving a project with anyone else can be inherently scary, but I was never anything other than excited to know she would be making this story its best. And did she ever.

Add in the rest of the team at Fawkes Press, and the insanely talented Fresh Design, and I couldn't be more ecstatic with this work.

You also wouldn't be reading this novel if I hadn't gotten an incredible amount of support from a community of oil pipeliners. The ideas for Summer Foster, her murder in 1999, and Butch Heller's incarceration on Death Row came to me early in the summer of 2018—before the final edits were done on my first novel. But Bartholomew Beck and the oil pipeline setting was a different matter altogether. My original main character was boring with a boring job in a boring place until my best friend Jesús (who I consider my brother) talked me into joining him on a job in Oklahoma for inspiration. We met with Jaime on our way to a test in Oklahoma City. And from the moment Jesús and Jaime struck their arcs, I realized I'd found a setting and culture infinitely more interesting than what I'd been struggling to write. Beck and Veronica came to life quickly after that.

There are dozens of welders, helpers, labor hands, and operators peppering the pipelines of Texas, Oklahoma, and the rest of the country who I will forever call my friends. I could try and name them all, but I'd be forgetting many.

I will single out Jaime (Jesús' brother-in-law for the entirety of my time researching out on the pipeline) and Edgar (Jaime's helper), who were particularly helpful, in terms of doing the job and answering my questions and providing inspiration.

After learning as much as I could in the field, I had to begrudgingly call my research complete and start writing the novel. When the first draft was finished, I relied on some fantastic beta readers and critique partners.

My first beta reader is always my mother, Julie. Though she's legally obligated to tell me my novels are good, I trust her to tell me what works and what doesn't. She's read and forgotten more novels than I will ever get around to thumbing through, so she's a walking library. My sister, Nikki Martindale, and my good friend Amber Guffey are two other beta readers I will trust with everything I write.

For this novel, I also sought out the expertise of Crystal Phares, a member of the Texas High Plains Writers. She provided detailed notes on the first draft and really helped me decide what to expand upon, what to keep, and what to cut. I also had the pleasure of working long-distance with Farhaanah Fawmie, a critique partner I found in Sri Lanka. She was instrumental in showing me places where my plot needed tightening.

The most substantial changes in this story came after a

critique session with Tex Thompson, M.D. (Manuscript Doctor). Her notes on the story's structure and characters—including one big ah-ha moment—are what took this story from a strong work-in-progress to a story worthy of a top-quality publisher.

I also owe a ton of gratitude to everyone involved in the production of *Lore*. To say their podcast and television show was inspirational to this thriller writer would be an understatement of epic proportion. My fiction can never be as creepy as the truth behind the Hinterkaifeck episodes, but without listening and watching them, Hinterbach and its history would never have made it onto the page.

BOOK CLUB DISCUSSION GUIDE

Let the Guilty Pay
Rick Treon

This book club discussion guide for Let The Guilty Pay *includes discussion questions and other ideas for getting the most out of your reading group's experience with the novel. The questions are aimed at helping your book club approach the text from fresh angles, and we hope they enhance your experience discussing the story.*

When he was sixteen, Bartholomew Beck's thirtysomething neighbor, Summer Foster, was brutally murdered in a small Texas town. He told police he saw the murder, testified for the prosecution, and later wrote a bestseller on the case. He tried to turn that book into a true-crime writing career. But twenty years after the murder, his career has stalled and he's making ends meet on a Texas Panhandle oil pipeline.

Beck is adjusting to his new life when he finds the body of an enigmatic female coworker stuffed in a pipe—and staged to look like Summer Foster. That, plus a public falling out with the victim, puts Beck at the top of the Texas Rangers' list of suspects.

Meanwhile, Austin-based journalist Veronica Stein is working on an exposé aimed at exonerating Butch Heller, the man Beck helped put on Death Row for Summer's murder. That's a problem for the man whose name has become synonymous with Heller's guilt for two decades.

In exchange for dropping her investigation, Beck gets Veronica a job on the pipeline so she can write an undercover piece about Jillian's murder and help prove his innocence. But as facts are revealed about both murders, Beck learns the power of truth and the price of redemption.

Questions and discussion topics

1. What does the first chapter tell you about Bartholomew Beck? How did his encounters with Jillian and the deer shape your initial impressions about him? How did those impressions change throughout the novel?
2. How would you describe Beck's relationship with Jorge? He calls his boss/host his best friend, but how do you think Beck's solitary writing life has impacted the development of their friendship since they were in college?
3. How about Beck's relationship with reporter Veronica Stein? How did you react to Beck's attempts at manipulating her to his advantage? How did you feel when you learned their dynamic was not as simple as it appeared?
4. What are your thoughts about the structure of the novel? Did you enjoy getting to see the day of Summer Foster's murder unfold? Did the characters'

points of view and the excerpts from Beck's true-crime book, *Cold Summer,* enhance Hinterbach as a setting?

5. Look back at how Hinterbach was portrayed by Beck in *Cold Summer,* in particular comments by the local men of faith. What does Beck's description of the town and the possible "role" of its residents in Summer Foster's death say about Beck's interpretation of the events surrounding the murder? In light of what you learn toward the end of the novel, do you think that was done on purpose, or did Beck include those passages subconsciously?

6. Discuss how the facts portrayed in the excerpts of *Cold Summer* were sometimes at odds with how the characters behaved and some corresponding scenes played out in reality. Did that disconnect provide any hints to Beck's and Veronica's deceit in the present timeline?

7. Throughout the novel, Summer is a victim of a series of sexist, violent men. What are your thoughts on her reactions to those attacks? Do these attacks add to the tragedy of her story?

8. Summer's alleged killer, Butch Heller, is seen by most as an alcoholic and petty criminal. He is those things, but did being in Heller's head add any complexity to his character? Did you sympathize with him by the end of the novel?

9. What was your reaction to Summer's abusive ex-boyfriend, Franklin Jones, as a suspect when he was discussed in Veronica's news story early in the novel? How did that change once you got inside his head?

10. Did you enjoy learning about how things operate on Texas oil pipelines through the narrative? Could you have done with less of that knowledge? Did you want to know more? How about the overall pipeline culture

(trash talking, drinking, level of knowledge required
to do the job, etc.)?

11. About halfway through the book, Beck discusses how
he's "too nice," and how deciding to be that way has
impacted his adult life. In the end, he says he's proud
of being "too nice." What was your reaction to that
speech based on what you knew about Beck at the
time? What, if anything, did it foreshadow?

12. At what moment did you realize Veronica's connection
to Butch? How did you react to that revelation?

13. What was your reaction to reading the scene during
which Summer is killed? Did you see it coming? If so,
what clues led you there?

14. Was Summer destined to die, based on the mindset
and future intentions of other characters? If Summer
hadn't died that night, what future do you think she
would've had?

15. Discuss the punishment each character received for
their misdeeds. Did you enjoy how the author handled
those punishments? If not, why?

If you enjoyed this book and would like to support the creation of further Bartholomew Beck thrillers, please do one or more of the following:

- Leave a review on your favorite book review site
- Tell a friend about the book and author
- Ask your local library to put Rick Treon's work on the shelf
- Recommend Fawkes Press books to your local bookstore

Readers make our work possible!